Released

EJ Pay

ISBN: 978-1-7331202-6-5(Paperback)
ISBN: 978-1-7331202-5-8(eBook)

Any reference to historical events, real people, or real places are used fictitiously. Names, characters, and places are products of the author's imagination.

Cover design by Mindee Dziuba www.joobahstudio.com

Printed by Amazon

First printing edition 2020

www.ej-pay.com

For my Ashleigh

My Evelyn

My Chelsea

I love you

PROLOGUE

Thieves break in and steal. They take something from you and leave an emotional wound. But what happens when a thief steals a part of *you*? A part of your life? How do you keep on living when seven years are stolen? Please tell me. I have to keep living.

I am Evelyn. I am also Pearl. At least I was, anyway. I am part of a civilization of two-worlders who can live both on land and in water. I live and serve with the army of Atlantis. But seven years ago, I was trapped in the body of an ancient power source named Pearl. I entered her ten-year-old body when I was seventeen. I had been trying to save the world from the evil octopus woman, Ceto, who wanted to use the pearl's power to flood the earth. Little did I know that when I touched that stone, I would lose myself to Pearl's life in Ancient Greece. For seven years, I learned about Pearl and became a part of her. She became a part of me. I grew and I learned, and I fell in love – a love I lost when I was kidnapped for my powers and eventually reentered my own life as Evelyn.

I finally found my way home, back to the twenty-first century, with the help of Namaah. Namaah is all around us, always. She is the air. She always has been and always will be. Namaah helped me feel the power I had inside. Together, we used that power to bring down the evil politicians in the ancient city of Atlantis. We brought them down and brought Atlantis with us, through time, through space, resting the ancient city on the bottom of the Atlantic

Ocean, near the Bermuda Triangle. Pearl was released from her beautiful and powerful pearlescent prison – her spirit reunited with her twin brother. I was returned to my own body, just as I had left it, 2,400 years later.

No real time passed for the people I left seven years ago. Only a few hours went by. But I was left to pick up the pieces of my lost seven years while Atlantis continued to battle against Ceto in the modern world. That isn't a loss I take lightly.

Here I am now, a young woman caught between two lives, forced to make my way in a future stolen from me. A future, a life, seven years stolen by Queen Nyobi Kadul. This evil goddess who has dominated her part of the sea for thousands of years is responsible for my loss and Pearl's and threatens all of life as we know it. Queen Nyobi Kadul planted the curse that led to Pearl's entrapment and, eventually, to mine. She gave birth to Atlantis' enemy, Ceto. They must be stopped. They must be destroyed.

I will make it happen.

CHAPTER 1

Tap. Tap. Tap. Tap. Tap. Tap. Tap. Tap. Tap. Tap. Tap. Tap. Tap. Tap. Tap. Tap. Tap. Tap. Tap. Tap. Tap. Tap. Tap. Tap. Tap. Tap. Tap. Tap. Tap. Tap. Tap. Tap. Tap. Tap. Tap. Tap. Tap. Tap. Tap. Tap. Tap. Tap. Tap. Tap. Tap. Tap. Tap. Tap. Tap. Tap. Tap. Tap. Tap. Tap. Tap. Tap. Tap. Tap. Tap. Tap. Tap. Tap. Tap. Tap. Tap. Tap. Tap. Tap. Tap. Tap. Tap. Tap. Tap. Tap. Tap. Tap. Tap. Tap. Tap. Tap. Tap. Tap. Tap. Tap. Tap. Tap. Tap. Tap. Tap. Tap. Tap

Sigh.

I'm driving my roommate insane. Celia will find any reason to demean me. If we are late because she had to wait for me, I will never hear the end of it. The assignment to keep an eye on me is testing her willingness to follow orders. But Celia is nothing if not loyal to the cause of Atlantis. Or to the cause of making herself look important. She may hate every minute of watching over me, but I know she loves having an assignment that sets her apart. She will report my progress to Lady Pescara, directly. If I do well, Celia will take the credit. If I screw up, she gets to yell at me. Unfortunately for her, I have bigger problems than keeping her happy.

"We are going to be late, Evelyn," Celia finally snaps at me from the doorway. "I swear. You say you are going to rejoin Atlantis, but you take forever to even get to the beach. It's bad enough that you still haven't breathed water since you got out of the hospital. Now you are trying to take me down with you!" I roll my eyes and sigh.

"Celia, we aren't going to be late. Besides, if you are in such a hurry, why don't you just leave without me?"

"Ha!" she scoffs. "I'm sure you would love that! Then you could be as lazy and slow as you want." She takes a step into my room, pointing her finger while she speaks. "But *I* don't go against orders, Evelyn. *I* know when I have a responsibility, and for now, *you* are it. Let's go!" She leaves my room and I make an unnecessary sweep of the room to see if there's anything else I should take. I have no problem taking my time if it means irritating Celia.

I finish packing the rest of my things and head for the hall. Celia stomps through the kitchen to our apartment door. I grab a bagel on the way out. Celia goes crazy over it. Driving her crazy is one of the few joys left in my life. She avoids white bread like the plague and is always after me for my poor eating choices. And my timing. And my study habits. And my words. And…and…and…

But she is right about one thing. I still haven't breathed water since I returned from Ancient Greece. I couldn't breathe when I reentered my own body. Jack was left behind to watch and wait for me. It's a good thing, too. I was too stunned, scared… I don't know what I was. I just know I couldn't breathe water anymore. If Jack hadn't been there, I would have died underwater in Poseidon's temple – one more casualty in a centuries-long battle for control of the seas.

Everything else about me is the same. I still have the muscle I built up while living in Atlantis. I have the same memories of life in the ocean. I've played around a bit with wave control, a skill I had before. I assume I will still be able to communicate with sea life and work with water temperature in the ocean and tides if I need to. I just can't breathe like an Atlantean.

I've been working with Celia and our captain, Jack, to retrain my body and my brain to accept water breathing again. We've been to pools and waded out in the bay, but when it's time to let go and embrace the water, I freeze. I have so many fears about breathing it. After years of dreaming that I would drown, it nearly happened. I don't want to risk finishing the job. My mom says I've just been out of practice, that the lost ability is all in my head. Jack agrees with her. Celia tells me I'm pretending because I don't really want to go back to Atlantis - that I'm too afraid to fight in the war. They are all right.

I do feel fear. I feel it every day. I feel it every night. I dream in fear. There are always flames and screams and betrayal and the tortured faces of my loved ones. Sometimes I scream out loud in my sleep. Celia comes in and wakes me up. She acts irritated, but even she looks like she pities me. I hate that.

Those seven years in Ancient Greece were enough to strike fear into anyone. The realization of immense power. The murder of Pearl's twin, Domideus. Being kidnapped. Falling in love only to have his love torn from me. Letting that burning power drive me to ultimate freedom. But what kind of freedom is plagued by nightmares in the dark and shuddering fear in the light?

I follow Celia out of our apartment complex to her blue BMW and work on the deep breathing my mom has been trying to coach into me. I don't need to give Celia another reason to be irritated, so I keep quiet. I click my seatbelt and look to the FIU campus as we drive away. If everything goes as we've planned and I have hoped, I won't be seeing these buildings for several months. I'm trading them in for the ancient watery ruins of Atlantis. The ruins I created.

When we reach the shoreline, Jack is already there, waiting with my mom. She took a sabbatical from teaching at ASU to be with me. Uncle Russ, the FIU president and a general in Atlantis, has helped her get work teaching in the underwater schools. Though Atlantis is primarily a political and military base in the underwater world, it is filled with college students who are squeezing in a degree while they battle for freedom for the planet. My mom teaches these students any subjects that need to be taught, helping them prepare for life after war. She refuses to join the army herself. She says it's because she can't face fighting Ceto, her sister-in-law, that she couldn't do what was needed in the end. But I think what she really wants is to give me a place to go when I can't handle the fighting. She's hoping I'll change my mind and leave the army, choosing a life of safety instead. But too much is at stake. If I make it back to Atlantis today, there will be no turning around for me.

Celia pulls into a parking spot and jumps out of the car, heading straight for Jack. I take my time, still trying to steady my breathing, and pull my bag from the back seat. The bag looks like your everyday run-of-the-mill backpack, perfect for a day at the beach. But it holds everything that ties me to land and sea. A picture of my parents, my favorite wetsuit, the family album my mom gave me when I first came to FIU. It's wrapped in plastic and cannot even be opened underwater. But I can't be without it. I can't be happy unless I know my happy memories and the strength of my Cherokee ancestors is with me. I shoulder the backpack and focus on the cut of the strap as it digs into my shoulder. The pressure is a reminder that I am back in my own body, living in my own time. I feel so alone in all of it, it's so surreal, I have to pinch myself every once in a while to remind me of where I am.

I close the car door and feel the warm breeze against my cheek and pause to catch my breath. When I lived in Ancient Greece, the air was my constant companion, a living legend and superpower named Namaah. She took human form to keep watch over me as I tried to find freedom. Her power is what helped me return to my present, human life. But I haven't even tried talking to her since returning home. I'm afraid she isn't there, that she won't be able to speak to me anymore or I to her. I just want to feel her presence. I hope she knows that.

I walk over to where Celia and Captain Jack are talking. He turns as soon as I come close and a smile spreads across his face. He wraps his arms around me in a big hug, something I wasn't

5

expecting. I haven't seen Jack since he last came to visit me in the hospital a few weeks ago. I don't know how he can still smile at me and hold onto me so tight when he knows my heart is so torn. Did he forget that I loved someone else, almost married someone else, just a short while ago?

"How are you?" he asks when he stands back. "It's so good to see you here. How are you feeling about today?" I give a noncommittal answer, saying that I'm ready to give it a go. He doesn't seem convinced.

As soon as she sees an opening, Celia jumps in, telling Jack about getting me ready for reentry. She assures him that I can hardly remember anything about Atlantis and the ways of the Atlantean army. She embellishes everything, making herself sound like a saint and me her inept follower. She assures him she has done her best, but we can only wait and see if I've gleaned enough of her wisdom to pass muster. Jack gives me knowing glances while Celia reports everything to him and I smile. He knows Celia is full of it as much I do. I don't have to defend myself with Jack. He believes the best in me.

Right when I'm getting really tired of listening to Celia, my Mom shows up. She jogs over and wraps me in a hug.

"How are you feeling today, Sweetie?" she asks when she takes my bag.

"I'm alright," I tell her. How can I put into words everything that is in my head? If she could feel my anxiety, confusion, and pain, she would keep me from trying to return. But staying on land is not an option for me. I have an enemy to conquer.

"Are you ready?" she asks.

"As ready as I'm going to get," I respond. Lady Pescara says it's now or never. Ceto and Nyobi have been working together in the Mediterranean Sea, uninterrupted, for long enough. The army of Atlantis will be moving out soon, with or without me. Our enemies are waiting for us. They must be stopped, and I must be a part of it.

Jack turns his back on Celia and faces me and my mom.

"I know how Evelyn is feeling today," he says. "She's ready to kick some evil octopus butt." Jack reaches for my arm and gives it a squeeze. His smile is so big. How can he have so much trust in me? Maybe he's just trying to placate my mom.

"Well, I'm definitely ready to get going," I say. "I've been gone for long enough." I'm trying to sound confident, but my voice cracks and my breath rattles out of my chest. "I miss Dad." Mom smiles and rests her hand on my shoulder.

"And he misses you," she says. My dad is a full-fledged merman now, unable to live on the land. He spent so much time locked in Ceto's underwater prison, that his change is now complete. I thought he was dead until Ceto brought me to meet him. I've hardly had time to get to know him again. He is another reason I am so eager to get back to the underwater city.

"I've got some classes to teach this morning," Mom says as she kisses my cheek. "I need to get to the city. Let's meet up for dinner with Dad tonight. Does that sound good? We'll even eat in the soldier's dining hall."

I know what she's doing. It's the same tactic she has used my whole life. Act like I will be successful, like it's no big deal because in her mind I've already won, then walk away to let me shine. She isn't going to hear my concern; she already knows it's there. She is so confident that she will leave me to it. At least I think she's confident that I'll be successful. Maybe she is just too nervous to stay. What if I fail? I think she would actually be happy about that. Without the water breathing, I wouldn't be able to fight in a war and we could live safely together on land. But then I couldn't see my dad again. No, she is going to leave so I don't have more eyes and more pressure than I already have on my shoulders.

"Thanks, Mom," I say. "Dinner sounds nice." She knows I'm lying. I know I'm lying. Everyone probably knows I'm lying. I am afraid that I will never make it to that dinner in Atlantis.

"Until tonight then," Mom says, kissing my cheek again. She turns away and heads to the water, wearing her coral one piece with shiny water leggings, the natural olive of her dark skin creating a gorgeous contrast. She is still carrying my bag. It probably helps her feel calm. I know she is trying to be brave for me.

"Well, are you two ready to head into the water?" Celia's face is beaming. I pull my eyes away from my mom and my stomach turns. I don't want to fail in front of Celia.

"Actually," Jack says, "Lady Pescara has given me orders to remain with Evelyn today. I will be helping her until she is ready."

"That could be a loooonnnggg time," Celia laughs, "but I can be patient." She flicks her perfect braid behind her back. I want to smack her.

"Fortunately for you," Jack says, "Lady Pescara has left this task just to me. You are to return to Atlantis now and give your report."

Celia's face falls, her glib smile twitching at the corners. She is doing all she can to bite back any arguments. But no matter how much she wants to stay and flirt with her captain, she will obey the order. She wants to look perfect for everyone. She takes a deep breath, revives her smile, and stands a little straighter.

"Ah, I see," she says, turning to me, "Good luck today, Evelyn. But don't worry if it doesn't work out. The army will be back in a few months, and you can try to rejoin us then." She squeezes my arm with a little more than friendly encouragement and turns her beautiful blue eyes to Jack, "I'll see you later, Captain. I'll tell Lady Pescara you are doing your duty and Evelyn is trying to do hers."

"Thank you, Celia," Jack nods. "Please make sure my group is ready to go. They have their orders already, but it will be good for someone to check up on them just the same." Giving her some responsibility is exactly the kind of thing Celia relishes. And it takes her attention off of me for a moment.

She lifts her chin and flashes her brilliant smile. "I will take care of it, Captain." She salutes Jack before she turns and heads to the water. I watch her go and envy her swim gear. In her long wetsuit, she looks like a beautiful creature made for the water. Her strokes are graceful, and her form is flawless when she dives below the waves toward the drop that leads to our underwater headquarters.

Several minutes pass before I realize that Jack hasn't said anything. I turn my face to him only to find that his green eyes are staring just at me. A small smile lifts the corner of his mouth and a playful light brightens his face. My heart skips a beat and already I feel guilty for it. I know this is reality. I know that Jack was in my life long before Gileaus, that we were starting to have something special. I know that I'll never get Gileaus back, but I don't know if I can erase his memory so soon.

"What are you thinking about?" he asks.

"That's a loaded question," I say, embarrassed. "I'm not sure I know the answer."

"How are you *really* feeling today?" he asks. "I know you told your mom and Celia that you are ready to go, but I know you better than that. You'll say what you think other people want to hear. But are you sure you're ready to try this out? Celia is right, you know. You can wait to rejoin the army when we get back." That's all the encouragement I need. I'm not about to do anything that Celia suggests.

"Ha," I laugh. "You know you can't make it without me." The even greater truth is I won't *let* the army face Nyobi and Ceto without me. I want, I need, a piece of that revenge.

Jack smiles and takes my hand in his, stroking the backs of my fingers with his thumb. I try to steady my breath. I'm still not sure I'm ready for him to hold my hand, but it does feel good to feel desired. My head is spinning. I want to get my life back. At least that's what everyone else wants for me. I don't know which life I miss most, but that doesn't even matter. This is the life I have been given back. So, I take a deep breath and embrace it, linking my fingers with Jack's.

We take our time, making small talk on the walkway between the parking lot and the sand. Our fingers are still linked together, but I'm not really paying attention to the conversation. I'm paying attention to Jack, trying so hard to recall the feelings I had for him before I was taken away. I tell myself this is what I want.

Jack was built for the water. Tall, muscular, with long arms to propel him through the sea, sun-bleached hair and green eyes. He is handsome and he is kind. Most girls would feel lucky to have him. I pull my long, dark hair into a bun at the base of my neck, freeing my hand from his. I let out the breath that I didn't know I was holding. It's time for me to fight for my future.

"Shall we try, Evelyn?" Jack asks me. I nod. "I'm right here with you," he says. Jack was with me before and he is with me again. I can trust him. He smiles, but the smile does not quite reach his eyes. Is my struggle written all over my face?

"I know," I whisper. "I'm ready."

I step out in front of him, slip off my flip flops, and step my toes onto the sun-warmed sand. It greets my feet in a warm welcome home. Today is the day. Today, I am going to breathe again.

CHAPTER 2

Like a dog licking its owner who just came home from a long trip, the waves lap at my legs. I feel their spirit, and I laugh at their welcome. I can communicate with the waves. I can coax them into moving higher or lower than they normally would. I respect the waves. I don't ask anything of them unless it is necessary because I don't want to abuse the power I have in our relationship. I think the waves appreciate that about me – a two-worlder who won't ask anything that isn't in the best interest of the sea. The waves feel real affection for me, and I love their greeting.

I walk until I am waist deep in the salty water. Jack follows, moving quietly behind me, not reaching for my hand or saying anything. His presence is reassuring, but I am grateful for his silence. He won't push me to breathe if I am not ready. I want to be ready. I close my eyes and let out a deep and satisfying sigh. I inhale the salty ocean air and fall back into the water.

I don't try breathing right away; I just float on my back. The salty current plays with my hair, running through the strands like grandparents' fingers doting on a favorite child. I let myself feel the peace and ease of the ocean's gentle touch – a touch that can turn deadly if controlled by the wrong people. I flip to my stomach, swimming beneath the waves, my eyes adjusting to the scene below the waterline. Seashells roll along the sand as the current moves in and out of the shore. Tiny fish dart out of the way of boats in the distance. Bubbles float from my skin, back to the surface of the water, unwilling to go any further with me. This is the life I have missed for so long. I remember the feeling of home that I had here. My chest aches and I come up again for air. Jack is still standing in the waist deep water, watching me. He hasn't decided if I'm ready either.

"How about we just enjoy ourselves for a while," he suggests. Nothing has ever sounded more glorious to me. I splash Jack in the face and dive back down beneath the waves. It is so nice to let go of some tension.

We spend the next hour playing in the waves near the shore. A few more beachgoers arrive, but not many. With school in session now, there are only some retired couples and moms escaping to the beach during the week. It feels so good to be back in the ocean's water again.

"I'd like to try now," I tell Jack. I feel so close to home, I don't want to wait anymore.

"Okay," he says, smiling with confidence. "Let's do this."

We swim farther and farther out. We leave the waves behind and swim in the swells. My body rides up and down on each swell while I make my way out to sea. I had forgotten how much I love this place. Jack and I are just about even with the end of the pier when we pause. This is where I will try to breathe water again. The butterflies in my stomach are strong. Everything will be okay. Jack is with me if I can't breathe, after all.

"I'll go down first and wait for you," he says. He swims closer to me. Our legs kick each other as we tread water. "You can do this, Evelyn," he says. He swims forward, kisses my cheek, then disappears beneath the water before I can react.

My head swims even more now that his lips have touched me. So many thoughts fight for my attention. But I don't have time to think about those things now, I have a job to do. I shake my head and take a deep, cleansing breath. I exhale slowly and listen to the sound of my breath leaving my lungs. It sounds like the ocean. I am ready.

I inhale once more and dunk my head beneath the waves. Jack is waiting for me just below the surface and we are face-to-face. He smiles and I smile back. A few bubbles escape from my nose.

"I'm ready when you are," he says. I hear him as clearly as if we were above the water. That's a good sign. I smile and reach out to Jack. He takes my hand in his and squeezes my fingers, but I squeeze his fingers like a vice. I pull him closer and he wraps his arms around me. I need the pressure of having him there. It's a warm and comforting safety net. Squeeze me tighter, Jack.

Let go of the nerves, Evelyn, you can do this.

I close my eyes and exhale the air left in my lungs. I don't give myself time to think about whether or not this will work. I force peace and calm into my mind, and I inhale. I wait for burning, but I feel none. I exhale again and inhale. I feel the salty sea entering my throat and lungs. I feel the tingling sensation of saltwater working its way through my body. I open my eyes. Jack is smiling again, and his face is painfully close. I smile back, my heart pounding in my chest. I reach my fingers to his face and twist them in his hair. I pull him to me and kiss him forcefully, letting go of every bit of tension I've kept trapped inside for weeks. Right now, I get to let go and celebrate. I am breathing underwater again!

I am so excited that I push away and let out a shout. Several tiny fish pause when they hear me. I laugh and Jack laughs with me. I swim away from him and dive deeper into the ocean. The increasing pressure of millions of gallons of ocean water feels good to me – like I am being hugged.

Jack and I swim and dive in the water, deeper and deeper below the surface. I move slowly down, and Jack follows. We finally make it to the continental drop off – that vast and intimidating space that will let us plummet into the open sea and down to the city of Atlantis. I pause and float for several minutes, taking in the familiarity of the experience.

"How are you feeling now?" Jack asks, reaching for my hand again. I smile at him then return my gaze to the open water.

"I feel amazing," I reply. "I feel more like myself than I've felt in ages. This is so different from when I first breathed water. I was so full of anger then, I just wanted to escape my life."

"Because of James and Gwen?" he questions. I nod.

"Yes. Because of James and Gwen. But this time, I want to remember everything."

"Let's both remember it then," Jack says. He turns my face to his and pulls me closer to him. Before I have a chance to say anything, Jack's lips meet mine. His lips are rough, but his kiss is gentle. His arms are strong, but not forceful. He kisses me and I kiss him back. For just a moment, I let everything else leave my mind and focus on the warmth of his lips against mine. It feels so good to be kissed again.

The water is colder than it was when James kissed me beneath the waves. But this time, everything is warmer. I feel Jack pulling the heat from the water and focusing it around our bodies. I don't know if it is something he is thinking about or just a product of the moment, but the increased temperature is more than noticeable.

As the last of the bubbles escape from our lips and we are completely at ease with the water and each other, Jack pulls away. It takes a minute before I am willing to open my eyes. I am living in a dream, and I want to hold onto this moment forever.

"Was that okay?" he asks when I meet his gaze. I smile at him. I loved the kiss. I love his nearness. I care so much for him. I ignore the pressure in my heart when it reminds me of Gileaus.

"I loved it, Jack," I tell him. "Thank you for asking me." I pause before I say anything more. I touch his cheek, my eyes never leaving his. I need him to understand. "I want it to be okay for more than just one moment or one kiss," I tell him. "This is the life I am choosing. Will you be patient with me while I fight for it? There is so much going on in my head. But this *is* what I want."

"But you're worried about your feelings for Gileaus," he whispers.

"Yes, Jack," I say, "I am. But that is over. I *want* this with you." I can't help the crack in my voice. I can't help the tear that escapes from my eye to mingle in the salty water all around me. I can't help it and I want to help it. In this moment, I want to be with Jack. I want to forget Gileaus. I want what is in front of me that I know I can have.

"I understand," Jack says. "What if we take it slow, Evelyn? You are worth it to me. I can wait patiently for you to give your heart only to me. I almost had it before." He kisses me softly then pulls his lips away. "I won't pressure you, Evelyn. If you want a kiss, kiss me. If you want to be held, come to me. When you are ready to love me, tell me." He kisses me again then swims back, letting the colder water wash away our warmth. I wish he would come kiss me again.

"Until you are really sure, we'll take it slow. I'm just happy to be back in the race." He turns to face the open water. "So, we'll keep kissing to a minimum and hand holding only when you can't help but want to hold it." He winks and I laugh at him, glad he can lighten the mood. It may take a while for me to really get on board, but it is nice to know he's giving me the space he knows I need.

"Yes, to both," I say. He swims forward and kisses my cheek, letting his face linger near mine for a moment. I close my eyes and take a sharp breath. I am dizzy and wanting more, forgetting what we just said. But Jack pulls away slowly, letting me want him, not destroying the moment or taking advantage of it. I smile and whisper, "Thank you."

Jack winks again and turns to face the sea.

"Well," he says, "Since we won't be kissing, are you ready to head to Atlantis?"

I laugh out loud, shaking my head, and tell him I'm ready. We hold hands and step off the ledge beneath our feet. We float for a moment then sink onto the transport fish who are stationed and waiting for us to come. I think about all they must have heard, and I blush.

For a brief moment, I think I have landed on Pisces' saddle again. The smooth leather surface that meets my legs is so familiar to me. But the thought passes quickly. My companion fish, Pisces, is dead. He died for me.

Hello. I feel a new warmth coming from the giant sea creature beneath me as she whispers to my mind. *I am Chelsea,* she says. Having a sea creature speak to me again feels like home. But Chelsea is so unique, I don't know what to focus on first: introductions or her rare species.

Hello, I answer as I adjust myself in her saddle. *I'm Evelyn.*

I know who you are, Chelsea says. The feeling of her speech is different than with other sea creatures. Like she is speaking with an accent I am familiar with but cannot place. There is a twangy quality to her voice, and I have to concentrate to understand her.

I have been waiting for you, she continues, *I've been assigned as your battle companion. There have been many new recruits since you were last here. Many people wanted to serve with you, but Lady Pescara and Captain Jack chose me for the job.* I feel

18

pride sweeping through Chelsea. She is young, like me, but she is so pleased to serve, to be a part of something so much greater than herself. I feel her budding sense of adventure and courage mingled with uncertainty. I'm glad to have such a strong companion.

I glance over at Jack and he smiles. "That is because Chelsea is the best fit for you," he tells me. "You two will do amazing things." Jack and his fish dive into the water and my mind returns to Chelsea.

Are you ready to go now? She asks me. In time, she will be able to sense my readiness, and I will be able to sense her movements before she makes them. For now, we work on getting to know each other.

Yes, Chelsea. I'm ready, I tell her. Her heart races and she dives down. She is fast and strong, but these are not the only things unique about her. She is not the same species of companion fish that I am accustomed to seeing and riding. She is the largest, most magnificent seahorse I have EVER seen! She isn't a regular seahorse, either. Her large, warm body is gold with long, flowing tendrils of orange and pink growing all around her. At the end of each tendril, a leaf-like growth fans out in iridescent fuscia. Small, pink scales are scattered in clusters across her face and body. I have seen only one seahorse that looks like her before.

Chelsea, I ask as we dive deeper. *Do you know Lachlan? I knew him when I was in Atlantis before and you look so alike. Are you from the same area?*

Chelsea's chest swells and she puffs out against my legs.

Lachlan is my cousin, she tells me.

Your cousin?! I ask. *But he is so much smaller!* I instantly regret my surprise. Chelsea is embarrassed by her size.

Yes, she whispers. *I have a genetic defect. I grow and grow. I won't stop growing for the rest of my life.*

Chelsea, that isn't a defect, I tell her, recovering quickly. *That is incredible! You are the most breathtaking creature I have ever seen.* And it is the truth.

Do you really think so? She asks. I let her feel my awe and some of her fuscia leaves turn to catch the little light in the water around us.

I do think so. I say. *In fact, I* know *so!* Her embarrassment subsides and her confidence returns.

I scratch her neck and lean closer to her head as we swim. Her tendrils tickle my face and brush through my hair. I am surrounded by floating color – hidden, in the midst of her beauty. Chelsea is the most stunning creature I have seen, in or out of the water. Her skin is velvety, and her muscles are strong. I feel the power of her body as she carries me through the water. She may be young, but I know already she is an incredible asset to the army of Atlantis. Her appearance alone would make opposing forces stop and stare.

Chelsea tells me more about herself on our way to Atlantis. She is the youngest of seven siblings and the only one of her size. She isn't a seahorse like I thought she was. She and Lachlan are sea dragons, cousins to the seahorse family. Their family traveled with other sea creatures from the rocky reefs of Australia to join Atlantis. Both of her parents have died since sea dragons only live for a few years.

The specialists think I may live longer, she tells me, *because of my size. That's at least one good thing about being so big. There are a few other things that I can do that other sea dragons can't.*

Before I can ask what her other special qualities are, I sit up and peer out from her leafy appendages. Atlantis is coming into view. My questions never make it to my lips and my stomach turns in knots.

A great dome surrounds the city. It looks like a snow globe, but I can see that it is the current controllers working. They are creating a barrier for the city, something to protect Atlantis from its enemies. Chelsea and I follow Jack and Perseus to the entrance guards. I don't hear what Jack says to them, but the guards nod and give orders to the current controllers nearest them. With strong arm movements that bespeak their talent, they arch away from the guards, creating an opening in their current force field. Jack and Perseus swim through with Chelsea and me close behind. I turn to look behind me as we pass and see the dome seal shut again, protecting us in its hazy glow. When I face forward again, we are at the gates of Atlantis.

The last time I saw these gates, they were in their stone and bejeweled glory, rising like beacons set to guard the ancient metropolis. But now, the walls on either side have collapsed, providing no protection to the underwater city. The rotting gates which would be buried in sand if not for the two-worlders who keep them functioning, hang loosely from their hinges and creak in the ocean water. The ancient buildings that once ringed the inner walls of the city have floated off their foundations and settled in the sand that makes up the new floor of Atlantis.

As Chelsea and I pull up alongside Jack and his fish, my vision blurs and fractures. I see over and over again the shining gates overlaying this decayed entrance. I see the walls made of precious stone that kept the regal city hidden from view. I remember the first time I rode a ship toward this place, toward my destiny. Namaah was with me then. Gileaus was with me too. It was the last time my lips touched his.

Chelsea and I float in front of the once glorious sign. It is now nothing but a rotted, lumpy, disfigured mess, a shadow of its former self. Like me.

Atlantis: Home of the Ancients
Headquarters of the Modern War

"Evelyn," I hear Jack beside me. "Evelyn, are you okay?" I nod. I don't want to talk about everything I am feeling right now. Too much has been lost for this city and for me. Queen Nyobi Kadul, Ceto, even Gwen in her attempts to be free from her mother's shadow. All have brought destruction to this once great city. It's their fault these gates and walls are a rotted and useless protection for the city. I clear my eyes, narrowing them into slits, and wait. I will seek revenge for all that has been lost. Understanding my intent, the gates to Atlantis swing open and take us in.

CHAPTER 3

"Ceto has been with the Queen for weeks off the coast of Jaffa! We MUST take action NOW! We have waited long enough!" Uncle Russ pounds his fist on Lady Pescara's desk. Several captains and generals surround the merwoman and leader of the Atlantean army. Each has a look of frustration on her or his face. Several shake their heads. I have been back in Atlantis for under an hour without a chance to see my dad and already I am thrust in the middle of a war council.

"The prisoner assures us these are rumors," Lachlan interjects. The tiny seahorse's booming voice sends ripples through the water.

"And why do you think you can trust him?!" an aged merwoman demands. "He has been working for the darkest creature in all the ocean!"

Lady Pescara rises from her seat behind the desk. Her mermaid tail shimmers beneath her. Waves of silver hair float in the water behind her back. A deep blue sash crosses her torso, laying on the seaweed top she wears. Medals of bravery and leadership cover the sash, casting a brilliant display of color and light throughout the room. There is no question who rules in this place. All voices hush and all eyes turn to their leader.

"Then it is fortunate that we have someone who can help us decipher the words of the prisoner," Lady Pescara says. "Evelyn," all heads in the room turn toward my seat near the door. I feel like I'm in a classroom and the teacher asked me a question but I haven't been paying attention. I knew I was reporting for duty. I didn't know I had an assignment waiting for me.

"It is lucky that you were able to join us today," Lady Pescara says. Her eyes are serious. No smile touches her face. I don't think one ever would. "You have experience that the rest of us do not," she says. I don't know what she means unless it is a reference to my time in Ancient Greece. I doubt there is any need for that here. "You will speak with the prisoner and ascertain whether or not Ceto is indeed with Queen Nyobi Kadul in the Mediterranean Sea. Your answer will determine our next move."

I look at the group of narrowed eyes, all staring at me. Some are still shaking their heads.

"I am ready to help in any way I can," I tell my leader, "but what is it that I can do that those already in this room cannot?" The leaders who have been shaking their heads mutter to one another. Lady Pescara shoots them a warning look and they quiet.

"Evelyn," she says, "you are uniquely qualified because you have previous experience with the prisoner."

"Ma'am?" I ask. I don't think I want to know who the prisoner is.

"A few weeks ago, our troops were finalizing their reports on Ceto's fortress," she tells me. "While they were securing the last of the rooms in the treasury, they came across some of Ceto's followers. They were trying to steal her treasure, no doubt to help her buy more followers. Our soldiers were able to capture three of them. The rest got away. Our regiment arrived in Atlantis with the prisoners only a week ago."

"Who were the prisoners?" I ask against my will.

"Two of the prisoners were new recruits from the other side of the Atlantic Ocean," she says. "One is someone you know. James O'Brien."

My heart stops. James. My James. Did Jack know he was here? I look to my side, but Jack is avoiding my gaze. He definitely knew. Why didn't he tell me? Why didn't he tell me that the James who betrayed me when he made out with my best friend and roommate, Gwen, is a prisoner in Atlantis? The same James who betrayed Ceto to follow Gwen in a subplot to destroy both Atlantis and Ceto. James who was the most brutal of the guards to the prisoners in Ceto's fortress. That James. That James was captured, and I have to interrogate him. I hope they keep a guard in the room. For his safety.

I face Lady Pescara again and feel Jack's eyes on my back. He knows I'm mad. He should have prepared me for this.

"Where is he?" I ask. "I will learn whatever I can from him."

Lady Pescara nods. She approves, not that I need her approval anymore. I have enough motivation for the entire army. James is on my list of enemies.

"The girl betrayed Atlantis," a female captain interjects, "she cannot be trusted." The head shakers mumble their agreement. I have no idea what they mean. I have done everything for Atlantis. Lady Pescara addresses me again.

"Evelyn," she says, "Several of my choicest leaders are concerned that your behavior in the battle with Ceto were acts of treason. We debated the evidence on hand and from your accounts as they were relayed to us by Captain Jack." I don't dare turn to look at him, afraid I won't be able to keep myself calm. I keep my eyes focused on Lady Pescara.

"It was determined by special council that you were acting in behalf of the army of Atlantis," she continues. "It was a difficult decision to reach, and as you can see, not everyone agrees with the council's findings." Lachlan's eyes are on mine. He believes in me. I can see it in his steely gaze. His conviction ripples through his small, sea dragon body. For the first time, I notice tinges of grey in his plumage. Is he aging quickly like Chelsea's parents did?

"Lady Pescara," he booms from his tiny body, "I will gladly take the blame for any of Recruit Marin's actions as it was I who encouraged them." Lady Pescara looks down on the sea dragon.

"General Lachlan," she says, "your actions are not in question here. You have already explained yourself to the council and been found guiltless. We have not yet heard from Miss Marin's own lips and desire to do so now, before we take her to the prisoner."

"Evelyn," she says. She holds her hand out toward me. "Will you come to the front of the room and submit to the questions of the war council?"

"Is there time for this?" I ask. "Don't you need answers I can provide to you by talking to the prisoner? What is more important to you? Separating truth from lies in James or hearing truth again from me?" Lady Pescara lowers her hand and raises her chin.

"I must have the trust of Atlantis' leaders," she says. "As you heard, General Lachlan was already able to appear before the council and answer questions to their satisfaction. I will grant a few questions from the council convened here with me today so they can reassure themselves of your loyalty. If you refuse, you will not be allowed to see the prisoner and you will not be trusted to join our forces in further conflict. What do you choose?"

My eyes move about the room and meet the gaze of everyone there. Lady Pescara's silvery blue eyes show no emotion, only determination. Uncle Russ's eyes are pleading. Lachlan's eyes are apologetic. The old merwoman's eyes are questioning and the captain's eyes are distrustful. The remaining officers in the room look at me steadily, waiting to see what I will do. Some seem sympathetic, others are skeptical.

"Then let's have the questions," I say, "so I can get to the prisoner and find the information you are looking for." Before I swim to Lady Pescara, I step on Jack's toe a little too hard. He makes a small noise and I swim to the front of the desk. Everyone takes a seat in the rows of chairs in front of Lady Pescara's desk.

They are a serious and formidable group. Lady Pescara floats by my side.

"We have time for only a few questions," she says, "only enough to bring peace of mind. This council will not waste time going over territory that has already been discussed." She looks to each person in the room. "You may ask your questions."

The old merwoman rises from her chair, "Lady Pescara," she says, "would it be beneficial to first hear of the account in Recruit Marin's own words? Any discrepancies to the council's findings will be easily discerned and several questions answered without the need for a lengthy ordeal." Lady Pescara nods.

"Thank you General Bleyl," she says, "if it is pleasing to the council, we will turn the time over to Miss Marin to hear her description of the events. All in favor?"

"Aye."

"Any opposed?" The room is quiet. "The Ayes have it. Recruit Marin, please share with the council what happened on the evening in question. We want your description of the events in the battle with Ceto. Remember to be thorough but quick. We have no time to waste." Lady Pescara sits again in her chair and everyone looks at me. I find Jack's eyes. He looks sheepish enough. I straighten my shoulders and begin.

"The day before we were called to battle," I say, "I was approached by Gwen Mizrahi." There is mumbling in the room. Gwen was my roommate and best friend, but she is also Ceto's daughter. "Gwen had a plan to reach the power source before her mother did. She didn't want to flood the earth like her mother, but she did want to rule the oceans.

"I knew I had to find help. But as I swam back to Atlantis with Gwen's guard, whom you know as General Lachlan, he stopped me and told me of a plan of his own." Everyone shifts their eyes to Lachlan. He keeps his eyes on mine, encouraging me to continue.

"Lachlan knew about Gwen's plan to destroy her mother and rule the ocean. He knew about Ceto's plan to flood the world. He also knew that the leaders in Atlantis would not listen to him because of his species and his size." Several officers lower their gaze. Lady Pescara nods to Lachlan.

"And he was correct," she says. "We were too confident in our information and plans. If he hadn't acted when he did, we would have had a vastly different outcome." Lachlan nods to his general.

"Lachlan told me he had an army of outcasts ready to follow me," I say, "I'm not anything special, but Lachlan knew Ceto was my aunt and that my parents, Kai and Marisol Marin, were some of Atlantis' most devoted citizens. He believed I could help the army." Lachlan rises from his seat.

"I knew you were special, Miss Marin," he says, "I knew you would help us, and you did." More mumbles throughout the room.

"We aren't here to hear how special Recruit Marin is," the female captain from before calls out. "We are here to determine for ourselves her role in the attack and whether or not she is a traitor." Lachlan spins to face her, ready to argue, but Lady Pescara stops him.

"Yes, Captain Sidhu," she says, "I second your thoughts. General Lachlan, please return to your seat. Evelyn, please continue." Lachlan lowers. He is red with frustration.

"As soon as I left Lachlan," I continue, "I went to find my mother."

"Why did you seek her out?" Captain Sidhu asks. "Why not go straight to Lady Pescara?"

"I don't know," I answer. "She is my mother and she was staying with Lady Pescara. I knew she would believe me and would know what to do.

"I woke Lady Pescara, looking for her. When she wasn't there, I headed for the hospital where Lady Pescara said she was visiting an injured friend. But when I arrived, that friend was actually my father." A few of the officers clear their throats. Everyone thought my father was dead. That was until we discovered that he was really trapped as one of Ceto's mind-controlled prisoners.

"And what did your mother say when you finally told her about the traitor to Atlantis?" Captain Sidhu asks.

"She believed me," I answer. "She believed me, but an enemy of Atlantis, disguised as my father's nurse, tried to stop me from leaving. There was fighting, but I escaped. So did my parents. They told me to go to Lady Pescara. By the time I reached her, the army had been assembled for battle. I tried to talk to her, but she wouldn't listen." I glance back at Lady Pescara. Her fingers are pressed together at her lips. She nods.

"I was in battle mode," she says. "I was moving an army and wouldn't stop for anything. I'm glad you did what you did." She looks at me. I nod to her.

"I met my parents on the training field. Lachlan came with his army and they followed me."

"How did you know where to go?" General Bleyl asks.

"I didn't," I answer. "Well, not with a map or anything. I was following the pull inside of me."

"The pull inside of you?!" Captain Sidhu says. "What does that mean, Recruit Marin?"

"My whole life the ocean has called to me," I say. "I thought I just wanted to be where my father went missing, but it was more than that. I was being called by the Atlantean Power Source. I was called by Pearl. She had a job for me to do."

"And what job was that?" Captain Sidhu asks.

"I didn't know at the time," I answer, "but she needed me to free her from her prison." The Captain opens her mouth to ask another question.

"Lady Pescara," Uncle Russ interjects, "all this questioning is taking away from the issue at hand. Permission to let Recruit Marin finish her explanation uninterrupted."

"I agree with you General Salvesen," Lady Pescara says. "Evelyn, you may continue with your description of the battle. There will be no further interruptions."

I nod to the mermaid general and face the group again.

"I followed the direction my body naturally wanted to go and landed face-to-face with Gwen and Ceto. The army of Atlantis wasn't far behind and soon everyone was fighting. Eventually, I went to the surface of the sea to counteract the hurricane Ceto was brewing above the waves. But the battle continued below, and I knew I still had to find the power source before Ceto or Gwen did.

"My mother joined me at the surface and she and the air took over the battle above the sea. I made it back to the underwater tunnels without being detected. I swam all the way to the underwater ruin of Poseidon's temple where I found the power source.

"Within moments, the room was filled with fighters. Gwen was there. I knew she wanted the power source and I knew I had to save it. I reached out and took hold of the pearl before Gwen could. The room filled with light and I was transported into the Pearl's body. She was a living, breathing, cursed human in Ancient Greece, not just a source of power and strength. I had to save her from the curse she was living in. It didn't take long to realize I had to save myself, too."

"When the light burst in the room," Lady Pescara says, "You vanished. There was general pandemonium for several minutes. Then the fighting resumed. Our forces pushed the enemy army out of our city and back to the open sea. Captain Jack remained by Poseidon's temple in case you returned."

"I'm glad he did," I say. "I couldn't breathe when I came back. Captain Jack saved my life." More mumbling fills the room. Some muttering their relief at the outcome. Some grumbling that they don't believe the story. I look to Jack and he smiles. I guess I can't be too mad at him over James. He did save my life, after all. Lady Pescara rises from her chair and the room grows quiet again.

"Miss Marin has completed her account of the events," she says. "Ladies and Gentlemen, time is of the essence. Are there any further questions or will we proceeded to send Miss Marin to the prisoner?"

An older merman rises from his chair. "I am satisfied, Lady Pescara," he says. "Recruit Marin's account aligns with the findings of the council. I move to have her escorted to the prisoner."

"Motion noted," Lady Pescara says. "All in favor?"

"Aye."

"Any opposed?" The room is quiet again. Captain Sidhu doesn't look happy, but she is still for now.

"Motion carried," Lady Pescara says. "Captain Jack, please escort Recruit Marin to the prison. The prisoner in question is in cell 2-4-3. Recruit Marin," she turns to me, "It is the request of this council that you interview the prisoner. Find out from him what he knows of Ceto's location and her plans. We must know if she has reached Nyobi Kadul and if they are working together. Learn what you can of Gwen. What are her whereabouts? What are her plans? Is she siding with her mother or is she still plotting against her? Learn what you can. Our actions depend on the answers you bring to us."

I nod to Lady Pescara, "I will, my lady," I answer. Captain Jack moves to the door and I follow. The officers in the room rise from their chairs as I pass by. Uncle Russ squeezes my arm. Lachlan puffs out his chest. I smile at them both.

I follow Jack out of Lady Pescara's office and into the cold halls of the justice building. The building was an old temple in Ancient Atlantis. Not the central temple where Poseidon was worshipped, but a temple built by a nobleman. It is one of the buildings resting on top of the sand of new Atlantis. Poseidon's temple was buried.

I follow Jack down the stairs and into the open streets of Atlantis. Neither of us speaks. I can barely breathe, but I cannot hold his hand. I'm not quite ready to fully forgive him for letting me be blind-sided. When we finally make it to the prison and past the guards who watch over it, I am not prepared for what I see. There, leaning against the bars of his cell, and staring at me like he is the one in control, is James, my former boyfriend, my nothing. He is nothing to me but a means to an end anymore. But that doesn't explain what I do next.

I swim to his cell as he opens his sneering mouth to speak, but before he can say a single word, I reach through the bars, grab his shirt to pull him close and punch him squarely in the face.

CHAPTER 4

"I'm not sure why you think I'm going to tell you something different than I told your merman guards. Especially now." James glares at me through the rusting iron bars of Atlantis' underwater prison, rubbing his cheek where I hit him. My knuckles are throbbing, but I don't massage them. I can't let him know that I am hurt. I want him to feel the threat.

"I don't want you to tell me something different as long as what you told them was the truth," I say. Jack stands to the side, eyes narrowed at my old boyfriend. He looks torn between protecting me and not protecting James. James laughs, glancing at Jack for a moment.

"We could have been so much together, Evelyn," he says, pausing. Then he risks another punch as he swims closer to reach through the bars and touch my hair. He's just trying to get a reaction from me. Or from Jack.

It works.

"Keep your hands away from her!" Jack says. He moves to the cell and grabs James by the wrist. "You earned your place in that cell. Now stay there!" Jack shoves James' hand back through the bars. I don't move away.

"Oh, a little protective, are we?" James asks. "You two wouldn't happen to be together, would you?" Neither Jack nor I reply. James laughs. "Fine. Fine," he says. "I won't touch her, but don't expect me to cooperate either. I may be a prisoner here, but I'm not stupid. I have nothing more to say."

I put my hand on Jack's shoulder. "I've got this," I tell him. "Just let me do the talking."

"Yeah, pretty boy," James taunts from his cell, "Evelyn is a pretty good talker. I've heard her talk for a long time. Can't say I got much out of it, but I heard her, just the same. She's a good kisser, too."

Jack steps forward again, his hands balled into fists, but I stop him.

"He's just trying to make you mad, Jack," I say. "Let me handle it." Jack sighs and moves back to his post against the wall, running his fingers through his hair.

"That's a good boy, Jack-Jack," James says from his cell, "do as you're told." Jack glares at James then looks at me. I roll my eyes and shake my head. He's got to let it go if we are going to learn anything here.

"James," I say.

"Yes, Evelyn?"

"Where is Ceto now?"

"It's like I told the stringy seahorse and his entourage of buff mermen," he says, "I don't know. The last time I saw her, she was sitting on a throne, but by now, she might be sitting at a table eating shellfish."

"Is she in the Mediterranean?" I ask.

"Maybe, yes. Maybe, no," he answers.

"What about Gwen?" I ask. James is quiet for a second.

"What about her?" he asks.

"Where is she? Is she with Ceto? In the Mediterranean? Or is she on her own?" James shakes his head.

"I don't have anything more to say," he tells me.

"This is a waste of time, Evelyn," Jack says. "Let's go back to the council."

"Give me a few more minutes," I tell him. James laughs and sits on his cot.

"It's like I said, Evelyn," he tells me, "I don't have anything more to say."

"I know," I answer. I don't need him to say anything else. I have an idea.

When I was in Ancient Greece, Pearl told me I was a part of her, and she was a part of me. I learned to use her powers there. I could read minds and make people hallucinate while I was trapped in her body. I want to see if those powers are still with me. It may not work, but it is worth a try.

I focus my attention on James and close my eyes. I search inside my head for the power I grew accustomed to 2,400 years ago, but I can't find it. Then something pulls from inside. I search my heart and discover a remnant of Pearl's power there, waiting to be found.

Hello, I whisper to my heart. The beating answers me.

Hello, Evelyn, she says. *I'm glad you knew to look for me.*

So am I, I answer. *Shall we work together like we used to?*

Yes.

Excellent.

I open my eyes and cannot help the smile that creeps onto my face. It makes me laugh.

"What's so funny?" James asks. I just shake my head.

With my heart open and searching, I send out tiny white tendrils toward James. He can't see them. Neither can Jack. They are pieces of me and pieces of Pearl.

I send the pale strands to James' mind. He is quiet and still, waiting for me to say something. But I have nothing to say. I have everything to see.

I enter his memories, searching for what I am looking for. I see the battle months ago and see James escaping with Gwen. I see Ceto's army traveling east. Gwen breaks away from her mother at her earliest opportunity and James goes with her. They hide near Ceto's fortress. The day James is captured by the army of Atlantis, he is taking money from Ceto's treasury but is intercepted by Ceto's followers who were sent to do the same thing. They threaten to take him back to Ceto if he doesn't take them to Gwen.

"Ceto is with her mother now," they tell him. "A queen even more powerful and dangerous than she is. Tell us where Gwen is, and you'll have the chance to live. Don't tell us, and we will force her location out of you."

James considers their offer. He is trapped. He doesn't want to turn Gwen in, but he is not always loyal to the women in his life.

"She's hiding in the ancient tombs," he tells them. Ceto's followers smile and reach forward to take James, but there is a noise from outside the treasury. Ceto's followers swim back through the maze of tunnels of Ceto's fortress city, leaving James behind. He has to get to Gwen to tell her to run, but he is too late. He is captured and taken prisoner by the Atlantean army.

"Ceto is in the Mediterranean with Queen Nyobi Kadul," I tell Jack. "Gwen has been hiding in the tombs beneath Ceto's city fortress, but she has probably left since James didn't come back. She may have been captured, though. James told Ceto's followers where to find her."

James' nostrils flare and he is still as a statue.

"How do you know that?" Jack asks me. I turn to face him.

"I didn't live in Pearl's body for seven years for nothing," I say. "I have remnants of her power still."

"What does that mean?" James growls under his breath.

"It means I read your mind," I tell him. I turn my back and swim out of the room. Jack follows closely behind.

"You read his mind?" Lady Pescara asks as I stand across from her. She is seated as Jack and I deliver our report.

"Yes, ma'am," I answer.

"And how exactly did you do that?" she asks.

"When I was trapped in Pearl's body," I tell her, "I learned to use her power to control and enter the minds of others. A piece of that power is still there. It's not as strong as it was in Ancient Greece, but it is still there."

Lady Pescara is quiet for a moment before answering.

"How long have you known you could do this?" she asks.

"I didn't know before today, ma'am," I say. "This was the first time I thought to try."

"And you can control people with your mind?" she asks.

"I could in Ancient Greece, Lady Pescara," I answer. "I don't know if I can do that here. The power is not as strong in our time." Lady Pescara rises from her desk and paces the room, her large fin propelling her through the water. I feel the force of her tail each time she sways. She is stronger than I realized.

"This is dangerous information," Lady Pescara says. "How many people know about this?"

"My mom knows I had the powers in Atlantis," I tell her. "Jack and you and I are the only ones who know I have it here. And James." Lady Pescara pauses.

"And James?" she asks. Her eyebrows furrow and she glares at me. "You told him you read his mind?"

I am embarrassed. Why did I have to throw it in his face? James is a prisoner and I told him my tactic.

"The prisoner was antagonistic," Jack says, "Evelyn reinforced his position as prisoner."

Lady Pescara looks at Jack then back at me. "Evelyn," she says, "I'm sure I don't have to tell you that letting him know your secret was a grievous error."

"Yes, ma'am," I say. "I apologize." My face is burning red and I can barely hear my own voice. Lady Pescara sighs and paces again.

"We will have to keep him quarantined," she says. "We will ban any contact with other prisoners and carefully choose and monitor his guards. I don't want this information to get out."

"Yes, Lady Pescara," Jack and I both answer.

Lady Pescara sighs and returns to her desk.

"Evelyn, I will take this information back to the council," she says, "leaving out your newly acquired skill set. You will have to report for duty with Captain Jack and the rest of your group of 50 by the end of the day. You have an hour to reacquaint yourself with Atlantis and visit your father. That will be all."

My father. Dad. My heart skips a beat and I smile. I can't get out of this office fast enough; I'm so eager to see him again.

Jack and I bow to Lady Pescara and leave her office.

"Your dad's office is on the lower level, Evelyn," Jack says. "Do you want me to take you to him?"

"No, thank you," I say. "I'd like to go alone."

"Okay."

Jack gives me a quick kiss on the cheek. I lean in for more, but he puts his finger to my lips. "Slow," he whispers. I lean into the feel of his finger on my mouth, close my eyes, and kiss it. Too soon, the pressure leaves and Jack swims to away to work with his group of 50. I have to take deep breaths and clear my head before turning away. The hallway on the lower level of the building is lined with doors. The doors are a new, metal design, created to withstand the caustic waters of the Atlantic Ocean. They are a stark contrast to the Ancient block and marble doorways they are attached to. Each door has a placard on the outside with the name of an official mounted clearly. I swim down the row, reading each placard.

General Salvesen, Master of Recruits

General Bleyl, Master of the Courts

General Lachlan, Master of Sea Creature Resources

Kai Marin, Secretary

I stop at the last door. My dad's office. He is secretary not only for Lady Pescara, but for the other council members. I remember enough about Atlantis to know that this isn't his office alone, he has a group working with him, but he is the main point of contact for the highest-ranking officers. Because of his years of imprisonment and mind manipulation by Ceto, he is no longer capable of serving as a soldier or an officer in the army. His body is too weak. His mind has dealt with all it can.

I stop in front of the heavy door kept ajar as messengers bustle in and out. A secretarial desk, piled high with wax-coated papers and piles of notes, is the first place I stop. But my dad isn't sitting behind this overflowing desk. A merwoman named Catarina (her name etched on the edge of her desk) is there shuffling through papers, pushing her glasses up her nose. All but one of her long, dark braids are tied behind her back. The single, rogue braid floats in the open water above her head. Catarina looks up at me over the tops of her glasses.

"How can I help you, honey child?" she asks in a distinct southern accent.

"I'm looking for Kai Marin," I tell her. "He's my father." Catarina jumps out of her seat.

"Your father?!" she says, swimming over her desk to get to me, "Well, let me just give you a hug, you sweet thing." And before I know it, I am squeezed in her pillowy arms. "Your daddy has told us all *so* much about you." Her voice drops to a whisper like she is telling me a secret. I have to strain to hear her. "And about his time in Ceto's fortress, bless his soul." Catarina pauses and shakes her head. She sighs and flashes me a smile again, eyes brightening. "Well, we certainly can't let you wait a moment longer, no we can't."

She takes me by the hand and pulls me through the water to the back of the secretaries' office and taps her fingers on a glass-windowed door. Shadows move behind the frosted glass and the door opens. Without a thought, I let go of Catarina's hand and wrap my arms around the merman's neck, hugging him tight. I feel the jagged bones of his shoulders digging into my chin, but I don't care.

I welcome the sensation. His boney arms wrap around my waist, squeezing me close. It is such a different feeling than hugging Catarina whose ample arms were so warm and inviting. I'd hoped he would have been healthier by now. But he isn't, so I squeeze him even tighter, willing the life back into his body. Catarina sniffs.

"Oh, my girl," my dad says. "My sweet, beautiful Evelyn."

I cry and he holds me. When I can't take the pain of his shoulder in my face anymore, I pull back and look at him.

"Dad," I say. "Dad I've missed you so much. How are you?"

"Wonderful now that you are here," he says. He kisses my forehead with dry lips then pulls away. "Thank you for bringing her to me Catarina. What a wonderful surprise in my day."

"You're sure welcome," Catarina says through thick tears. She wipes at her nose with a moss handkerchief she pulls from her shirt. "I love a happy ending." She turns from us and heads back to her desk. Dad shakes his head.

"Catarina is a kind-hearted woman," he says. Then he smiles at me. "Well, my wonderful girl, come sit down and we will catch up. Your mom will be here soon." I smile and go in.

Dad's office looks like an array of items taken from sunken ships. His desk is covered in barnacles except for a small, flat area where he can work. There are telescopes and globes lining the moss-covered shelves. The chair he offers me is decayed, though the cloth seat has been refurbished. One large window overlooks Atlantis and the open ocean. I can see the edges of the city from his office on the hill. Groups are practicing on the training fields, college students are swimming back to their barracks, groups are heading to the mess hall. The current controllers keep their shield moving to protect the city. Beyond the city, the Atlantic spreads into the darkness. The glow that keeps Atlantis alight does not extend to the empty water beyond. The black ocean feels like a home for hidden enemies.

I look at my dad. He was graying and thin when I first met him in Ceto's fortress. For me that was over seven years ago. For him it was just a few months. The haunted look that covered his face while he was under Ceto's mind control has faded away. There is knowledge in his countenance now, recognition of the world around him. He sees me now without the cloudy fog of her power. I wish his body had recovered as much. He is all jagged angles, flaking skin, though his color at least is starting to improve. He is walking a thin line between looking like a merman and resembling a sea monster.

"I've missed you, my girl," he says as he sits on the other side of his desk. "But I'm so proud of all you have done. For Atlantis, for everyone. Your mom has told me so much. You have been through so much." His voice catches in his throat and he cries, pulling out his own handkerchief from his pocket.

"Oh, Dad," I say, reaching across the desk to lay my hand on his arm. "Everything will be okay now. I'm home." But even I don't believe my own words. I don't know why I said them. But it feels like the right thing to say. My dad wipes his eyes and takes a deep breath.

"You're right," he says, tucking his handkerchief into a drawer. "There's no need to dwell on that until you're ready. I do

46

love you, Evelyn. I'm sorry for all you have endured." He pats my hand. I smile at my dad, looking so breakable. I want to change the conversation.

"How are you and mom doing?" I ask. It's not the best question, but it's the best I could come up with. It has to be awkward to be living with your wife again after more than a decade apart. Dad smiles.

"We're okay, darling," he says. "It's a big adjustment to live as man and wife, well, merman and wife, after all this time. We're both doing the best we can. She is with me here in Atlantis most nights now. We have a little house outside of the city. Lady Pescara is worried about our safety, but we need the time together and alone."

"I'm sure it hasn't helped that Mom's spent so much time on land with me," I say.

"Oh, Evelyn," he says, "neither of us would have it any other way. We'll be fine. You'll see."

There is a knock at the door.

"That must be your mom, now," he says. He rises from his seat and swims to answer the door. But it isn't my mom.

"Mr. Marin," a man's voice says at the door, "Lady Pescara desires to speak with your daughter."

"We were just waiting for my wife so we could eat dinner together," my dad says. The man at the door steps into the room. He is a two-worlder who has just started living full time in the ocean. I recognize the scales growing around his waist. His ocean leggings fit just below the scales. I wonder if that is uncomfortable for him. The blue sash around his torso tells me he is one of Lady Pescara's personal guards. He steps to me through the water, past my dad, and bows.

"I apologize for having interrupted your plans, Miss Marin," he says, "but Lady Pescara insists that it is urgent."

"If she could wait just a little while longer," I say, "I haven't seen my dad in months. I haven't even been with my parents together yet."

"Surely Lady Pescara can wait until after dinner," my dad says, "Just give us a little time before she whisks Evelyn away."

"I'm sorry, sir," the guard says, "I have my orders. It is a matter of war."

"Everything is a matter of war," my dad says to the guard. "Hang the war. I will not let my child go so easily." He takes my hand and faces the guard. "Where she goes, I go." The guard is young and strong. He could easily toss my dad aside, but he knows enough to maintain respect.

"I understand, sir," he says, "and I'm sorry for the interruption. But Lady Pescara has given me orders and I will obey them." He straightens then looks to me again.

"Recruit Marin. Please come with me." I don't want to risk an argument between my dad and the guard. I don't know what my dad's body can handle. I don't want to leave, but I do want to diffuse the situation.

"Of course, I'll come," I answer as I stand. I wrap my arms around my dad, trying to create a memory of each boney piece. "Maybe the business will be quick. I can join you and mom soon," I try to reassure him, but I don't believe the words I'm saying. Lady Pescara wouldn't be willing to call me back so quickly, not now, not when I'm finally with my dad again. Whatever she needs won't be quick. I squeeze my dad again, mindful of his angular body, before letting him go.

The guard leaves the room and I turn to follow him. I stop and reach for my dad. I put my hand on his cheek and look into his sad eyes. "If it takes too long, can I have a rain check on dinner, Dad?" he smiles at me, takes my hand, and holds it to his heart.

"Yes," he says. "Rain check." He kisses my fingers. "I love you, my girl. I always have. I always will."

I kiss his cheek because I can't talk without crying. I swim away and out of his office. Catarina is blocking the doorway, pretending to be filing something. The guard has a difficult time getting by without pushing against her.

"It's a shame you couldn't have more than just a few minutes time with your daddy, Miss Evelyn," she says when she straightens. I smile at her as I pause in the doorway.

"I agree, Catarina," I say when she hugs me. "I hope I'll be back soon. Take care of my dad for me, won't you? He needs to eat more." Catarina nods and sniffs. I let her go, bumping into my mom as I swim out.

"Evelyn!" she says, embracing me. "I am so happy for you! I knew you could get here. Let's grab your dad and go get some of that mess hall food they're handing out. You can tell us all about your day." When she pulls back and looks at my face, her smile fades and her eyes grow dark.

"I'm sorry, Mom," I say. "It looks like we may have to take a rain check. Lady Pescara called me to her office." I pull myself from her arms to follow the guard. I can hear her talking to Catarina and my dad. Their voices fade. I wonder if my dad will tell my mom exactly what happened when the guard came to his office or if he will try to soften the story, making it sound like I'll be back and there won't be a big problem. I wonder if my mom will follow me and demand to be in the meeting with Lady Pescara. Before I can wonder any longer, I am at Lady Pescara's door again and there is no one but me and her guard.

"Come in," Lady Pescara says when her guard knocks on her office door. He opens it and announces me. "Thank you, Daniel," she says. "Evelyn, please come have a seat."

Daniel closes the door behind him, and I see that I am not the only person called to meet with Lady Pescara. Jack is already seated by her desk. I sit in the chair next to his.

"Do you have a passport?" Lady Pescara asks me. I crease my eyebrows and shrug.

"I did before I left seven years ago," I say. "Nothing else has disappeared, so I'm sure I still have it." An uneasy feeling makes my stomach queasy.

"Good," she says. "I have just received some alarming news. Several of our spies have returned from the Mediterranean. Their reports are disturbing. They tell me that Nyobi has an entire town under her control."

"I didn't know she was still so powerful," I say. "She's ancient." Lady Pescara nods.

"She is ancient," she says. "But with her daughter to help her, she is capable of more. Ceto found a relic belonging to the Queen and restored it to her. That, combined with the Queen's powers and Ceto's, gives her the strength she needs to control the town."

"What is she making them do?" I ask. Lady Pescara is quiet then looks to Jack. He turns to face me.

"Our spies tell us they are sending their own children into the sea," he says. "At least one child each day."

"Why is she doing that?" I ask.

"We believe she is amassing her army that way," Lady Pescara says. "Children are still moldable, easier to control, and won't fight against her in her weakened state. She can train them however she sees fit. She is bringing them to the ocean and turning them into her soldiers." My stomach turns. A child army.

"How can even they be in an underwater city without being two-worlders?" I ask. "Why are the people willing to let their children be taken?"

"That is what I want you to find out," Lady Pescara says. "You have a remnant of Pearl's power still living within you. You have experience with both Ceto and Nyobi. You are my only recruit who has lived in that part of the world."

"That was thousands of years ago!" I say. "It can't possibly be the same!"

"Nonetheless, you are at least familiar with the region," she says. "These people are the descendants of the people you lived with and loved, Evelyn. If anyone will be devoted to helping them and helping Atlantis, it will be you.

"I'm sending Captain Jack with you and your companion, Chelsea. She is a rare two-worlder who began her life as a sea-dweller. Her perspective may be useful as you navigate foreign waters. If I send a large garrison, they would attract too much attention to themselves. Not to mention how slow they would be. You will fly out today. Travel by sea, no matter how fast, is not as fast as air travel."

I look at Jack. There is no smile on his handsome face. He knows there is no other way and so I trust him. What other choice do I have? He will be with me. Chelsea will be with me. They can make up for whatever I lack. I hope Lady Pescara is willing to tell my parents for me because they aren't going to be happy.

"When do we go?" I ask. "How much time will I have to prepare?"

"You leave tonight."

CHAPTER 5

There is barely time enough for explanation when my mom and dad meet me outside Lady Pescara's office. My mom is yelling so loud that several people pause to see what is happening. But it's an open and closed case. I am a soldier. I signed up for this life. I am needed to serve Atlantis, and as a soldier in Atlantis' army, I have no choice but to obey. To disobey my orders would mean imprisonment for me and increased danger for the two-worlders I love.

Mom and Dad pull me back into Lady Pescara's office, but I slip from their fingers and take Jack by the hand. We swim together through the chilled water, silently obeying as we must. I hear my mom and dad calling to me and arguing with Lady Pescara. But it won't help. I know what has to be done. Hot tears burn my eyes. I dig my fingernails into Jack's hand, accidentally drawing blood, but he doesn't say anything about it. The pain has to go somewhere. The sooner we win this war, the sooner I can at least look for the peace I crave and the sooner my family can be whole again.

It doesn't take long for Jack and Chelsea and me to be ready to leave our watery home for the journey to land. Mom tries to follow, so guards have to keep her in check. My dad wraps his arms around her shoulders, his face a twisted picture of pain. Chelsea insists that I ride her to the top of the continental shelf. I don't think I could swim there myself – I'm too torn. I need someone else to take me there.

I climb onto Chelsea's back, wrapping my arms around her neck. Her colorful tendrils surround me and hide my face from view. I let my head rest there and communicate silently to the enormous creature.

I'm afraid, I say, my tears flowing into the Atlantic. *I don't know how I will face this.*

You won't be facing it alone, she reassures me. *Jack is here and I will never leave your side. We are in this together.*

Chelsea sends waves of warmth to me and lets me ride silently to the top of the continental shelf. Her presence is comforting as I cry quietly into her beautiful mane. I'm glad she is with me.

When we reach the top of the continental shelf, I climb down from her back. Jack dismounts from his own companion and pats his neck. His companion is a fish like Pisces, not a two-worlder, so he has to stay behind. I know it will be difficult for Jack until they are reunited.

I turn my attention away from Jack and look at my own companion and my heart skips a beat. Chelsea is glimmering from nose to tail; each leafy tendril is lit up like a flame in the dark water. She is gold and shining more than any other sea creature I have seen on land or in the sea. As I watch her in awe, Jack swims next to me. He puts his hand on my shoulder and we watch my companion take her human form.

The light shining from Chelsea expands and fills the water. I feel its warmth as she sheds her cold-blooded body and embraces the warmth of a human. Soon, the leafy tendrils change their shape. The reds and pinks and golds that have swirled around her body move in tightly around her body. Her equine and dragon-like head shrinks and reshapes into the head of a human. The tendrils that encircle her head lay down to become soft, flowing, red hair. Her scales turn into freckles and her blue eyes retain their hue in her human form. Her body glows brighter and brighter. Jack turns his back to her so she can have privacy while her body becomes that of a young, human woman. I open my bag and pull out the swimsuit packed there for this purpose. Chelsea takes the purple one-piece, steps into it, and slips it over her human legs and arms.

When her transformation is complete and she is dressed, I nudge Jack. He turns around and smiles at the beautiful young woman before us.

"That is quite the change, Chelsea," he says. "I've never seen anything like it. You're magnificent." Chelsea blushes and nods her head.

"Well, it's nice to know it works out well when I don't have any choice in the matter," she says. "Shall we go?"

We all turn our gaze up to the sloping sea bottom before us and begin the swim to shore. None of us says anything, our minds are too full. When we arrive onshore, there is a van waiting for us with everything we need inside for the journey. We change into dry clothing, pull out the passports and tickets that have been collected for us and settle in for the drive to the airport.

I watch out the window as the world passes by me. Numbness seeps into my bones even though Jack's arm is around me. I am leaving a long day behind and the beloved city and life I am ready to give my own life for. How many days and worlds will I live through and leave before I can finally have peace?

CHAPTER 6

"Evelyn!"

"Pearl!"

"Evelyn!"

"Athena!"

Names are shouted all around me. Evelyn – my real name. Pearl – the name of the girl whose body I was trapped inside in Ancient Greece. Athena – the name I used to protect myself and Pearl while hiding from our ancient enemies.

In the crowd of voices, I recognize one, and it tears my heart in two. "Athena! Save me! Please, Athena! Don't leave me behind!"

His beautiful hazel eyes plead with me as he runs to my side, calling me by the name I had when we fell in love. His dark hand reaches toward me and touches my face. He runs his fingers across my cheek and up the back of my neck. They tangle in my hair as he pulls me close. His jet-black locks fall into his face – his beautiful face – as he pulls me closer and drops his voice to a whisper.

"Please, Athena," he says. "Don't leave me again. I gave myself for you. I cannot live without you." And he lowers his lips to mine.

"Gil. Gil," I whisper his name over and over between kisses. "I love you."

A gentle hand shakes my shoulder. I turn my head and open my eyes. Jack looks at me with a pained expression and a tear rolls down my cheek.

"We are about to land, Evelyn," he says softly. His hand reaches to my cheek and brushes away the tear. "You were dreaming." He kisses my forehead before turning away from me and waking up Chelsea.

I turn around and blink away the remnants of my dream. Gileaus is not here. I am no longer Athena. I am Evelyn. I say the words over and over in my head. I need to believe them. I need to wake up. This is my life now.

When the plane lands in Tel Aviv, I stare out the window at the world that awaits me. The last time I was in this part of the earth, I was surrounded by water, wagons, wooden boats, and rough-hewn stone. But the city around the airport shows no such signs. Instead, tall buildings built only decades ago, rise above the dry earth of the Mediterranean landscape. It is still not a city as modern as those in America, but it is no longer trapped in the ancient life that once flowed here.

We take a taxi from the airport to Jaffa. The whole time, Chelsea and Jack admire the changing landscape and foreign culture around them. The further we get from the city center, the more we see of ancient architecture. Glass and metal buildings give way to mud, brick and clay businesses that have served families for countless generations. The dry air doesn't hint to just how close we are to the sea until we finally catch the scent of salty ocean water on the cool breeze.

As we near Jaffa, cars and bicycles and pedestrians fill the streets. Open-air markets line the roadway and bustle with tourists and locals. I smile when I see the stands selling beans and lentils, fruit, and rice. Those stands lived in my time, sure with some variation, but open and humming with energy, nonetheless. I used to buy their food when I lived across the Mediterranean. I cooked their recipes and fed their ancestors. My heart and eyes open to the people around me. These are the descendants of those who traveled and worked and lived here thousands of years ago. I learned to love them then and I love them still.

Eventually, our taxi stops at the entrance of a narrow alleyway. The cobblestone street is encased by buildings the color of sandstone with brown and red tile rooves, leaving no space wide enough for the car to pass through. Jack pays the driver and we gather our belongings from the trunk. A boy, maybe 12-years-old, with a handcart is nearby and offers to carry our things to our hotel. We load our bags into the cart and follow the boy through the tight, stony streets.

The sounds of children playing and people doing business are all around us. Women lean out of their windows in the walls above us and gossip with their neighbors. Sometimes they look down at us, glare in our direction, then close their vibrantly painted shutters tight. Our boy with the cart tells us these are the gossipy women, too

59

caught in their old ways to like Americans. Children stop their playing to watch us as we pass by. Some try to sell us trinkets and food. I buy a bag of roasted nuts from a little girl in an oversized, threadbare dress and a long braid. She smooths the wrinkles of her skirt when she pockets the money. Chelsea buys a necklace from a little boy who is already growing out of his creamy white shirt. His smile is bright and his hair shines like polished mahogany. He gives her a bow and runs away when she pays him, eager to show his earnings to his friends. A few lines of laundry blow in the breeze over our heads. From the street I can see the patchwork colors of hand-crafted repairs and hand-me-downs made over into something new. The lines squeak when they are pulled by the women. Light, dry clothing disappears. Dark, wet clothing takes its place. Our cart rattles on the ground. Dogs, fighting over a fish, growl at each other. The sound of waves crashing against stone is the background to all this beautiful music.

When we finally stop at our hotel, we are only steps away from the Jaffa shoreline. The domain of Nyobi herself. Flags of blue and red and yellow line the shore and hang from the entrances of the businesses, making the whole place feel like a holiday.

Our hotel is a little bed and breakfast operated by a local man and his family. The boy with the cart talks to the man in a language I don't understand but has a tone of familiarity to it. The man listens to the boy chattering on and pats him on the shoulder.

"You are right, my Zaher," he says to the boy. "These are the Americans we were waiting for. But you'll not get off early for bringing them here. Unload their bags and get back to your post. A day's wage isn't earned in a single trip."

Zaher mumbles more in his native tongue and turns to Jack with his hand outstretched. Jack smiles and reaches into his pockets for some coins and bills to hand to him. Zaher's eyes grow wide and he runs away quickly with his cart and his tip, laughing on his way. We watch him go, making all kinds of racket on the cobblestone path, then turn to our host.

"You'll spoil him that way," the innkeeper says. "He must learn to work and earn his keep." But then he smiles and shakes his head as he watches his son disappear.

"I am Habib Jamal," he says in his thick accent, "and this is the house of Tahn. We welcome you." He bows to us and we return the bow.

"Thank you for having us here on such short notice," Jack says to Habib. "I'm Jack. This is Evelyn and Chelsea. We hoped to see the coast of Jaffa on our break. We're glad to have such a nice place to stay."

"It is our honor," says Habib. "I hope your stay here is everything you hoped it would be. Inbar!" he calls into the house. "Inbar! Our guests have arrived!"

A moment later, a soft and round woman in her mid-forties appears at the door. Her black hair with a few strands of silver is covered by a shawl. A smile spreads across her face.

"Ah, the Americans," she says. "We haven't had Americans in our home for a year or more."

"The Americans don't care whether or not other Americans have stayed here, Inbar," Habib whispers to his wife. "They just care that the place is clean and ready for them and that the food is good."

"Then the Americans will be quite pleased, won't they?" Inbar whispers with reproach to her husband. Then, turning to us she says, "Your rooms have been ready since this morning and I have a nice meal ready for you inside. I'm sure your travels here have been long and tiring. Habib will carry your things and I will show you to your room."

"Thank you," Jack, Chelsea, and I each say in turn. We pick up our bags as Habib takes the largest of them and we all follow Inbar into the house.

The home smells like cinnamon and nuts. I wonder if we will be eating anything I am familiar with while we are here. It isn't Greece, but their diets must share some similarities. We follow Inbar up a narrow staircase as she tells us about their home. The staircase is only wide enough for one person at a time. The walls are a rusty brown color and have a faint smell of earth to them, but the scent of earth is laced with the sharp and sweet spices of our dinner. My stomach growls.

"Habib and I have lived here since we were first married," Inbar says. "We took over the inn when my parents passed. It is where I was raised and where we have raised our children.

Hopefully, we will have grandchildren with us soon. Many generations of my family have lived here in these walls."

"It's amazing to live in a place where your ancestors lived," I say.

"It is a blessing to be sure," Inbar says, "though it does come with its disadvantages. Maintenance for one. If you could have seen the issue with the pipes we had a few years back…"

"Inbar," Habib hisses from behind us. "Enough about the pipes. The Americans don't want to hear about our pipes."

"The Americans will want to know about our pipes when they know we have fixed our pipes and they will not have any problems with the pipes," Inbar hisses back. "Ah, here we are. Ladies you will be staying on this floor. The young gentleman will be staying on the ground floor near our room."

"You could have mentioned that before we brought all the bags up here," Habib says.

"Nonsense," Inbar answers. "The young American doesn't mind carrying heavy things up and down the stairs. It shows off to the young ladies. And you know we can't have them on the same floor. They aren't married, Habib!"

Habib mumbles to himself as Chelsea and I take our bags and he heads back down the stairs. Inbar opens a dark, old wooden door and motions for Chelsea and me to go inside.

"Thank you very much," I say as I enter the room and set my bags down. "This is lovely."

"It is nothing," Inbar replies. "Your dinner is on the table there by the window. Call for me if you need anything. Breakfast will be ready when you get up in the morning." She hands the room key to Chelsea and heads back down the stairs, taking Jack along with her. We hear her voice trailing away, telling Jack all about the price of the pipe repair.

Chelsea closes the door and we take a moment to inspect our room. It is an old building – nearly ancient – and the feeling is like being transported back to my past life. The rough stone walls have been covered in plaster and painted yellow with intricate designs in blue and purple and red. Two beds are on the opposite wall from the door. A small window sits between them. To the right is a fireplace with wood already laid and ready for our use. The left side of the room is wide and open. A small, handmade rug sits in front of a large, hand carved armoire. Images of fishermen and their catch are etched into its surface. Beyond the armoire is a small bump-out that extends over the street. In its little alcove is the table with two chairs and food waiting for Chelsea and me. We clean our hands in the small washbasin by the armoire and head to our meal.

"I haven't eaten human food in so long," Chelsea says, "I don't know if I can stomach it."

"Don't worry," I tell her. "If you need my salad, it's all yours."

"Thank you," she says, and we sit down to our dinner. The little alcove has windows on all three sides. The small west window has a view of the ocean. Chelsea and I sit together, facing the sea.

The horiatiki salad only varies a little from what I remember from my time in Argos. The only difference is the oil and vinegar. They just aren't the same. Our main dish is a pot of warm tomato sauce with poached eggs inside. This is the first time I've ever had anything like it, and I am in heaven. A round, crusty bread loaf is the perfect way to finish the sauce. Chelsea tries everything, but she takes me up on my offer to eat the rest of my horiatiki. She isn't quite ready for the heavier foods.

"I wonder if Jack is eating as well as we are tonight," I say as I finish the last piece of bread.

"We could always text him and ask," Chelsea says, "but that means I would have to get my phone and it is way over there. My bed is so much closer. Besides, he is probably learning more about those pipes." I smile and shake my head.

"I definitely think we should wait until morning to ask him," I say. "How about we eat dessert and go to bed."

"You have never said anything so sensible," Chelsea says.

I pull the little basket from the other side of the table and lift the cloth napkin from the top. The smell of warm cinnamon makes its way to my nose. So many memories accompany this smell, but this time, the memories don't consume me. I remember the smell of James' cinnamon gum. I remember the night I made this dish for Dom and his mother in Argos. I remember fleeing. I remember finding Gileaus. I remember losing him. I remember Atlantis.

But all of that was a thousand lifetimes ago. So, I force the memories out of my mind, pour a little syrup over the cinnamon and nut dough balls and take a bite. I let the sweetness fill my mouth and hear Chelsea say, "Oh my gosh, Evelyn. These are amazing."

"Yes, they are," I say. I reach for a second ball and rest my eyes on the ocean. From where we sit, I can see for miles. Tourists are clearing away from the shoreline. Only a few swimmers are still in the twilight ocean water. I see the head of a young man, nearly half a mile away from where I sit. He bobs in the water, looking to the shore. I cannot see his features, but my mouth goes dry and I choke on my dessert. I cough and Chelsea hands me my water.

"Are you okay?" she asks.

"Yes. Thanks," I say, draining my glass. "It just went down the wrong way." I cough again then look to the ocean where I saw him. The water is empty. He has gone to shore, back to his hotel, then. He wasn't who I thought I saw – he's just another tourist. "I'm tired," I tell Chelsea. "I think I need to go to bed."

We clean up our table and leave the plates on a tray outside the door. We get ready for bed and climb gratefully into the fresh linens. Chelsea is passed out within minutes of her head hitting the pillow. As I drift off, I see him again in the water, bobbing up and down. I swim out to meet him and wrap my arms around his neck, sinking into the water with him. I kiss him over and over. My Gileaus.

CHAPTER 7

My sleep last night was unsettled at best. I spent most of the night tossing and turning, having nightmares about Gileaus in Atlantis. He was screaming and there was nothing I could so to reach him or save him. I awoke with a pounding headache at the start of a new day.

We had breakfast and have now started our walk through the streets of Jaffa. Chelsea and I have our swimsuits under our clothing and Jack is wearing his swimwear as shorts. We look like tourists out to explore the beautiful Jaffa shoreline.

"You must not spend all of your time at the beaches," Inbar scolded this morning as we left. "You have plenty of beaches in America. Just like children to miss the best parts of the city. You must visit Saint Peter's Church at the very least. You cannot come all this way just to miss that. What will your parents say?"

We promised her we would see more than the beach – that we just needed some time to unwind from our long journey and overcome our jet lag. It was enough to pacify her for the moment, but I am sure she will take us around Jaffa herself if we don't tour it before long.

"The human world creates such beautiful things," Chelsea says as we walk the ancient pathways. She is trailing her fingers along the walls, absorbing the feel of every nook and cranny in the ancient mud. "I've seen plenty of ruins under the sea, but they are so much better preserved on land. I would be happy to live my life here."

"It is pretty awesome," Jack agrees. "I'm impressed that people made all this by hand, and it's lasted for hundreds of years."

"Thousands," I correct. "Thousands of years."

I admire the buildings here. They remind me of my life in 400 BC when these buildings would have been here. I reach out my fingers like Chelsea and let them brush against the rough-hewn stone of the buildings. But with each ridge and valley of brick, I feel the hands of the slaves. I see them working to cut the stone. I feel their pain and their suffering and their imprisonment that built these beautiful places. I feel their pride in their work despite their circumstances. Knowing they were creating something lasting, useful, and beautiful gave them some satisfaction, even in their rough and meager existence. But that satisfaction was fleeting as each night they returned home, bloodied and exhausted, without enough to eat, watching their children suffer with hunger and disease. I drop my hand, unable to look at their past anymore.

We step down stone stairs and walk onto the rough, white sand, the beach much smaller than the beaches in Florida, and set up our space for the day. Laying out towels, and removing shoes and outerwear, we sit and enjoy the scenery. I sit between Jack and Chelsea and feel Jack's fingers brush mine as we look over the water and I rest my head on his shoulder. His gum is minty, and the scent is refreshing. I would kiss him right now if Chelsea wasn't sitting right next to us.

We are in a little bay with a few other tourists and locals. The blue of the ocean dulls the blue of the sky where they meet at the edge of the horizon. To our left, the tower of Saint Peter's Church stands like a sentinel overlooking the port of Jaffa. The buildings that surround the tower create an outcropping that reaches all the way to the water. The trees and greenery behind the church make the white stone that much more of a contrast in the landscape. The same stone creates the stairs that lead to the sand. A breakwater in front of the port protects the church from an angry ocean. On the right side of the bay, the beaches of Tel Aviv and more of the city push against the sea. A mix of modern and ancient architecture, it is the perfect blending of two worlds.

"I could stay here forever," I say, breathing in the salty sea air and feeling the gentle Mediterranean breeze. Chelsea mumbles in agreement and turns her face to the sun.

"It won't stay this beautiful if we stay here forever," Jack says. "It's time to do what we came to do." He is right, of course. I reluctantly lift my head from his shoulder and stretch my arms high above my head, looking around the beach.

The beach has enough tourists and holiday seekers to obscure a few swimmers who don't resurface from the bay. Jack is right. It's time to go.

Jack stands first and offers his hand to Chelsea and me. When we stand, we dust off the sand from our feet and legs. Jack shoulders our travel pack and we leave our other things on the ground. Chelsea's freckled face is already pink. We will have to remember sunblock for her even for the short trips in the sun. We walk through the warming sand; I'm in front with Jack and Chelsea right behind me.

As soon as my toes touch the water, I gasp and take a step back. The water in the Mediterranean is MUCH colder than the water off the Florida coastline. I knew it would be colder, but I was not prepared for this. It isn't freezing, but it is COLD! Jack laughs at me and Chelsea as she, too, jumps backward.

"What's the matter, ladies?" he asks. "Not what you were expecting?" He chuckles as he wades into the water. "You'll be fine. Just use your water warming strength. It won't take long to feel at home." He dives into the sea and Chelsea and I are left on the shoreline, goosebumps covering our shivering legs.

"Well, I'm not about to let him go without me," Chelsea finally says with a shaky breath. She inhales deeply and runs into the water at full speed, yelping the entire time. She takes another big gulp of air and plunges down, leaving me alone. I grumble to myself. I am going to have to suck it up and go for it.

I take a few paces back and get ready to run into the water. I race full speed ahead, laughing at myself for feeling so cold. I get as deep as my thighs and dive in. But right before my face hits the water, I see him, the young man from last night. The shock of the cold water hitting my chest is nothing compared to what I feel when I see his face. He is no more than ten feet away from me and his hazel eyes stare straight into mine as I dive. He opens his mouth to say something and takes a step toward me. I miss his words. Chelsea and Jack are already swimming into the deeper water, but I have to make sure I'm not hallucinating. I stand up where I am, the swells of the Mediterranean lifting and lowering me in the sea. But when my head breaks the surface, there is no one there. I look from side to side, checking to see if he swam somewhere else. There are tourists everywhere, but no Gilcaus. I shake my head and grumble to myself. He isn't here and I am freezing. I need to focus so I don't go totally crazy. It has to be jet lag. I dive down again and work hard to catch up to Chelsea and Jack.

"You alright there?" Jack asks when I swim up beside them. The Mediterranean is not deep. We have been swimming for several minutes and are only ten feet or so below the surface of the water.

"I'm fine," I say. "I thought I saw something before I jumped in, but I was wrong." I rub my arms trying to convince them that I'm cold. "It is so cold!"

"Pull in that heat, Evelyn," Jack says. "I don't want you getting hypothermia. Chelsea, how are you doing? Is the water too cold for you?"

"No," she answers. "I think if I keep in my human form, I'll be okay. It would be hard in my normal body, but I think I'll be okay even then. It's not like we are swimming by a glacier."

"Thank goodness for that," I say. Jack laughs at both of us then looks around the water.

"We won't be going more than a few hundred feet below the surface here today," he says. "It's not like being in the Atlantic. You'll probably be staying in your human form this trip, Chels. Let's keep touring then and both of you keep yourselves warm."

We swim further, looking for signs of Nyobi's kingdom. None of us think we will actually find her hiding place today. This is a clue-finding mission. Tomorrow, we will start talking to locals to see if they know anything or what the local legends are. We want to know what we are up against before we go too far into Nyobi's territory. After nearly an hour of swimming, Jack stops us.

"We have to eat something," he says. "We may be searching for a while." He opens the travel pack and pulls out several packets. I take mine and open it eagerly.

"Peanut butter?" I say as I run my finger through the goopy, brown contents. Chelsea looks perplexed at the inside of her packet. She shakes her head and mumbles to herself.

"Yep, peanut butter," Jack answers. "Packed with calories, fat, and good nutrients to keep you going for a while. You can eat the wrapper, too. It's what we've got for now, so let's eat and keep going."

I use my fingers like a spoon to eat the peanut butter from my packet. It is so weird to have land food in the sea. When I look at Chelsea, I can see she is not at all happy. She is floating in front of me, looking green in the face while she stares at the scoop of peanut butter on her finger. She tries to lick a little bit of it but ends up gagging.

"I hate peanut butter," she says and this time, it's my turn to laugh.

"Well, we don't have many other options right now," I tell her. "How about this: Jack and I will share your peanut butter and you can eat our seaweed wrappers? You'll still get some of the peanut butter, but at least you'll have the seaweed to balance it out."

"Deal," she replies and thrusts her packet toward Jack and me. Jack and I scoop out the peanut butter and hand our empty packets over to Chelsea. She eats those happily, making a gagging face whenever she tastes too much peanut butter. I just hope it's enough to get her through the day until our next break.

In a few minutes we are on our way again, searching lower and lower in the sea for signs of life. Several fish swim around us as we travel. Varieties and colors I am not used to seeing in the ocean are everywhere. Crabs, eels, some anemone, all adapted to this unique environment. They do not speak to us and we do not speak to them. They are wary of our presence, though I can tell they have seen two-worlders here before – a hint that we are headed in the right direction. Eventually, I spot a broken piece of pottery. It is old, but still may lead us further in the right direction.

"This is a good start," Jack says while he investigates my find. "Let's keep it up for another hour before heading back to shore."

"What if we head back to shore now?" Chelsea asks.

"Why?" I ask.

"Well, we've been down here for hours. It might be a better use of our time to see things from a higher vantage point – something to help us see more of the ocean? Like climbing a tall hill or something? Maybe we could see something from above that we can't see here."

"I think you're right," Jack says. "Let's give this just a little more time and we'll head back in. We can take Inbar up on the tour offer tomorrow."

We swim a little while longer but find nothing more, so we head back to the shore. By the time we arrive, the sun is setting, and we are exhausted. We gather our things and head back to the inn.

"Someplace high?" Inbar asks when we talk to her over dinner. "Something with sweeping vistas and amazing views of the city?"

"We are actually looking for amazing views of the sea," I tell her.

Inbar clucks her tongue and sighs. "Americans. Teenagers. I offer you a real tour and you want more ocean and beaches."

"Why not give them both?" Habib asks. "The tour and the ocean view?"

"And just how do you think I should go about that?" Inbar asks.

"Let's just say I have a friend who can help us out," Habib says. "Can you three be ready to go, first thing in the morning?"

"We can," Jack answers. "What time should we be ready?"

"Ah," Habib says. "How about 7 or so? If you will come to breakfast by 6:30, we should have plenty of time to fill our stomachs with my wife's good cooking and still get some sight-seeing in." Inbar slaps Habib's hand and rolls her eyes before smiling and chuckling to herself. She mumbles under her breath about her cooking and he gives her hand a gentle pat.

"We'll be ready," I say.

The three of us head to bed early, exhausted after our long day and still overcoming jet lag. As Chelsea and I walk up the stairs, I can hear Habib and Inbar talking in their room below.

"What did you mean when you told the Americans, 'I have a friend who can help?' What time do you have for making friends with connections?" Inbar asks her husband in a not-so-soft whisper.

"Trust me, my love. I know more than you think." He answers. I hear him kiss her face and the sound of the switch as they turn off the light.

CHAPTER 8

Chelsea, Jack, and I are ready to go before breakfast is ready, so we help set the table and get the food out. Habib joins us right at 6:30 and is beaming from ear to ear.

"I'm not sure why you are happy so early in the morning," his wife says to him. "It's normally nothing but 'grumble, grumble, grumble' from you."

Habib kisses his wife on the cheek and gives her a little pinch. She swats him away and brings a large bowl of fresh yogurt to the table.

"It is not normal for me to have an outing for a day," Habib says. "I am eager to get on my way and visit an old friend."

"Hmmm," Inbar mumbles and follows it up with some carefully chosen words in her own language. Habib responds with another kiss on the cheek then sits down to the table.

Breakfast is wonderful. Yogurt, fruit, cheeses, nuts, bread. It's the kind of thing I wish I could eat every day – the kind of thing I did eat every day in Ancient Greece. We help clean the table and kitchen when we are done, despite Habib's push to leave a few minutes early. Inbar smiles at each of us and pats our cheeks.

"Ah, you good American youth," she says. "I see you have better manners than my husband there." Their son, Zaher, runs through the kitchen, kisses his mama, and runs out the front door with flatbread in his hand. Inbar barely has any time to respond.

"And there is the reminder of my husband's manners," she says with a shake of her head. "Now, you good children take yourself out and enjoy your day. I will finish up here."

We thank Inbar for the breakfast and for taking such good care of us. We grab our day packs and follow Habib out the door.

Habib talks as we walk but my mind is on the city. In the brightness of the early morning, shopkeepers are getting their wares ready for their customers, mamas are shaking out towels as they cook the morning meal, children have started their sweeping and playing and some, like Habib's son, have already started to work helping tourists navigate through the city. We pass through an open-air market that is just beginning to bustle with the sounds of vendors prepping their wares.

"This is one of the best markets in Jaffa," Habib tells us. "We must pass through here on our way back to the inn." I take in the stands decorated in colorful wares: beans, lentils, fruits, clothes, lace, pottery, and other handmade goods are set up for display. As we reach the edge of the market, a different stand catches my eye – it is filled with hamsa medallions.

I pause near the stand and watch the vendor pull out her wares.

"Evelyn," Jack says when he comes up next to me. "Do you see something you like?"

"Yes," I say. "Habib says we will return, right?"

"Yes, of course," Habib answers. He eyes the medallions that have caught my attention. He smiles and nods. "Yes, we have many fine artisans here, some of the best in the region. Inbar wouldn't forgive me if I didn't take you to see their stalls."

I smile and turn to face him. "I'll be glad to see these again," I say. "I would be in trouble if I didn't take some souvenirs home with me." I leave the stall behind and Jack and I catch up with Habib and Chelsea.

"There are plenty of bicycle carts and tourist vehicles for getting around the city," Habib tells us after another thirty minutes on foot. "But what is the point in all that? The city speeds by and you don't get to see the beauty of the people."

It's true. We have seen so many locals already this morning. Habib has stopped and introduced us to several whom he knows. We don't speak the language, but we smile and bow our greeting, happy to see more of the people here. All around us, tourists are beginning their morning outings on bicycles and in carts, missing out on the people of Jaffa. I am grateful to Habib for this introduction to the modern people in this ancient city.

As we walk through a neighborhood of homes, we overhear a woman and a man arguing. We cannot understand what they are saying, but Habib stops to talk with them. Both the man and the woman are holding the shoulders of a young boy about the age of Habib's son. They are holding him tight and trying to get him to go with them. As Habib talks with them, it is clear their son does not want to go with them. At home, no one would stop and talk to someone as they dealt with their child on a street corner. We are too caught up in appearances, don't want to be seen interfering, don't want to be nosy. But life isn't like that here. The people talk to each other. They are a real community. Maybe the boy is trying to keep from going to see his grandmother or start a new job – something a typical boy might fight against – and now he gets to hear Habib's opinion.

After a few minutes of talking, Habib returns to us, shaking his head. The boy and his parents pass by us and out of the neighborhood. The boy looks at us, pleadingly, his eyes begging us for help. But his parents have him held tight. There is no getting out of his situation.

"What was that all about?" Jack asks Habib when the boy and his parents are gone. Habib's face is worried, his mouth in the first frown I've seen it in all morning.

"They are devout followers of the Kadul tradition," Habib tells us. Jack, Chelsea, and I all pause and look at each other. "They take their children to the temple of Kadul each year," Habib continues, "just their sons." We all start moving again, eyes no longer taking in the views, ears intently listening to Habib.

"What do they do at the temple?" Chelsea asks.

"They teach their young sons the art of warfare. The art of being a soldier. There was a place for that kind of teaching in ancient times, the tradition is not an entirely unfounded one. But in recent months, many of the boys have not returned. Their parents say they have left them for further training, but many of us are beginning to suspect something worse."

"But what do you think is really happening?" I ask. Habib's face darkens.

"No one knows for sure," he says, "but there are rumors of… terrible things."

"Well, what can be done about it?" Jack asks. "How do we find out what is happening and how can we help that boy?" Habib turns his sorrowing eyes to Jack's.

"There are things you do not understand here," he says to Jack. "This is not America. If we interfere, we risk bringing harm to our own families. There are many groups and factions of government and secret organizations who work underground here. They have spies and moles in every branch of government, both locally and nationally. They have members in our military and police. If the disappearances of the children do not arouse the attention of the authorities, or if the disappearances help their causes, then there is nothing left for anyone else to do about it. There are some of us who try to reason with the families, but it doesn't help. They get a glossy look on their faces and repeat the same excuses over and over. 'We honor our fathers. We save our people. It is his calling and ours.' All that kind of nonsense."

Chelsea, Jack, and I look at each other with solemn expressions. We have a pretty good idea of where that boy is headed. If only we could find the place ourselves. My stomach is sick, and I feel the lump of food I ate this morning sitting like a rock.

"Where is the temple?" Jack asks Habib.

"It is further than I care to go," he answers. "And I would never hear the end of it from Inbar. We'd best be on our way." Habib turns his back to us and continues to walk through the neighborhood and onto a bustling street. He is quiet now and we all follow behind him, too somber for words. Jack takes my hand and I lean into his strength. We have to save these boys.

We finally make it to the base of the stairs in front of Saint Peter's Church. The old stone stairs show the wear of centuries of use. Grooves have been worn into their surface from the hundreds of faithful who travel here. The steps are sprinkled with tourists taking selfies with the white bell tower behind them and parishioners heading in early to get a good seat for mass. I follow Habib up the stairs with Chelsea and Jack following closely behind. Though he has not said anything more since the scene in the neighborhood and has kept his expression downcast, Habib's face brightens as he reaches the top of the stairs. He stretches his arms out to greet a Franciscan friar who waits for us there.

The two kiss cheeks and exchange greetings. This time, I think the words are Italian.

"Habib, veccio mio, e da un bel po che non vedo il tuo volto. E coperto di rughe e faccio fatica a riconoscerti," the friar says with a twinkle in his eye. Habib gives the man a good-natured nudge in the belly.

"Wrinkles?!" Habib laughs. "Be careful what you say old friend. My age shows on your face as well!" The two men laugh and Habib points to us, "I have brought you some visitors," he says.

"Sono dei lottatori," the friar answers with a questioning look on his face. "Sono affidabili?"

"Yes, they are strong and trustworthy youth, Russelo," Habib answers again in English as he turns his face to us. "They wanted to see the ocean, Russelo – a view from above. I told them I could give them a view to remember." Russelo nods and grunts, letting a broad smile open on his face.

"I am happy you have come," Russelo says to us. His accent is thick and warm. He reaches his arms out, embracing us each in turn, and kisses our cheeks in greeting. We smile and introduce ourselves. It's the first time I've ever been kissed as a hello and I love it. I need to get Jack to do this, but he looks a little unsure. I smile at him and nudge his ribs with my elbow. Chelsea is grinning from ear to ear.

"Habib and I have been friends since our parents sent us to the same English boarding school years ago," Russelo says. "I think they had an idea of our being politicians in our lifetime." Both Habib and Russelo laugh. "But Habib fell in love with a beautiful woman and I fell in love with God's work," he continues as he rests his hands on his round belly. "Yet we both landed here, near the Holy land and each other. God certainly had better plans than our parents did."

"And for that I am grateful, old friend," Habib says. The two men grasp right forearms in a firm shake.

"Now, enough reminiscing," Russelo says. "You have a view to catch and I have a mass to prepare. Come with me and none of us will be disappointed."

Russelo leads the way with Jack, Chelsea, Habib, and me following behind. He makes small talk as we enter the beautiful church's sanctuary doors. As I step inside, I feel the cool temperature of the marble that covers the walls. I don't remember the last time I was in such a beautiful space.

Then a stinging in my chest reminds me: Atlantis was this beautiful.

Veined marble of varying colors lines the walls creating eye-catching displays for the magnificent artwork throughout the building. Paintings of Christ, Mary, and heavenly angels add to the quiet nature of the sacred structure. A few parishioners are seated or kneeling in reverent prayer. For a moment, I am caught up in awe. What I would give to spend weeks exploring the details of this place. The paintings, the statuettes, the carvings. To see a mass led by Russelo and witness the faith of the people. But I am not here to admire and study the best of humanity. I am here to save it.

Russelo tells us of the histories and rarities in the church as he leads us. He knows we do not have long to stay, but he cannot help but point out his favorite pieces: paintings of the Virgin Mary with the Christ Child are frequently pointed out. Eventually, Russelo leads us to a dark, narrow, hand-carved door.

"This is the part of the church that no one ever sees," he tells us. "Not many people are interested in narrow hallways and old staircases. It does not even have a lock, and nobody has ever been caught trying to explore. But this is my favorite part of the church. I am so pleased to have someone to share it with."

He opens the aged latch and the old door doesn't even creak when it swings on its well-oiled hinges. We follow him through the dark, narrow hallway and to the bottom of narrower stairs that climb around the long, hanging ropes of bells. The stairs make a 90 degree turn every few steps, so we are constantly moving up and around. Jack looks a little green, like his stomach is starting to do flips. The climb is dizzying, but I keep my eyes on Russelo to steady myself.

"When I first came here," Russelo tells us, "I used to get a little sick from the winding staircase. It's taken some getting used to, but the view at the top takes away any discomfort, I promise you."

There is a ladder at the top of the stairs and Russelo climbs it without hesitation, his friar's robes moving out of the way like they know what to do. He opens a small trapdoor at the top of the ladder and goes through. A moment later, his face appears, smiling, in the small opening.

"Come, come," he says, and we each head up the ladder after him. When I reach the top, I cannot believe my eyes. I move out of the way to let everyone else onto the roof and we stand in awe of the view.

The sun shines on everything. The city to the right looks white in the mid-morning sun. The water gleams in the light. A few boats rest behind the breakwater while many more have made their way out to the deeper water of the Mediterranean. I scan the sea for signs of a city beneath. Atlantis is so far below the surface, no one would be able to spot it from above, but the Mediterranean isn't as deep as the Atlantic Ocean. I'm just hoping to find something to give us a clue about where to go. Russelo points out various parts of the city: the market we passed through, his favorite restaurant (they always give him food to take to the poor), the breakwater that preserves the church. Eventually, he and Habib start talking together again of old times and the rest of us are left to scan the view.

We are all quiet for several minutes when I decide to try talking to the ocean air. Talking to the air above the ocean is one of my two-worlder skills. It helped me battle Ceto in Atlantis when she was trying to force a giant hurricane onshore. We aren't actually on the ocean, so I don't expect too much, but whatever I can get will be useful.

Beautiful air of the Mediterranean, I whisper. *I am Evelyn Marin and I have come to seek your guidance. Are you willing to communicate with me?*

Evelyn? The air whispers back. *Is that really you? It has been so long. How I have missed you.*

The accompanying breeze moves the hair from my face. The familiar touch and sound of her voice brings tears to my eyes. It is my Namaah.

Namaah, I whisper. *I have missed you so much.*

Jack's eyes grow wide when he sees my face.

"Namaah?' he whispers, and I nod. He knows my history. He knows how much I love and have missed Namaah.

And I have missed you, Namaah whispers back. *I watched you enter the sea again. It has been so long. Why did you not speak to me then?* I can feel the tender heartbreak in her voice. More tears leave my eyes.

There was so much, Namaah, I tell her. *I lost so much. Returning to the water took all my strength. I'm sorry I was so lost.*

My sweet Evelyn Pearl Athena, she says to me. *You have lost much in your young life. I am sad for you, but I am here for you now. What is it that you need from me?*

We are searching for the kingdom of Nyobi Kadul, I tell her. Suddenly, the breeze grows icy and Chelsea and Jack both look at each other with concerned faces, rubbing their arms to keep warm. They cannot hear what Namaah is saying to me. They only know that I am speaking with the air – a skill that neither of them has.

Why would you seek out that villainous creature, Evelyn Pearl Athena? Namaah asks with growing intensity. *Is it not enough that she took so much of your life and your love away? Will you pursue her now with vengeance and risk losing all that you have left? Do not let her hold such sway in your life, my young one.*

I do not seek for revenge, Namaah, I say. But even as I say it, my heart beats wildly. *The oceans and the world are in even greater danger now. In Atlantis, we have learned that Nyobi's daughter, Ceto, has joined with her. We hear rumors that they are amassing an army of youth from the Mediterranean coastline. We fear that they may have the power to destroy all the earth.*

Then why do you come here with only two to assist you? she asks. *Why not meet her in the open seas, far from land? Why risk your life here and now? Why put so many land dwellers in danger?*

Lady Pescara asks it of us, Namaah. She wants to know the truth of the rumors. She wants to know exactly what we are up against. We do not intend to make a battle so close to the shore.

And another spy could not do that for her? Namaah asks. *She had to send* you? *Are you sure you are not bait for her?* Namaah's words sting, but I feel her concern. She wants my safety, but I want safety for my family and all of Atlantis.

Other spies would have been sent, I tell Namaah. *But they were not equipped as I am. They do not have a history here in this place.*

Nor do you have a history here, Namaah responds. *You lived in Greece, Evelyn. You never lived as far east as this coast.*

Yet, I did come when Atlantis was still a thriving city in the Mediterranean, I say. *How far away was I then?*

Still more than 500 miles, she says. *You are* not *the best person for this job, my child.*

I stand quietly for several minutes, unsure of how else I can convince Namaah to help us.

"Well, my young travelers," Russelo says as he steps forward to where we are standing. "Have you found the view you came for?"

"It is so beautiful up here," Chelsea replies to him. She looks nervous, but there is no need. Russelo doesn't know I am speaking to the air, but she tries to cover for me anyway. "Is the sea always so green?"

"It is," Russelo says. "Though it can brown a great deal when the winter storms come through." Then he points far across the horizon. "Can you see that patch of green that fades into the brown way, way out to sea? Maybe 75 miles or more away from the coast?" Our eyes scan the sea to find the change in color.

"I see it," Jack says to Russelo.

"That little patch has been worrying me," Russelo tells us.

"What is it that worries you, my friend?" Habib asks.

"Well, we hear so much about the care we take of the earth God made for us. So much about global warming and the damage we are doing to our mother earth," Russelo says. "That little patch of darkness has been growing for several months. When the winter storms left, that patch stayed. I fear that we are polluting the Mediterranean. I fear that displeases God."

"I can understand your fear," I tell Russelo after a moment. "Our oceans are so beautiful. We must protect them." Russelo nods in agreement.

"Do you know what causes the change of color?" Jack asks.

"I have heard rumors," Russelo says. "Unfortunately, much of what is said is myth. Not much is based in the scientific or faithful worlds. It isn't worth repeating, though just a week ago, a government environmental worker came to mass here. I asked him about the sea."

"And what did he say?" I ask.

"He told me there was a disturbance under the water," Russelo says. "He said a great deal of debris must have sunk to that part of the Mediterranean during the stormy season. The deposits are moving in the current and kicking up the sand from the ocean floor. It is a pity that we are so careless with our gift from God."

"What about the rumors you have heard from the locals?" Chelsea asks. "How do they explain the changing ocean?" Russelo laughs quietly.

"There is great tradition steeped in centuries of suspicion here, my young friend," he says. "Locals here have worshipped pagan gods and false deities for generations. The majority of what the locals say is founded in their beliefs." Now Habib's face darkens.

"It is the rumor of the goddess, Nyobi Kadul, is it not?" he asks Russelo. Russelo nods.

"It is," he says. "Many here are saying the old sea goddess is angry and destroys the Mediterranean as a punishment for human behavior."

Chelsea, Jack, and I exchange glances. We may not worship pagan gods, but we are familiar with the damage they can do.

"But all of that deters one from the real problem," Russelo says. "Human interference. We must care for the earth we have been given. Saint Francis taught us that."

We all stand quietly looking out at the sea for a few more minutes before Russelo tells us he must leave to prepare for mass. He descends the ladder first, followed by Habib. As Chelsea, Jack and I head to the small door, we whisper to each other.

"That has to be the location of her city," Chelsea says. "Her armies must be kicking up the silt and debris while they train."

"I think you're right," Jack says. "I think we will be renting a boat tomorrow."

Chelsea climbs down the ladder. As I step my foot on the top step to head down, a cold blast of air hits my face.

Do not go there, my child, Namaah warns. *Lady Pescara must find another spy. You will be in too much danger!*

Thank you, my friend, I whisper into the air. *I will be careful.* I kiss my fingers and blow it into the wind. Namaah blows colder. I head down the ladder, out of the ocean air, and into the stillness of the church. I will be careful, but I know now for sure that we are headed in the right direction. We are headed to the kingdom of Queen Nyobi Kadul.

CHAPTER 9

The rest of the day yesterday was spent walking through the market and setting up our boat and diving rentals for the rest of the week. The man who rented them to us wanted to know where we were from, where we were going, how long we would be there, how experienced we were. He acted like he was trying to protect his equipment, normal, but the way he kept looking at us made Chelsea and me nervous. We were ready to leave and find another rental when he suddenly changed his tune, assuring us he was just doing his duty. Jack paid the man and we set up our pickup time for today. On the way, I visited the jewelry stand covered in hamsa medallions. I couldn't help it. I picked out a little one with a black pearl in the palm. It is attached to a beaded blue necklace and sits lightly on my chest. Even though it isn't the same medallion I wore in Greece, just having a hamsa near me again is comforting. I feel like I am back in Pearl's body, drawing on her memory and her strength.

A teenage girl met us in the rental shop this morning when we picked up our boat. In very broken English, she told us her father had to travel to another city for the day and she would be getting our rental ready for us. I was glad not to see her father again.

The day is clear and windless. Namaah has not spoken to me once since we stepped on the boat, though I know she is here and watching. I filled Jack and Chelsea in on the rest of my conversation with Namaah yesterday. I can tell Jack is worried about it. He keeps looking to the sky and asking me if she has said anything more. Today's answer: no.

"We're almost there," I tell Jack as our boat skips over the water. "Kill the engine."

The water is calm, the air is still motionless. A few other boats are on the water. One or two are pleasure-seekers, diving off the edge and splashing around in the dark water. The rest are local fishing boats where aging men teach their sons the family trade. The fishermen glare at us and the other tourists. They don't like having their water invaded. I avoid their gaze as much as I can. Until I see the boy.

"Jack," I whisper with my back to the fishing boats. Jack looks up. "The fishing boats. Look at the boy with the fishermen. He isn't their son." Jack looks past my shoulder and furrows his brows.

"You're right," he says. "At least we know we're on the right track." He puts his head back down, finishing his prep and a knot forms in my stomach. That boy. The boy whose parents Habib argued with in the street yesterday, is sitting on the fishing boat. A glazed-over look covers his face and a hamsa hangs around his neck. He is going to be sacrificed to a child army and there is nothing we can do about it. Jack sees the look on my face and comes closer.

"We can't blow our cover, Evelyn," he says.

"I know," I whisper back. "It just makes me sick."

"We're all sick of dealing with this," Chelsea says. "So, let's get down there and find what we came to find."

We put on our diving gear, doing all we can to maintain our cover with Nyobi's servants so close. Chelsea stays in her human form. I may be recognizable to Ceto, but Chelsea can be a surprise if we get trapped. Less than a minute is all it takes for her to transform into her sea body.

We swim down further and further into the water. The light at the surface fades the deeper we go. Soon, it is too dark to see, and Jack pulls out his dive light. As the beam shines through the murky water, it glints across something.

"Wait. Did you see that?" I ask.

"Yes," Jack answers. The three of us swim forward while Jack swings his light from side to side. It shines on something again and he focuses the beam on it. When we reach the object, we grab it and turn it around in our hands.

It is a small, hamsa medallion that was sinking to the bottom of the Mediterranean. A hamsa just like the boy had around his neck. A hamsa almost like I purchased in the market yesterday. But the center of this hamsa isn't a black pearl, instead it's a green stone that looks alive. It moves and changes color in the palm of the hand.

"It hasn't been sinking for long," Jack says.

"Maybe the boy tried to get away," Chelsea says, and we are all quiet for a minute. It's a grim reality. This deep in the water, the boys cannot survive without air. There were no tanks on the fishing boats. The medallion had to be what was letting him breathe in the water. He was too young to be a two-worlder. We are not ready to face it, but we are not yet ready to turn our backs on it either. This is evidence that the rumors are true: boys are being sacrificed to a life of warfare. Jack pockets the medallion and we keep going.

Soon, we see more evidence of life below. We swim past a sandal and a ring. We add those items to our collection of found things. They will be more proof that we found the city.

Twenty minutes go by with no other sightings of people or things. Chelsea swims ahead of Jack and me. She pauses and puts her hand up, making a fist to signal for Jack to turn off the dive light. At first, everything is dark. But after a few seconds, I see what Chelsea sees. A few hundred feet below us, the ocean is glowing. The light is dull and spread over a large area. There are flickers here and there and I can feel the water warming beneath my feet.

"It's a city," Chelsea says. "We've found Nyobi's city." My heart catches in my throat. I want to swim like mad and break down every door in the city, to find Nyobi, to find Ceto. I want to destroy their everything.

"We have to make sure it's the real thing," Jack says. "Be careful." We cluster together a little tighter and swim down toward the light. But the closer we get, the stranger everything becomes. The light is bright, but it is shining through a wall. Not a wall of brick or stone, but a wall of eels, octopi, and sharks. The dome that covers and protects Nyobi's city is made up of a mass of swimming sea life using their own bodies as the shield of defense.

There is an opening in the wall of slithering bodies. Two guards wait in front of the opening, spears in their hands. Several travelers, some two-worlders, some sea life, are lined up in front of the guards, waiting to get into the city.

"Time to get rid of these," Jack says. He takes off his oxygen tank and Chelsea and I do the same. We will only draw attention to ourselves if we look like regular humans accidentally stumbling across Nyobi's city. We stash the tanks in a small outcropping of rocks, burying them in the sand. I take Jack by the hand and together we swim to the line with Chelsea behind us. As the line leads to the main entrance of the city, we hide among the many travelers heading through a checkpoint.

"What do you think they are checking for?" Chelsea asks me. I shake my head.

"I'm not sure. Maybe us? I don't know what to expect," I answer. The line is full of people from all walks of life and all cultures. We enter the line and listen for clues in the conversations around us. Each language becomes clear and understandable to our ears under the water. This is a first for me. I didn't know we would be able to understand other languages here.

One man tells a young boy, "This is what you have been training for. You will make us so proud."

"Yes, father," is the boy's quiet response. He fidgets with the hamsa around his neck. His father pulls his hand away.

"Do you want to drown, my son?" he asks. "If you lose that medallion, you will no longer be able to breathe." The boy drops his hand to his side, staring forward as bravely as he can. "Swim firmly," the father says. "Show them your strength." The son lifts his chin and puffs out his chest. His father pats his shoulder, approvingly. "The mighty queen will bless our people for providing such a worthy candidate. You will make our family proud, my son."

Another couple, a man and a very pregnant woman stand nearby.

"It will be alright," the man says to the woman. "You'll see, the queen will help us. She watches over our shores. I have always submitted my obeisance to her as has my father before me. Surely she will bless our child." His wife nods as she swims with difficulty alongside her husband, one hand resting on her round belly with each stroke.

A group of teenage boys swims together, they each wear the same hamsa.

"You're just messing around with me," says one.

"No, I'm not," replies another. "Just wait until you see her. Green skin and a bunch of legs. Her hair is crazy, too!"

The first rolls his eyes. "If you are wrong, you owe me homework for a year."

"Ha!" is the reply. "Easy. And if I'm right, you stay here with us."

"Yeah, yeah," says the first. "I stay here with you guys and never see my family again. Blah blah blah. Won't this line move any faster? I have homework for you to do." The other boys in the group all exchange glances. They are all hiding something from their friend. Are they working for Nyobi and Ceto? Are they bringing in more recruits? And if so, for what? Are they being paid? Are they being offered protection?

We make our way through the line and to the guards who stand at the gate. Each guard is holding a trident. They don't look like they hold any kind of power, but the points are a sharp warning for anyone without permission to pass.

We watch and listen as each group or individual passes through the gates. Each gives their reasons for being at the great city and each is let through. Finally, it is our turn.

"What business have you in the Queen's city?" the larger guard asks Jack. The guard's voice is low. He has a fully developed fin and arms stronger than anyone I've ever seen. Jack takes me by the hand.

"We desire the queen's blessing for our upcoming marriage," Jack says. "We have traveled far to seek her majesty's grace." It's all I can do to keep a straight face. I want to hit him for talking like that. This had better work, or I really will hit him later.

The guard eyes us for a moment, probably thinking we are too young to be talking about marriage, probably thinking we are running away together or something. Then he looks at Chelsea.

"What about her?" the guard asks.

"She's my sister," I tell the guard. "I couldn't leave without her." The guard nods and moves his trident to the side.

"Very well, then," he says in his booming voice. "Move along."

"Where can we find the queen?" Jack asks as we move through the gates. The guard just laughs.

"It isn't my job to hold your hand and take you to her," he says. "If you don't know where to find her, maybe you don't belong here." He bends down so his face is even with Jack's. Jack stiffens then stands a little taller.

"Never mind," he says. "We will find her on our own." The guard grunts then turns away. We're in. We've made it into her city.

"That was too easy," Chelsea says. I let go of Jack's hand and we swim to the side of the waterway. We pause between two buildings that look like they came from entirely different eras. One stone, one steel. This city has been added onto for centuries.

Hundreds of people and sea life fill the streets. Many have objects with them to be blessed by the queen. Others have hope-filled voices, "The queen will help us if we help her." I hear over and over again. I can't think of anything Nyobi has ever done for humanity to warrant this faith in her. All she has ever done is take and take. Maybe it is fear that has fueled these generations of devotees.

"So, where are we heading next?" Chelsea asks. "Main road or side streets?"

"The main road is our best option," Jack answers. "Let's follow the crowd and see how close we can get."

"And what if we are recognized?" I ask. Jack and Chelsea both turn to me.

"You are the only one in real danger of that," Jack says. "But I have a disguise for you and Chelsea anyway." He reaches into his bag and pulls out two wraps of seashell and fine linen. "Here. Try wrapping this around your hair and face like some of the other women here. I picked them up in the market yesterday." He hands the material to us.

The fabric is light and gentle in my hands. The tiny shells that decorate the border have been hand-woven in with an embroidery design. It's beautiful. Chelsea and I put the long shawls over our heads and wrap them around our faces and necks. It feels like a strange combination with wetsuits. Chelsea's eyes get big and she starts shaking her head.

"I'm no expert, but don't these make us stand out more?" she asks.

"You look like a faithful follower in a wetsuit," Jack answers. "It's the best we have right now. We will fit in better if we look like we might really be local." Chelsea adjusts her shawl a little more, trying to make it look like she is used to wearing it. Neither of us is doing a very good job.

"Let's just stay together as long as we can," I say. "These shawls will only get us so far. We have to be ready for anything."

So, we head back into the crowd of people moving along the waterway. There are very few people moving the opposite direction. It looks like nobody wants to leave. Or nobody is allowed to leave. As we move closer to the heart of the city, the guards change from mermen to sea creatures. Octopi and eels, a couple of sharks, all with their eyes narrowed in on the crowd. I feel more and more exposed and watched, so I move behind Chelsea and Jack. They block me from the view of most of the guards. Finally, the line of people slows down. I look up and see that we are all headed into a large building, I'd even call it a castle.

The castle is one of the ancient buildings. Up until now, most of the structures looked like they were built in recent years – real glass in windows, walls covered in plaster and still in one piece, new doors hung in doorways. But not here. The castle is stone built on stone in the ancient standard. I can see portions of the exterior that still have the marble façade attached, a memory of what the ruins used to be. But that façade is chipping rapidly away.

We move together up the steps of the building as the crowd of followers pushes us forward. We are pushed into a large, circular room, covered in marble. Warm lights shine from the ceiling. Gold and jewels cover the walls. There is no furniture in the room except for a large throne and on that is the most hideous creature I have ever seen.

She is human. Or she was human once. Her face is aged and wrinkled and green. Her lips are a fiery red but dull and lifeless. Her eyes are like black jewels shining out from her sagging face. They are the only thing about her that sparkles or moves. Except…

Her hair.

Her hair moves. But not the movement of long locks allowed to flow freely in water. Her hair moves like a creature. Like eels. Her hair is a swath of eels moving silently around her head. They weave in and out of a jagged, silver crown. Every few seconds, one cuts itself on the points. The queen winces and the eel bleeds.

A merman guard brings a person forward and bows before the queen.

"This man desires to place his son in your service, Majesty," the guard says as he stands again.

"Where is the boy?" a voice asks, but it isn't the queen. I raise up just a few more inches to confirm that it is a voice I know.

There, next to her mother, is Ceto. She stares at the guard and the man, waiting for a response. Her face is the beautiful version of her grotesque mother's. Ceto's hair moves in the water, forming beautiful waves in the space around her. Her human form is still shaped well, her tentacle legs fan out beneath her. Her legs mirror her mother's. Nyobi is also part octopus. But her tentacles have lost the shine of youth and are dull and flaking. I wonder how this decrepit, deteriorated, fabled beauty feels about sitting next to her obviously beautiful daughter. I cannot see Gwen, but I wonder if my old roommate is here as well.

"Let us see the boy," Ceto says again. The boy steps forward. He is the young man we saw on our way into the city, the one so eager to please his father. Ceto asks the boy questions about where he lives and why he wants to serve her. His answers reveal that he is here at his parents' bidding. His voice trembles but he stands erect.

"You will make your parents proud yet," Ceto says to him with a smile. She nods at the guard who leads the boy through the crowded room and out a door in the back. The boy's father bows deeply, thanking Ceto and the queen for taking his son. Then he turns from the throne and leaves out another door, like he knows where to go, like he has been here before to send other sons to their new home. I get a closer look at his face as he passes. His expression is blank.

I watch him leave and my heart skips a beat. I poke Jack in the side and point to the door. In the line is the man from the rental shop.

"He's one of their followers," I whisper; my heart is pounding. I put my hand to my chest, afraid that the sound is so loud everyone will hear it. "He will tell Ceto about us. She will find us, and we will all be captured. I can't stay here."

"Where will you go?" Chelsea asks. "Everyone will notice if you leave the way you came without talking to the queen first."

"We have to try to get out one of those back doors," Jack says.

"But which one?" I ask. There is an entire row of doors behind the throne, all of them blocked by worshippers.

"The first one we can get to," he answers. He puts his arm around my waist, and I grab Chelsea's hand. Together, we make our way slowly through the crowded space. Most of the people are unaware of our movement. They are all focused on the monstrous queen and her daughter. We finally reach a side door when we hear a panicked voice in the room.

"I won't go! I won't go!" the voice calls out. It is a young boy with a voice and face I recognize.

"Zaher!" Chelsea gasps. "They have Zaher!"

Habib's son is pulled through the waiting crowd and placed before Nyobi and Ceto.

"Another son for you, my queen," the guard says to Nyobi. Again, Ceto is the one who answers.

"A reluctant son," she says. She swims to Zaher and fingers the medallion around his neck. She begins her questioning and Zaher continues his belligerence.

"We can't leave him here," I whisper to Jack and Chelsea.

"And you can't be seen," Jack whispers back. "You have to get out of here fast while Chelsea and I get Zaher."

"How do you expect to get him out of here?" I ask. "I can at least use my water temperature control to help you."

"You aren't the only one with that ability, Evelyn," Jack tells me. "Chelsea and I will do as well without you getting caught. You have to go now. Meet us outside as soon as you can get there."

"I have no idea where I'm going," I tell him.

"Evelyn," he says, "Ceto can't see you or know you are here." The guard holding Zaher starts swimming to the door where the other boy was taken. Zaher is kicking and fighting him. Ceto flicks her fingers in the boy's direction and his flailing body goes limp.

"That will subdue his temper for a while," she whispers with a smile. I try to swim to Zaher, but Jack holds me back.

"Evelyn, Chelsea, and I will get Zaher and find our way out of here. Let us do our job and you do yours. You need to get out of here."

"Why can't I go with you?" I ask.

"This is an order, Evelyn," Jack says. "You are to obey immediately, not to question." He takes me by the elbow and forces me through the door closest to us, pulling it quietly closed when I'm through. I try to force the door open, but is it locked from the outside. I feel my shawl fall to the floor below, but I can't reach for it. In the darkness, I can't see anything.

I am alone.

CHAPTER 10

I try forcing the door open again and again, but to no avail. It won't budge. I don't want to call out and risk having Ceto hear me. Jack will have to deal with me once we get back to Jaffa. If we get back.

I touch the wall and follow it until it joins another wall. The room I am in is narrow and the walls are smooth and cool like marble. I move forward through the dark water, my fingers trailing along the wall as I go. No furniture or art pieces obstruct my way. I hope I am in a hallway with another door. I pass many closed doors with no sound coming from the other side. Still there is no light.

After ten minutes or so of swimming this way, I see a faint green glow ahead of me. It comes from under a door at the end of the hall. I swim forward, listening as I go. When I reach the door, the light from below illuminates my surroundings. The door is solid oak with a thick and smooth finish. The doorframe is metal, maybe gold, and carved beautifully. Octopi, seaweed, and jewels are etched into its surface. I find the door's handle and push gently against it. It moves.

My heart jumps with excitement. Even if this doesn't lead outside, it does lead somewhere. I am that much closer to escape. I open the door slowly. It doesn't make a sound in the clear water. I pause for a moment to listen, wishing I hadn't left my shawl on the ground, but there is only silence.

As I open the door fully, the light of the room blinds me. Light glitters in the space. I blink to cure the blindness and see what the room holds. I freeze at the sight. I am in a treasury.

Jewels and golden figurines sit on marble tables and pour out of coffers. I move in slowly, knowing a treasury cannot be left unguarded. The room is still quiet, and I feel completely alone. I scan the space for another way out and spy an opening at the far end of the room. I make my way toward it, listening closely.

As I move through the space, the riches grow more and more exquisite. And more and more unique. I see the gold and jewels give way to a large collection of pearls. Pink pearls, white pearls, black pearls, and a million colors in between. Some pearls are small, others are larger than an apple. I stop by a table filled with black pearl jewelry. In the center of the table is a piece I recognize. It is my hamsa.

I cannot help myself. I reach up to the tourists' hamsa around my neck and pull the beaded strand off. I set it on the table, next to the hamsa I wore thousands of years ago. The gold that melted in my hand and brought me home is back in its intended shape, the hand that sees and protects. My fingers move slowly over the golden hand and I pick it up. It is empty where its pearl eye once was. My fingers brush against the empty metal and the hamsa calls to me.

My Pearl, My Pearl, My Pearl! A searing pain rips through my chest and I double over with the force of it, my hand clenching the hamsa to my chest.

My Pearl, My Pearl, My Pearl! the hamsa cries again and again. *Return my Pearl to me! I cannot be whole without her!* The hamsa stops its calling and emits the sobbing pain of one who has lost much. The searing pain in my chest subsides and I am left holding the beautiful medallion in a crumpled heap on the floor. After a few moments of deep breathing, my heart slows down, and I can look more fully at my medallion.

The fingers are etched beautifully, the gold unharmed by centuries in the ocean. It shines as brilliantly as it did the night Atlantis fell into the sea. But the center of the palm where my pearl once lived is tarnished and empty. It looks like a sore is eating away at the golden flesh. The chain that kept the hamsa around my neck in Ancient Greece is still there. I lift it, considering, and place the chain around my neck.

There is no response from the hamsa. It is quiet now and sits on my chest like any piece of jewelry would do. I sit up, regaining my strength, and finally stand. I swim to the back of the room, toward the opening. But as I am about to lift the latch, one more thing catches my eye. It is a piece of jade, large and polished. It has no fitting for jewelry, but I don't need to see one to know what it is. It is the jade Abraxas wore in ancient Greece.

I reach my hand toward it, but another hand reaches mine first.

"Who are you?" a voice asks as the hand grabs my wrist.

I try to pull away, to make it to the door before the guard can call for backup, but he is strong. I turn to face him and stop fighting altogether. I could never fight that face. I could never run from it. I've loved it for so long.

"Gileaus," I manage to whisper. "Gileaus, is it really you?"

His hand reaches to my cheek, brushing the hair that clings to me. He tucks it behind my ear and turns my face toward his.

"Who are you?" he asks again. "How are you here? How do you know the name of Gileaus?" he is whispering, but his voice is still uncertain.

"Gileaus, it's me," I tell him. "It's Evelyn... Pearl... Athena." Why can't I say which person I was when he loved me? When will I know who I am?

"It can't be true," he says. "You can't be real."

"I am real, Gil," I say, using the name I used to call him. "It's really me." I pull close to him and rise to kiss his beautiful lips, but he backs away.

"I am not Gileaus," he says. "Gileaus is a man of legend. He hasn't lived for thousands of years." He pulls his hand away from my face and lets go of my wrist, turning his face from me. "But you are *the* Pearl? *The* Athena? You are the legend intertwined with my ancestors?" He turns again to look at my face, searching it for the clues of my real nature. Tears sting my eyes.

"But...you... look...," I whisper.

"Just like him," the young man answers. "I know. Tell me, how did you come here? Why have you come? Have you come to release me or trap me?"

I shake my head, trying to understand what he is saying.

"I can't tell you why I'm here," I say. "I don't know who you are. But you look so much like him."

"I am Helios," the beautiful man before me says. "I am a descendant of Gileaus. For over two thousand years, my family has been trapped here, serving the queen Nyobi Kadul."

"Then, you are not Gileaus." I whisper to myself. "He is not here. He is truly lost." I step back. "You can't be his descendant. Gileaus died! I killed him before he could marry!" I reach my hand to my head and push against the pain in my skull. Helios reaches his hand to mine.

"I am not Gileaus," he says, "but my history is rich with his life and love. Please, tell me how you are here. Please tell me why you have come. Please tell me who you are. I am the only one left of my family. The queen and her daughter have destroyed them all. I am all that remains. I must know the reason I have been left alone. I must find purpose to my existence."

"I'm Evelyn," I manage to say. "Gileaus knew me as Athena. Others knew me as Pearl," my voice cracks. I don't know if I'm ready to face my past like this. "I didn't know you existed until this moment," I say. Helios' hand is holding mine. He is so like Gileaus, I cannot make myself turn away. I would do anything for my Gil.

Oh, how much I love him. "How are you real? How can I help you? How are you trapped?"

There is an echo of movement in the hallway outside the door. Helios turns his face to the door then back to me.

"The guard changes now," he says. "Wait in the corridor and I will come to you." He ushers me through the back doorway and into another dark space, closing the door behind me. I listen closely and hear him talking with the guard who entered the room. They talk about the congregation of people in the queen's throne room, how today's group is bigger and crazier than ever, and Helios takes his leave. I hear his strokes coming toward my door and my first instinct is to hide. I press my back against the wall, behind the opening door, trying to conceal myself.

The door opens and Helios steps through. He touches something on the wall and the hallway fills with light. I breathe a sigh of relief and move away from the wall. He closes the door and places a finger to his lips. Shhhh... He takes me by the hand and leads me through a series of hallways and doors, pausing at each opening, listening for the sounds of others. Once or twice, I have to conceal myself as a merman or sea creature stops to speak to Helios. I don't know why I don't panic. I am letting a servant of my enemy lead me through her castle. But something inside tells me I can trust him. I can trust Helios.

We finally make it to an outer door and Helios rushes me through it. We are outside, behind the castle now. An octopus guard turns to see Helios holding my hand. My heart stops, but Helios knows what to say.

"Ah, Davide," he says. "I am glad you are on guard today." Is Davide a friend? Will Helios sound an alarm? Will Davide take me to the dungeon? Has Helios trapped me?

"I was just showing my girlfriend through the castle," Helios continues. I hear Davide laugh. Helios sees him chuckle. Davide nods his head to the side, letting Helios know it is safe to pass. Davide will keep our secret.

Helios gives Davide a fist bump to one of his tentacles and takes me around the guard and onto the market lane. Several minutes pass. We are still holding hands.

"I don't understand what is happening." I finally say to Helios. "Please tell me what I am missing." He pulls me aside and we sit on an ancient bench, overlooking a neglected sea garden. "I thought Gileaus was killed when Atlantis fell."

"He was almost killed," Helios tells me. "But Nyobi wanted him alive. She killed his fiancée."

"Zenia," I say, remembering the giddy blonde who sat with me at my final meal in Atlantis. "But if Zenia was killed, how does Gileaus have descendants?" Helios shakes his head.

"Nyobi forced him to take her as his wife," Helios answers. "When the child was born, it was a male, so she let it live. In every generation since, the queen has trapped women into bearing the children of their descendants – all male."

"So, that's why you can live underwater in human form?" I ask. "You aren't a two-worlder. You're…"

"A descendant of an evil queen? Yes." Helios answers. "But it's a heritage I don't accept. I've seen what she does. She kills our mothers as soon as each male child is old enough to survive without her care. She is jealous and evil. I don't want that for myself or my children."

"How many children do you have?" I ask, hopeful that there aren't any yet.

"I have none," he answers, and I breathe a sigh of relief. "But that won't last for long. The queen has started looking for a bride for me. I'm sure you've seen the masses entering the sea."

"I have," I say.

"Well, the queen is preparing an army for herself," Helios says, "mostly sons, but sometimes a daughter is brought. The queen has been storing those up so she can pick one for me. It's gotten worse since her daughter showed up."

"Ceto," I say. Helios nods. "Ceto is your sister." Helios shakes his head.

"We share the same blood, but I have no family feeling toward her. She is almost as crazy as Nyobi. Ceto is on a mission to create some perfect race and a perfect world. Have you seen her yet… Athena?"

"Actually," I say," Athena is only one of my names." He gives me a questioning look and I tell him my history: my history in the sea, my history in ancient Greece and ancient Atlantis, my life and mission now, most of it anyway. I'm not sure I should tell him I want to destroy his ancestors.

"So, we are hoping for the same things," he says. "I want to be free from this heritage, Athena." he pauses, "Which name should I call you by?" I smile.

"Any of them will do," I say, "but everyone in this life calls me Evelyn." Helios nods.

"Evelyn is a beautiful name," he says. We are quiet for a moment, our hands still linked together.

Suddenly, we hear a ruckus from down the lane, near the castle entrance. We both look up to see a wave of guards breaking through the crowd and yelling.

"They are looking for someone," Helios tells me. He stands and moves in front of me, hiding me from view. Just then, I spy Chelsea, Jack and Zaher sneaking out from the top and down the back of the castle. Helios looks up to where my eyes are fixed and I stand, too.

"They are actually looking for several someones," I say. "I'm sorry, but I have to go."

"Let me help you," Helios says, still holding my hand.

"Okay," I answer. I hope I am not putting us all in greater danger. I can't get a good read on Helios and what his intentions are, but what choice do I have? He already knows I am here. He can already damage us if he wants. I decide to take that chance and we swim together to the back of the castle where my companions are hiding. We find them in an ancient burial ground.

"Evelyn!" Jack whisper yells from the garden. "I'm so glad to see you. I wasn't sure we would get out or find you at all." He reaches forward and embraces me. For the first time, he sees the man standing at my side. The man who looks just like the fiancé I told him about only a few months ago. The man who still won't let go of my hand.

"Who is this?" Jack asks as he pulls away.

"This is Helios," I tell him. "He is going to help us."

CHAPTER 11

Habib and Inbar are a mess. Inbar clings to Zaher and speaks a mile a minute with words I don't understand. Zaher was kidnapped from his post with the cart. The fisherman we saw when we stopped above Nyobi's kingdom brought the boy to her. Habib yells and gesticulates as he paces around the small front room.

"They took my boy!" he finally says to Jack. "They took my boy and gave him to Nyobi!" Inbar is sobbing and speaking in a rush of unfamiliar words. "I understand," Habib says to her. "Ready the boy and our things. We must leave here immediately. Madness has overtaken this place. No one is safe." Inbar pulls Zaher behind her and into another room at the back of the inn. We hear bags being pulled from closets, drawers being opened and a tearful mother fearing for the life of her child.

"Did you know Nyobi Kadul was real?" Jack asks Habib as he rushes to his office. "How did you know she was more than a myth?"

"There are many things you do not know about this place," Habib answers. He runs in and out of his office, gathering papers, putting important things into a large briefcase. "My family has been working against her for generations. All from land." He closes the briefcase and turns to Jack, pointing his finger between him and Helios. "And YOU have brought HIM to my home! The very spawn of the devil herself! You have no idea the danger you have put us in!" he shouts. Spit flies from Habib's mouth and covers Jack's face. Jack wipes the spittle from his cheek.

"Habib, we didn't know," Jack answers calmly. "Helios actually helped us get out of her city undetected. We didn't think we would be placing you or your family in any danger by bringing him with us. How could we have known you are an enemy of the queen?"

"Everyone is an enemy of the queen," Habib answers in a low whisper. He turns to me. "And you. How could you be so intimate with such a man." He points to my hand which is still holding Helios'. I haven't been able to let him go since I found him. I can feel Jack's eyes burning into me.

"Sir," Helios says to Habib, "I promise you there is nothing to fear from me. Nyobi is my ancient ancestor, yes, but she is my enemy as well as yours. I have no allegiance to her."

"Stupid youth," Habib says to Helios. "And you just assume that the evil queen will be fine with her own descendant leaving her kingdom? Your relationship with her has granted you certain privileges, but you have been made a pawn in the process. Nothing will keep her from looking for you." Habib turns back to Jack.

"How many people did you pass on your return here?" he asks. Jack shakes his head.

"I don't know," he says. "There were people everywhere." Jack's face is pale, almost green. He shakes his head. "They were everywhere," he says again in a whisper.

"Yes. People everywhere," Habib responds. "And how many of those people are the spies of the queen or are under her control?" Jack just shakes his head.

"You have made an egregious error," Habib says. "But there is no time to teach you to mend your ways now. We have no choice but to run. With the stir you caused in rescuing my son, there will be an army of two-worlders and Nyobi's pawns here in a matter of hours." Habib turns his face to the room where his wife has returned with bags packed. His eyes rest on his son.

"But you have saved my boy," he says. "I cannot deny that without your intervention, Zaher would have been lost." Habib sighs and looks at us again. "Get your things ready while I get the cart. We leave in ten minutes."

For the first time since meeting him, I let go of Helios' hand. Chelsea and I run up the stairs to our room to get our things together. When we return a few minutes later, Jack has his bags in hand and is glaring silently at Helios.

"Habib is packing his family's things into the cart. We will have to run to get to the wider streets again. Nothing can make it down this road. We will have to leave here in a few minutes," Jack says when he finally meets my gaze. "We have to stop to get a passport for this one to travel," he nods at Helios. "Habib has connections who can get us one quickly, but it will still add another half hour before we can get out of the city. You and Chelsea should go to the airport ahead of us. If anything happens, you two need to be safely out of here and together."

"I'm not leaving without you, Jack," I say as I step closer to him and set down my bags. "We are in this together. I won't leave you behind." I move to take his hand, but he pulls away, bending down to pick up the bags I've dropped.

"You don't have a say in this, Evelyn," he tells me. "I'm your captain and these are my orders. You and Chelsea will leave in the first car with Inbar and Zaher. Habib and I will take care of Helios and meet you in Florida." He steps out of the door with my bags. Meet us in Florida? No, I don't want to be away from him for that long – neither Jack nor Helios.

I follow Jack, brushing past Helios and leaving Chelsea behind. An icy breeze cuts across the back of my neck. Namaah is upset with me. She warned me not to enter the ocean. I don't know if she will help me at all now. I have to salvage what help I do have left.

"Jack," I say as he loads our things into the cart. "Jack, I don't want this." I put my hand on his shoulder and turn him to face me. "I don't know what is going on with Helios. I don't know why I acted the way I did with him. It was just so... much. I don't want to leave like this."

"I know it's a lot, Evelyn," he answers. "It's a lot for everyone. That's why I have to leave emotion out of it. My first order is to keep you safe and that is what I am doing. It has nothing to do with what you want or what you're feeling or what I want or what I'm feeling. It has everything to do with keeping you and Chelsea safe." I try to answer, but Habib pushes past us to load Inbar and Zaher's things. Inbar and Zaher are close behind. Inbar takes the handles of the cart, but Zaher, stops her.

"No, mama," he says, "it is my job. I will pull the cart." Inbar lets her son take the handles to the cart and looks frantically around.

"We must be going," she says, grabbing me by the wrist. "We cannot wait another minute."

Chelsea runs outside and takes Inbar by the hand. "It's going to be alright, Inbar," she says. "We will get there safely."

"It is time for you to go," Jack says. "We will see you soon." Zaher takes off with the cart and Chelsea and I walk with long strides behind Inbar. She will leave us behind if she needs to. I strain my neck to see Jack as I leave, but he is already back inside the inn, preparing the bags for the next cart. Our taxi is waiting for us at the top of the lane and we all pile in.

Every minute is a strain on my mind as we drive to the airport, unload our things, and get checked in for our flight. Chelsea tries to reassure me. She tells me that everything will be fine, that Jack and Helios will meet us in Florida, I'll see. But I don't answer. I can't see a way out of this. I feel so alone. Inbar hands out anti-nausea pills to Chelsea and me when we board the plane. I try to tell her that I don't get motion sickness, but she won't listen to me. She insists we must take it to avoid any problems on the journey back to Florida. I take the pill and within twenty minutes, sleep takes over and lets me travel home. It's the first dreamless sleep I've had in months.

CHAPTER 12

I'm groggy when we land in Florida. But as soon as we land, I check my phone for messages from Jack. He and Helios made it to the airport and on a redeye flight with Habib. Jack sent a picture of Helios staring out of the airplane window. *First time in the air* is the caption below. I smile at Helios, looking so out of place on an airplane. His dark hair curling like Gileaus' did thousands of years ago. My smile falters. I miss Gileaus and looking at Helios only makes the missing worse. And none of it helps me in my new relationship with Jack.

"Evelyn," Chelsea says as she looks over my shoulder at my phone. I jump at the sound of her voice. "You know it isn't him, right?" I feel her thoughts pulling away from my mind. This is the first time I realize we share mental communication on land as well as in the ocean. She's been feeling what I've been feeling and listening to what I've been thinking. I shake my head, feeling embarrassed and betrayed, and put the phone away.

"I know it isn't him," I answer. "Let's get going." I turn away from her quickly and head to the baggage claim area. Chelsea and I will rest in my dorm on the FIU campus before heading back to Atlantis giving us one night of rest to reset our inner clocks. Uncle Russ made hotel arrangements for Inbar and Zaher, so we say our goodbyes at the airport exit. Inbar cries and thanks us over and over for saving her son. It's awkward, but I'm almost as glad as she is that Zaher made it out of Nyobi's kingdom.

The next day, Jack and I sit in Lady Pescara's office.

"It's fortunate the fishermen were so eager that day," Lady Pescara says.

"The fishermen each wanted credit for bringing the newest recruits," Jack tells her. "I'm not sure they got what they were looking for." Jack smiles, but Lady Pescara is in no mood for jokes, even at our enemy's expense. She swims to the front of her desk and sits there, facing us.

Jack just finished telling her that a disturbance from the fisherman created a distraction that helped him and Chelsea sneak to the door where Zaher was taken. Once there, Jack acted like he was a new recruit in Nyobi's army trying to show his sister around, lost and clueless until they reached the soldier's bunks. Several guards gawked openly at Chelsea, eager to help her brother so they could make a good impression on her. Once they found the soldier's quarters, they found Zaher, and eventually found their way out – after causing a few more disturbances themselves.

"What you have learned about the area is shocking," Lady Pescara says with a grave expression. "We suspected mind control could be involved, but not to this extent. How could she control so many people and not arouse suspicion? Are the local authorities aware that so many children are disappearing?"

"There are many factions in the region, Lady Pescara," I answer. "I believe some may be controlled by Nyobi Kadul. According to Habib, many serve in government positions – some by choice, others by force. I did see something disturbing when I was in the palace treasury."

"And what was that?" Lady Pescara asks.

"She has the jade worn by Abraxas," I answer. "I believe it has something to do with what is happening on the Jaffa coast. When Abraxas wore it, he used it to control the minds of the people around him." Even while I answer, I can feel my hamsa burning beneath my shirt. But I'm not ready to talk about that yet.

"And with Ceto there, the queen has even more power at her disposal," Lady Pescara says. "Other sources tell us that the queen is aged and senile, that Ceto is in charge. What do you think, Evelyn? Now that you have seen them together."

I think about Nyobi's wrinkled, deformed face, the listlessness of her monstrous body, the eels on her head and the sparkle in her eyes. Knowing eyes. Seeing eyes. Then I picture her daughter, Ceto, sitting next to her ancient mother and running the palace. She is too confident. She doesn't know what her mother sees and what she is thinking. But Nyobi is aware of her. She knows her daughter's plans even more than Ceto knows them herself.

"I believe Ceto thinks she is controlling her mother," I say. "I think she believes that she is using whatever power Nyobi retains for her own benefit. She thinks she is in charge, that she will take her mother's place and her power."

"But her mother?" Lady Pescara asks.

"The queen barely moves," I answer. "But I don't think that is because she is incapable. I think she is still because she is watching."

"And what do you think she sees?"

I remember the eyes, the eels, the feeling. Did Queen Nyobi Kadul see me? Did she hear my thoughts? Did she lead me to Helios? Did she manipulate the situation so Jack and Chelsea could escape with Zaher? Or did she just watch it all happen, knowing it would benefit her in some way.

"I don't know what she is doing, my Lady," I answer, "but I do believe she sees everything."

"And you believe this jade is the link the queen uses to control other people?"

"I do."

Lady Pescara is quiet, thinking. She takes a deep breath and rises from the edge of her desk. Her tail glistens in the golden light of the watery torches on the wall. She swims behind her desk and sits down to a pile of papers.

"I don't want you to share any of this with anyone else," she says to Jack and me, "most especially about the jade. I suppose we cannot help people knowing about Zaher. And I want as few people knowing about Helios as we can manage."

"May I see him?" I ask. Jack stiffens when I ask. "May *we* see him?" Lady Pescara is writing on a seaweed parchment. She quietly finishes her note, then hands it to me.

"Take this with you to the prison guard," she says. "It grants permission for you to visit with Helios. That is, *after* you meet with another prisoner."

"What prisoner?" Jack and I ask together. Lady Pescara looks at us both before answering.

"I need you to meet with James again," she says. My stomach falls and I close my eyes, swallowing to keep from throwing up. I don't ever want to see his face again.

"Why do I need to talk to James again?" I ask. "Why do I have to see him at all? Didn't I already get the information you need?"

"Is there something our trained interrogators haven't been able to get from him yet?" Jack asks. "There's no telling what kind of influence James could have on Evelyn at this point."

"Hey," I say to him, "what is that supposed to mean?"

"It means that you get attached to people and that blinds you," Jack says in response. His words cut me, but I can't blame him. We haven't had two minutes alone since we brought Helios with us to Atlantis. "You want to believe the best in people and that everything will be okay, but that isn't always what happens, Evelyn. And people use that to take advantage of you." My mouth falls open.

"C'mon, Jack," I say to him. "Look, I know we haven't had a chance to talk about Helios or what it means for us, but now is not the time to jump to those kinds of conclusions!"

"What other conclusions are there, Evelyn?" he asks, "You were holding his hand until you were forced away from him. It was ridiculous. You have a problem when you meet up with old boyfriends and you're getting ready to go see another one!" Lady Pescara stops us both.

"It sounds to me like there is a problem with *your* relationship," she says. Jack and I both freeze, remembering that we are not alone. "This is why we have regulations against romantic relationships during wartime, Captain." Jack turns red, then white. We both know about the rules of wartime. Feelings can interfere with the job that has to be done. They cloud judgment. It is too difficult to regulate relationships when the fate of the world is at stake. We are supposed to cool our heels or fins and wait for peace before we start any relationships. But is peace even a real thing?

"Yes, Lady Pescara," Jack says, standing. "I apologize. I should not have pursued a relationship with Recruit Marin at this time. I will end it, here and now, to prevent further problems." My jaw drops. He can't be serious. Did he just break up with me to follow orders? Or did he use the orders to break up with me? Lady Pescara shakes her head.

"I'm afraid it's too late for that," she says. "The damage has been done. You have allowed this relationship to keep you from seeing clearly. The best you can do is move forward, aware that *your* feelings are just as much to blame as Recruit Marin's." Jack looks down, embarrassed.

"Yes, ma'am," he says. Lady Pescara rises from her chair and moves in front of me.

"You have a history with James," she says. "Yes, you are untrained in the art of interrogation, but you are familiar with the habits of the prisoner in question, his methods of communicating. In short, you can tell when he is lying better than anyone else can do on short notice.

"James has been giving us all kinds of information about Queen Nyobi Kadul and Ceto. Their plans for their army, the size of their forces, and the powers available to them. I want you to meet with him, Evelyn. I want you to be present while he is being interrogated. I want you to watch him and tell me if he is telling the truth. Try using your mind powers again, secretly. If we believe him and we are wrong, the world is ended. If we believe him and we are right, we win the war. Do you understand?"

I could tell her that I already know James is lying, that all he does is lie. But I cannot let my anger over our past affect my judgment like it is with Jack. This is serious. This is more than an old boyfriend and his lying ways. This is more than trying to get Jack to understand what I'm feeling. This is too important for my feelings to get in the way.

"I understand, Lady Pescara," I say. "I will go and do as you ask."

"Good," she responds and turns to Jack. "Captain, do you think you are fit to continue to command Recruit Marin or does she need a reassignment to another group?" Jack is quiet. He looks to Lady Pescara. He looks to me, pain written all over his face.

"I can stay focused, Lady Pescara," he says to her. But he doesn't take his eyes off of me. Lady Pescara sighs.

"I don't think you are right in this, Captain," she says. "I think reassignment is best. It will help both of you stay focused on the efforts at hand. Not to mention Recruit Marin has plenty of other things on her mind. She needs time to heal from her experiences. Do you understand this?"

"Yes, ma'am," Jack says, still not taking his eyes off me. I feel hollow inside.

"You'll receive your new assignment in the morning," she says to me. "Until then, visit with the prisoner and report to me. In light of what I have just witnessed, I believe it is best if you wait to visit with Helios until another time." I want to argue. I want to tell her that my feelings aren't important, that Helios is important, but I know it will come across wrong to both her and Jack.

"Since Jack is your captain until morning," she says, "it is his responsibility to accompany you to the prison today." She moves back behind her desk and addresses us both. "I trust I can rely on you both to learn from this experience. Do not allow your feelings to get in the way of what we are trying to do. Am I understood?"

"Yes, ma'am," Jack says. I nod.

"Yes, ma'am."

"Good," Lady Pescara says. "Evelyn, I expect to see you here again in four hours. Get the information you need in that time." I nod again and leave the room with Jack swimming behind.

CHAPTER 13

"He won't be able to see you, Evelyn," my dad says to Jack and me. My dad's secretarial duties are being handled by Catarina for the time being. For now, he is in charge of prisoner interrogations. It's his job to check for signs of mind control. He lived with it for so long under Ceto's thumb, it's a life and outlook he is all too familiar with. He has reason to believe that James is being controlled, though the signs are not totally clear to him. "The divider in the window works like a one-way mirror," he continues. "James won't be able to see you or hear you from the other side. You just watch and listen from here. It should be enough."

I step forward to the opening in the wall. An iridescent film separates us from the interrogation room. The film moves like a bubble would on land, undulating with color and shape. I look through it to the empty chair and table in the room beyond. Everything is distorted. The shape of the chair moves through the bubble, constantly altering its appearance. It's like being in a haunted house at the fair. The door of the ancient room opens and three figures step inside.

Though the image is blurry, I can tell that the person in the middle, flanked by two guards, is James. My breath catches and I feel the hamsa burning against my chest. She feels what I feel. James moves through the water with the same confidence he always showed on land. His reddish hair is longer now and moves freely in the water. His chin is high, and his shoulders are strong though his hands are tied in front of him. He looks around the room and walks to the chair in the center. He sits without being told to do so. His guards stand behind him. Dad leaves me and enters the interrogation room. He sits with his back to me and addresses my old boyfriend as their image circulates in the divider.

"Name, please," my dad asks.

"Mr. Marin," James responds. "It's such an honor to finally meet you. Evelyn talked about you often when we were dating. I'm sure she is excited to have her father back." My dad is unruffled by James' approach. He isn't surprised by anything. He is used to too many things.

My dad looks at James again and asks, "Name, please." James lets out one short chuckle.

"I see then," he says to my dad, "no conversation until the introductions. Okay. My name is James. Really, it's Michael James O'Brien, but James is what everyone calls me. Even the ones who aren't my friends." He rests his hands on the table and leans toward my dad; one of the guards grabs his shoulder and forces him to sit back. "It *is* a nice thing to actually be able to meet you. Evelyn missed you. Had a whole piece of her life removed when you weren't in it. I'm sure she's happier now. Aren't you, Evelyn?" he says to the bubble window. His face is distorted through the divider, and his eyes miss the mark, but he is looking for me just the same.

I know James can't see me. He is trying to act like he knows everything, acting like he has the upper hand. But knowing he is looking for me still sends a ball of anger into my gut. He has no place talking to me, ever.

"Who are you talking to?" my dad asks him. "Nobody is here but us." James sighs and relaxes his shoulders, so the guard lets him go.

"I guess I was just hoping," he says to my dad. "Evelyn and I haven't really been together in a while. Seeing her last week was good for my heart. Maybe not for my face," he strokes his jaw. "I miss her. There are a lot of things I want to say to her."

"I'm sorry, sir. Is it difficult to hear that someone is attracted to your daughter? I should have been more delicate with my words. I would love to speak to her, though." I feel Jack shift his weight behind me. He is uncomfortable. But this is war, what we signed up for. We have to try to hold off our personal feelings like Lady Pescara said. So much is at stake.

"And what is it you would want to say to Recruit Marin?" my dad asks. "Maybe I can get the message to her." James laughs.

"That might be a little awkward," he says. "Feelings and that kind of thing. It would be much better if I could tell her myself." My dad returns his attention to the parchment in front of him.

"I see that you actually spent time in Captain Margaret's squadron early in the war," my dad continues, "before you started to follow Ceto. How long did you serve there?" he lifts his head to look at James whose face is monstrous through the bubble. James shakes his head.

"Long enough," he replies.

"Long enough for what?" my dad asks.

"Long enough to see it wasn't the life I wanted," James laughs. "And long enough to learn how Atlantis works. Long enough to watch Evelyn, know her way of doing things here, how she acts, what she eats, how she fights. I know Evelyn is here. I know she's back from whatever she was sent to do in Jaffa. I know she really is on the other side of that bubble.

"How did you like Nyobi's kingdom?" James calls to the bubble mirror. How did he know where I was? How could he possibly know?

My dad is quiet for a moment before speaking again.

"Hmmm," he finally says. "What makes you so certain you are correct? Why is it even important to know what Recruit Marin is doing? Who are you giving your information to? Why do they care? Have they found out yet that your information is faulty?" James shifts in his seat and says nothing. He focuses on my dad, unsure if he's being played.

"Does that bother you, James?" my dad asks. "Does it bother you to know we already knew you had connections and we fed you bad information? That Recruit Marin never left Atlantis, never traveled to Jaffa? That we placed that information to get you to confess that Nyobi's city really is there? Does that scare you?" Wow, Dad. Way to lay it on. James' shoulders aren't quite so square

132

as they were when he first came into the interrogation room. He has stopped looking at the bubble window, no longer confident that I am on the other side.

"We can help you, James," my dad continues. "We can help you if you help us, but only if you help us. Who do you report to?" James continues his silence, glaring at my dad. "Is it Ceto?" my dad prods. "Is it Nyobi Kadul? We can keep you safe here, James. All you need to do is talk." James straightens his chin and meets my father's gaze.

"No," he says to my dad.

"No what?" my dad asks.

"Just no," James says again then sits back in his chair.

"No, you won't help us? No, you're not afraid? No, you're not in danger? No, you aren't working for the queen?" James just sits and shakes his head.

"What is he trying to prove?" Jack asks from behind me. I hear the edge in his voice. He wants to ask me how I could have dated somebody so cocky and if I have feelings for him now. But the James I knew and dated was not like this.

"He's changed," I tell Jack. "He's let all of this stuff, the war, the power, all of it, go to his head." Jack shakes his head.

"He's weak then," he says. I roll my eyes and stay focused on the conversation in front of me, trying to ignore Jack's jealousy behind me.

"I'll tell you what," James says to my dad. "If you can get your daughter to come in here and talk to me, I'll tell you everything you want to know."

"We have no guarantees that you would tell us the truth even if Recruit Marin were here to talk to you," my dad replies. "Perhaps you could give us something to go on. Then we could check it for veracity and consider your request."

"Check what?" James asks. "I've already answered your questions. You just weren't listening. I've told you everything you need to know."

"What is he talking about?" Jack says to me as my dad continues his interrogation. "What has he said other than 'no'?"

"No, he isn't working for the queen," I say. "No, he isn't working for Ceto. No, he isn't afraid. No, he isn't here for them."

"Then who is he here for?" Jack asks. I turn to face him, and grab hold of his arm.

"He's here for Gwen," I say. "He is still working for her." I rush toward the interrogation door. Jack is a pace too far behind to stop me from going inside. I reach for the knob just as Jack reaches for me.

"Evelyn, wait," he says. But he is too late. I let the door fly open, and my eyes meet James' as soon as I enter. There is a purple bruise on his jaw where I hit him. It's so satisfying to see. Jack is right behind me. My dad lifts his steady gaze to me and the guards raise their weapons, but I am only focused on one person and he is sitting right in front of me.

"Evelyn," James says. He sits up straight and squares his shoulders again. He tries to stand but the guards push him back into the chair. "I knew you were here," he says. "I knew you would believe me."

"Where is she?" I ask as I move toward James. Jack pulls me back, not letting me get close enough to strike. My arms are itching to reach out and scratch James' face. But Jack takes me to the other side of the table. My dad stands but I don't take his seat, there's too much energy for that, my eyes never leave James' face.

"You don't need to be so forceful with her," James says to Jack, "Evelyn is in no danger from me. I could never hurt her."

"I'm protecting you from her," Jack says. James raises his eyebrows then looks at me again. He is quiet for a moment, trying to pull out some of that charm that used to make me melt.

"But Evelyn," he says to me, "why would he need to protect me from you?"

"Where is she?" I ask again, pulses of electricity coursing through my veins.

"Where is who, Evelyn?" my dad asks.

"He's working for Gwen," I say.

"I'm not working *for* her, Evelyn," James says. "I am working *with* her. You can help us."

"Yes, James," I say, "because working with my ex-boyfriend and my ex-best friend is my dream. How could I possibly resist?" He reaches his bound hands across the table, but the guards keep him from reaching me.

"Evelyn," he says. "It isn't like that. I work with Gwen, but we aren't dating."

"Ha! You forget that I've seen evidence to the contrary," I say.

"That was over a long time ago," he says. "She knows that I just want to be with you. I'm helping her because I really believe that her plan is the best plan." He's making me sick.

"What do you think, Dad?" I ask. "Do you see evidence of influence over him?"

"I do," my dad says, "though it is different than I am used to seeing in Ceto's prisoners. His eyes hold a certain blank quality to them. He isn't really struggling to free himself from it. It's like he's okay with what is happening. That allows a greater pull to be held over him without much force.

"He is bent on winning you over, like that is his mission. Nothing else matters to him. He doesn't care that anyone else hears a single word. He doesn't process any of it. He just has an end-goal in mind and is working solely for that."

"Evelyn," James says, trying to reach for me again, "Evelyn, please. I love you. We can do this together. I just need you with me." I take a deep breath and step back.

"I've heard enough," I say. "Please tell Lady Pescara that we have another traitor in our midst. Gwen is close by, maybe hiding in one of our battalions. Maybe the same one James was in."

"Yes," my dad agrees. "The power being used is weak enough to be someone other than Ceto. Its wielder must be close to keep it going."

I shake my head at James. His eyes are pleading. He looks confused, but he is a willing puppet in another woman's army, so pathetic that I didn't even need to use mind power to see right through him. I turn back to my dad.

"Let's go find ourselves a traitor."

CHAPTER 14

Everything is chaos in Captain Margaret's squad bunker. Tables are tossed over and beds are being torn apart. Captain Margaret argues with a guard at the bunker door.

"What in the sea are you looking for?!" she demands. Dad and I swim up just in time.

"Margaret," my dad says as he takes her arm. She turns her dark green eyes to his face and pulls her greying arm away from him. Margaret has been living in the sea full time and has started taking on her sea-life form, but she isn't mermaid like Lady Pescara. She is taking on the qualities of a shark. Her skin shines and her eyes are growing dark. Her teeth have grown pointed in her years under the sea. She is one of the few Atlanteans who will eat sea life.

"What is going on here, Kai?" she asks my father. "This feels like another one of Lady Pescara's attempts at getting me out of her army." My dad shakes his head.

"Margaret," he says again, "Lady Pescara isn't trying to get rid of you. We have reason to believe there is another spy in your regiment." Captain Margaret jerks her head away from my dad and turns.

"*Another* spy? She asks. "And what makes you think that Kai? "Is it my shiny skin and pointed teeth?" She bites the water in front of my dad's face. He doesn't flinch. "Do you feel like the rest of the officers do? That I am different and therefore I must be dangerous?" Her face is getting red. Her shiny grey arms are turning pink.

"That isn't the case at all, Margaret," my dad assures her. "The boy we found has given us information that suggests he was not working alone in your group." Captain Margaret shakes her head and rolls her eyes, letting out an angry sigh.

"I'm sure he has," she says to my dad. "But I have done nothing to give Atlantis any cause to worry. I have only served with devotion, despite the bias against me. My camp isn't being searched; we are being attacked!" Then she turns her eyes to me. "I heard the boy knew your daughter, Kai. Maybe *she* is the one you should be searching." She glares at me.

"There's no conspiracy here, Margaret," he says. "We are just doing our job."

"Yes, I'm sure you are," she whispers. We are all quiet for a moment until one of the guards calls out.

"I found something," he says as he swims toward the lead guard. The guard takes the item, a paper, from the soldier's hand and looks it over.

"This looks like something for you," he says as he moves toward my dad. My dad reaches his hand out for the paper, but the guard stops him.

"No," he says. "This is a letter addressed to Recruit Marin. I cannot let you take it."

"Why not?" I ask. Captain Margaret smiles.

"Because it could be evidence that you are in league with spies," she answers. "And since you are the chief interrogator's daughter, letting him or you have the letter would be problematic, now wouldn't it?" Captain Margaret sneers.

"Protocol dictates that items seized in a search must be handled with care," the guard says. "Because of its value and possible contents, I cannot in good faith give it to you or your father."

"Well, what will be done with it?" I ask.

"He will take it directly to Lady Pescara," my dad answers. "We can find out its contents there."

"Let's get going, then," I say.

"Yes, let's," says Captain Margaret.

"I'm sorry, Captain," the guard says. "I have orders to remain here with you until your squadron is cleared."

"So, I'm a prisoner until I'm proven innocent?" Margaret spits at the guard.

"Not at all, Captain," the guard responds. "We are just following protocol."

"I'm sure you are," Captain Margaret says as she rolls her eyes.

"I will send the letter with lieutenant Spear," the guard says. "He will make sure it arrives safely to Lady Pescara." He hands the letter to the lieutenant and we follow the soldier back to Lady Pescara's office.

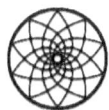

"Sit down," Lady Pescara tells me and my dad. We both sit quietly as we wait for her to read the letter. Lieutenant Spear stays by the door. I wonder if he is here to guard me and my dad. Does he think there is a conspiracy?

Lady Pescara is quiet for several minutes as she reads the letter. I cannot see what it says, but I recognize Gwen's hurried scrawl.

"By the time you get this, I will be long gone," Lady Pescara reads aloud. "Don't bother trying to find me. I know that you will probably hand this over to Lady Pescara anyway, so I won't bother telling you anything important. Just know you could have been a part of something big, Evelyn. Something really big.

"I've seen too many of your choices to trust you now. James was my willing decoy while I got out of Atlantis. He won't be helpful to you. I think I have enough information now to help my cause. When I think back to our first meeting in Atlantis, I try to remember any signs you gave me. Anything that would have let me know that you were on my side. But I guess you were only in it for yourself. I wish I could have that day again, Evelyn, to have another chance to convince you to join me. We could have done great things together.

"As it is, I will fight this battle without you. My mother and grandmother are strange, stupid creatures. They are so caught up in their quest for world domination that they don't notice me anymore. But that will be their undoing. With or without your help, I will prevail. I just wish you could have been a part of it.

"Your future leader, Gwendolyn Mizrahi." Lady Pescara sets the parchment on her desk and looks up at me.

"It sounds like your friend really thought she could have you on her side," she says.

"Gwen hasn't been my friend for a long time, Lady Pescara."

"Are you certain about this?" she asks. "It cannot be a coincidence that she showed up here while you were gone. That way you couldn't be used to interrogate them until you got back to Atlantis. Maybe she's been watching you – with another spy perhaps? Maybe she just knows you better than you think. Are you sure she hasn't been in your mind?" Lady Pescara's words cut into me and she looks me dead in the eye. Could she be right? Have I been an unwitting ally in Gwen's plan?

"Lady Pescara," my dad interjects, "you must see this for what it is. A deranged daughter of a dictator trying to lure in who she can and use them. Evelyn doesn't have any allegiance to Gwen."

"I don't doubt Recruit Marin's sincerity, Kai," Lady Pescara answers. "General Lachlan is a product of Gwen's former army. He has proved quite useful. He even told us about bringing Evelyn to Gwen just before the attack on our city. She may have started her mind control then. She may have planted seeds into Evelyn's mind that she wouldn't even be aware of."

"You think she's been in my head this whole time, that I've been letting her know what we're doing all along?" I ask.

"I think it is a very real possibility, Evelyn," she says to me. "We know how powerful Ceto is with her mind control. Your own father is evidence and witness of that. It is possible that Gwen has meddled with your mind and led you to believe things that were never true."

"You mean my time in Ancient Greece."

"I do."

After a moment of silence, I find my voice. "Helios," I say. "Helios is here. He is real, Lady Pescara. He knows he's a descendent of Gileaus. He is evidence that all of that really did happen. It wasn't a dream. It couldn't be." I start to cry, and it makes me angry.

Lady Pescara nods but keeps her look of frustration.

"You may be right," she says, "but I cannot let my judgment be clouded. Even Captain Jack told me Helios had power over you. This descendent of our enemy has not been vetted yet and could be part of a larger plan. I have to protect Atlantis. Recruit Marin, until we can prove that Gwen has no link to your mind, you will be relieved from your duties.

"What?!" I yell. "Why would you do that to me? I don't feel Gwen in my brain! I could feel her if she were there, couldn't I? Dad?"

"This makes no sense, Lady Pescara," my dad says. "Evelyn has been serving Atlantis since her return to the ocean. She risked her life to discover Ceto and Nyobi's plans. She broke into their palace. There is no evidence that her mind has been tampered with." Lady Pescara nods and looks at me.

"And she brought something back from the treasury. Kai," she says. "Evelyn, why did you return with that medallion around your neck? Why did you take it from Nyobi's treasury? Why did you steal it? What are the powers it possesses? What do you intend to do with it?" She points at the chain around my neck. The medallion has been beneath my clothing since I took it from Nyobi's treasury. I don't know why I thought no one would know or figure out what I had. My hamsa grows cold sitting on my chest. It feels so empty. It feels my emptiness and confusion. Why did I take it? Why did I steal something so valuable and powerful from our enemy and keep it to myself? Was I inadvertently getting it for Gwen?

"The hamsa called to me," I answer in a whisper. "It's the same medallion I wore when I lived in Ancient Greece. I couldn't help myself. It's a part of me. I knew I couldn't be without it."

"You couldn't help yourself," Lady Pescara whispers. "Have you thought about what you would do with it since you've been back? Have you left it lying anywhere or had the impulse to bury it or throw it away? It could be easy for Gwen to steal."

"No," I say, slumping back into my chair. "No. No. No. I've kept it on the entire time – ever since I got it. I feel more complete with it. I can't take it off."

"Lady Pescara," My dad says. "This is all conjecture. All of it is circumstantial. Evelyn is young but she is strong. It's outside of her nature to give into mind control, she is not weak. Please stop this line of questioning. There is so much more we could be doing to help the cause right now. Accusing Evelyn isn't going to help anyone."

"You forget that you also were not weak Kai," Lady Pescara says. "I agree that Recruit Marin is strong and assured of herself. But it is also possible that Gwen has created a plan to kidnap Evelyn, to lure her into a trap where she can take the Medallion for herself. Until I can know for sure, I have no choice but to relieve Recruit Marin of her duties and keep her under guard."

"Under guard? Why?" my dad asks.

"I believe Evelyn may have been drawn to that medallion, Kai," she says. "I believe it is immensely powerful and I believe that Evelyn's heart is true to the cause of Atlantis. If she can prove useful in a time of battle and if that medallion can give her added strength, I want her to have it. I will not take it from her. But I cannot let it or her fall into the hands of our enemy. This is for your safety and ours, Recruit Marin."

Dad and I both sit quietly. I have no idea what to say. I have no idea what to do. Instead of being able to help Atlantis, I have to be babysat because I *might* be kidnapped, and I *might* have some kind of mental tracker on me.

"Lieutenant," Lady Pescara calls to the guard at the door. "Send word for Captain Jack to retrieve his recruit," she continues. "He will be taking her back to her home on land."

"Lady Pescara," I say. "I need to be here. I need to help here. Please! Don't send me away." But my pleas fall on deaf ears. Lieutenant Spear leaves and a few moments later, Jack comes for me. It is an uncomfortable meeting as everything is explained and he is ordered to escort me from Atlantis. He is told to not have a relationship with me. He is asked to treat me like I am brainwashed or weak. I feel his body stiffen while Lady Pescara delivers his instructions. But Jack will obey the orders, I know he will, and he does.

Jack takes me by the arm and escorts me out of Lady Pescara's office. Her eyes are still pouring over the letter Gwen left for me. My dad is still trying to reason with her, but her face is red, and her eyes are angry. I know it will be useless.

Jack and I don't say a word as he leads me down the hall and back to our barracks. It doesn't take long for me to gather the few personal items I have here. At least I'll be able to open my family album on land, to see if my ancestors can send me any wisdom through their faces. Do they know what is happening to me? Are they watching from the next life?

Finally, Jack and I leave the city. As he takes me away, I keep playing what I can remember of Gwen's letter over and over in my head.

I know you'll give this letter to Lady Pescara.

If I could go back to that day.

If I could convince you to join me.

The first time we met in Atlantis.

Was she trying to tell me something?

Yes. She was.

"Jack!" I grab his arm in a tight grip.

"Ouch," he says. "What is it?"

"I know what Gwen is trying to tell me!"

"What do you mean?" he asks.

"In the letter! She was sending me a message in the letter! I have to go meet her!"

"You can't be serious, Evelyn," he says. "Do you have any idea what you are saying right now? That you want to visit a known spy who is trying to use you? Besides, Lady Pescara said she already fled from the city," he says.

"She wants Lady Pescara to think that," I reply. "She wants everyone to think that. Everyone but me." My medallion burns hot against my chest. I know I have figured it out. I let go of Jack's arm and swim away. Away from him and away from the gates of Atlantis. I curve around the walls of the city, Jack right behind me. He knows I am not swimming away from him. He knows I am swimming toward something, and he is swimming there with me.

After nearly twenty minutes, we finally reach our destination. I pause to catch my breath and look down into the water beneath me. There, covered by a hill of earth, are the remains of decades ago. Remains of a city destroyed by a submerged landslide. It is here where I met Gwen underwater for the first time. If I am going to find her, this will be the place.

"This is where we met," I whisper to Jack who floats beside me. "This is where I first saw her in the sea."

"You met in the open like this?" he asks. I shake my head.

"No," I tell him. "It was in one of the houses near the landslide."

"Which one?" he asks. "And are you sure you want to go there?" I shake my head.

"I don't know what I want," I tell him. "I know I don't want to see the world get destroyed. I know I don't want to see the ocean overrun by evil. I know I don't want to lose you." Jack tries to say something, but I stop him. "But Atlantis has abandoned me, Jack. My Dad can't help me, and it can't be long before my mom will be questioned for anything she might know. Even you abandoned me, Jack. You were ready to break up with me because your commanding officer told you to. I don't know where else to go. I have to see this through and see if it will help Atlantis. I have to try." Jack reaches out and takes my hand.

"Evelyn," he says. "I'm sorry about what happened in Lady Pescara's office. I broke the rules. I never should have started our relationship in a time of war. I should have waited for things to settle down, but I just couldn't." I turn to look at him and feel little fish swimming in my stomach. The green of his eyes is a little darker so far below the surface. He looks so…so…

He moves closer to me, his face looking into mine, and his arm wraps around my waist. His fingers lace through my hair.

"I'm sorry, Evelyn," he whispers into my ear. Then his lips brush across my cheek until they meet mine. The kiss is soft, like an apology. My heart beats faster and the hamsa vibrates with heat. We stay there for a moment longer, just letting our hearts beat together. When he finally pulls away, Jack kisses my forehead and looks into my eyes again.

"So, what are we going to do Evelyn?" he asks.

"We are going to find a villain," I say with a smile. And with hands clasped, we turn toward the crumbling city, together.

CHAPTER 15

We swim through the quiet darkness of this abandoned part of the city, looking for reminders of the path to Gwen. After a few minutes, we crest the hill. Just a few strokes beyond is a broken, familiar window with red markings fading around its frame. This is the place, the window I swam through with Lachlan last year, long before I lost myself in the depths of Ancient Greece. I pause for a moment then turn to Jack and gesture toward the window. I swim toward the broken opening and he follows closely behind.

When I enter the building, I pause to listen for voices. The last time I was here, there was a war council going on with Gwen's followers. But I hear nothing. There is no sign of movement, no evidence that anyone is here at all. I swim to the hallway and make my way to the familiar room where I first saw Gwen speaking to her small army, but this time it is empty.

Jack peers into the empty space with me but says nothing. He is waiting for whatever I know will be here. At least I think I know it will be. We leave the empty room behind and swim toward the large, spiral staircase at the end of the hall, not hesitating or listening for anyone. If Gwen is here, I want to find her and find her fast. I am done with playing. I swim up the stairs and into the empty top level. A few pieces of coral have made their home in the abandoned space, but otherwise, nothing has changed from what I remember.

"Where is she?" Jack asks. "Are you sure we are in the right building?"

"Oh, you're in the right building," we hear Gwen's voice speaking from the darkness. It is an eerie sound. "I just didn't expect Evelyn to bring anyone with her."

"Jack is the only one with me," I say to the shadows.

"If I didn't believe that was true, you wouldn't have made it this far," she says. "But my scouts keep me informed."

So, how much have her scouts heard? How much does she already know?

"Please," Gwen says as she moves out from the shadows and into the light, "come closer so we can talk. You can bring your boyfriend with you."

Jack and I swim toward the far end of the room where Gwen is waiting near a shaft of light, her face shadowed. It is difficult for me to get a read on her expression. Her dark hair looks black in the nighttime water. She has it wrapped in dreadlocks, so it looks like the snakes on her grandmother's head. Her eyes have grown even darker than the deep, chocolatey brown I remember. They are nearly black. The shadows across her face create a mask of gloom.

"So," she says, "why did you come here?"

"You left instructions with your pathetic scout so I could find you. Why make James beg me to come? Why not just send a note to me, directly? I didn't need such an elaborate plan to meet with you. I would have come." I reply.

"If everything had gone according to my plan from the start," she says, "You would have been among those who took James and he would have reached out to you earlier. But as it is, the message was still delivered. I am satisfied.

"I have the same reasons for wanting you here that I did the first time we met, Evelyn," she finally says. "I'm sure James delivered that part of my message."

"He did," I say. "Though I'm not sure he had much of a choice."

"James knew what he was doing when he came here with me," Gwen says. "My mother's original plan was to force me to persuade you to join her army. She used her mind-bending powers on me and sent me back to Atlantis, complete with a cover to protect my identity. But I am stronger than she knows, Evelyn.

"I was able to transfer her power over me to James. Don't worry, I had his consent. As the daughter of one queen and the granddaughter of another, I have more innate ability than either of them realizes. Even more than I realized. But I'm not forceful like Ceto or the queen. I like my followers to have a choice. But I couldn't do anything while my mind was blocked. James took that burden from me in the transfer of control. He willingly became my puppet to get to you."

Gwen has even more power than anyone knew she had. What is she capable of? What would have happened if she had been the one to take the Atlantean pearl months ago?

"My offer is still the same," she continues, "except now I am working against my mother *and* my grandmother. I want to take over the ocean, Evelyn. I'm tired of living my life in someone else's shadow. I want to make the seas great again. You are strong. I know you and know what you are capable of. I want you on my side."

"When you tried to recruit me before, you were wanting to create a new world order," I say. "You wanted to flood the land just like your mom did. Why is it just the ocean this time?"

"I realized that my goals were too big, Evelyn," she says in return. "I wanted too much and pushed too much. I was so blinded by my desires that I was blindsided by my mother. I'm wiser now. My time in the ocean has taught me what I need to know. I have my attention on both Ceto and the Queen. I am focused on what I can do without them. I've been watching and listening for months. I know their plans and their weaknesses. I am keeping my own plans in check until I can overpower them. Once that happens…"

"You'll try to flood the earth again," Jack says. Gwen barely looks his way before returning her attention to me.

"Once that happens," she says again, "I will bring order back to the seas. I will make them whole and healthy again. Of course, that requires teaching some land dwellers some lessons about caring for the earth along the way, but in the end, it will be the best course of action for everyone."

"What kind of lessons do you plan on teaching them?" I ask her.

"We will cross that sea when the time comes," she replies. I shake my head.

"I need to know more before I commit to anything," I tell her. "I want to know how you plan to make all of this happen. What kind of resources do you have at your disposal? How do you plan to overpower your mother and the queen? Do you have an army large enough to do it? Don't you think you would have better success if you were working *with* Atlantis?" Gwen lifts her chin and moves backward several feet.

"You must understand that I cannot give you all of those details, Evelyn," she says. "What assurances do I even have from you that this much will remain between us? How can I possibly share *all* that I know?"

"How can you expect us to make a decision to follow you without those assurances, Gwen?" Jack interjects. This time, Gwen turns to him to answer.

"You are not my primary interest, Jack," she tells him. "You are only here because Evelyn wants you here. My answering of questions has nothing to do with you. You get to come because Evelyn wanted it. Evelyn is the strength I am looking for." She turns back to me.

"What will it be, Evelyn?" she asks.

"Gwen," I say, "I have no idea what I'd be heading into. I have no way of knowing what your end-goal looks like or what you would or would not do to reach it. I can't commit to a cause I know so little about." Gwen pauses for a moment before responding.

"Then we've reached an impasse," she says. "I may see you again, but it won't be for a long time. You are always welcome to join me, Evelyn. I'd rather have you fighting for me than against me. Of course, fighting against Ceto would be enough for me." She turns toward the shadows she came from, talking as she leaves us.

"Don't bother trying to follow me," she says as she swims away. "You'll be disappointed in the result. And I suggest waiting around here for a while before returning to Atlantis. My guards have orders to hold you for a few days if you don't leave with me. They won't hurt you unless you give them a reason to."

"Hold us?!" Jack says. "Hurt us? You brought us here just so we could be your prisoners?" Gwen turns around.

"No, Jack," she says. "I brought you here as my guests. I wanted you to join me. That offer has been refused and I must protect myself."

"What about James?" I ask. I feel Jack stiffen when I mention his name.

"You don't need to worry about James," Gwen says. "I will take care of him. Goodbye, Evelyn."

Gwen swims into the shadows and out of sight. Jack hesitates just for a moment before trying to swim after her.

"OUCH!" I hear him yell from the darkness. He is back by my side in an instant.

"What is it?" I ask. "What happened?" Within a second a slithering, electric eel slinks into the room.

"That's what happened!" Jack says. "That thing shocked me!"

"Shhhhhheeee did warnnnnn you," the eel hisses as he moves closer to us.

"I don't believe anything she said!" Jack yells at the eel. A second eel creeps from the darkness.

"Thaaaat is your misssstake," the second eel says. All around the room, the hisses of eels fill the space. They slither along the floor and move through the open water to surround us. Jack and I move closer to one another as their circle around us tightens.

"Weeee heard eeeverythingggg."

"Youuuuu shhhhould have follllllowed her."

"Nooooowww we have to teeeeeeach you a lesssssson."

Jack and I float back to back as we face the onslaught of eels. It has been a while since we have fought together, but the feeling comes back to us. We've had plenty of practice on the training field. I open my arms wide and heat the water around me. It's a trick I haven't used in a long time, but it feels so good to try it out again here and now.

"How are you even alive here?" Jack asks the eels, stalling. "You're freshwater fish."

"It isssss as shhhhhhe ssssaid," they hiss.

"Shhhhheee hasssss many powerssssss and abilitiessssss."

"Becaussssssse of the princccccesssss Mizzzzrahi, we can live anywhere we choosssssssseeee...."

The water around me is uncomfortably warm. I can feel myself sweating in the heat of it. Jack's body is warming up as well. The heat I am coaxing from the water is raising his temperature. He will only be able to handle so much before we have to act.

Our backs press together as Jack swims into me. He opens his arms wide and moves them through the water, side to side. His power over current control sends the waves of heated water toward the electric eels. There are a few hisses of discomfort and even of pain, but none of the eels are moving away. They are still tightening their circle around us.

I put all of my energy into the water. I can feel the heat taking a toll on my body. I am getting dizzy and light-headed, but the eels are starting to slow their progress.

"Youuuuu cannnnnn't keep thissssss up forevvvvvver," they say. "You alllllready growwww weeaak…" I push the heat into the water with greater attention and force. The eels move backward again as Jack sends the water toward them in pulsating ripples, visible to my attuned eyes.

But these eels aren't going to give up that easily. They group together, even tighter in their circle. All I can see is their slithering bodies around me. One strikes out with its electricity then another then another. Each strike is a startling jolt and those jolts are increasing. Jack and I cry out with every sting and react with more heat of our own, but there are probably two dozen of these electric eels here and only two of us. We don't have much time left before we lose consciousness.

Suddenly, Jack's arms link through mine and he forces me onto his back. The strength of the move distracts me from what I am doing, and I stop superheating the water. The eels pour toward us and Jack dives down with me on his back, facing them as they chase us. Several eels hit us as we dive beneath the group. I let out a scream of pain, but Jack doesn't let me go.

More and more eels strike as they regroup above us. But Jack is using his current control to propel us through the water. It is tight getting through the stairwell and hallway on his back and more eels catch up. I feel them sting over and over, hitting us both with their hundreds of volts of energy. Jack winces and weakens. We are almost to the window, almost to our escape into the fresh and powerful current of open water. Just as we make it through the window, a large eel, sitting guard on the windowsill, reaches out and strikes with all his might. The pain is blinding. I cannot take it anymore. My world goes black.

CHAPTER 16

When I wake up, I am lying in my bed in my FIU dorm. My mom is sitting next to me, singing an old lullaby and holding my hand. Her thumb moving across my hand helps me open my eyes.

"Mom?" I ask. "Mom, what happened? Where is Jack?" I try to sit up, but movement is still impossible. A piercing headache shoots through my skull and I lie back against the pillows, squeezing my eyes tight against the pain.

"My love," my mom says to me as she leans over me. She moves a few loose strands of hair from my face. "Jack is okay. He had to go back to Atlantis and report to Lady Pescara."

"But," I say and then I cannot think of anything else. I touch my fingers to my forehead and wince again. It feels like I'm being struck by Gwen's eels all over again. My mom takes my hand and brings it again to my side.

"You have some pretty rough burns, Evelyn," my mom whispers. "Try not to touch them." It's then that I feel the stickiness on my arms. Something is pulling at the hair. I open my eyes enough to look down. My arm is swollen and red with several bandages stuck to it. A few Band-Aids are on my right arm with something tacky coming out from under them, but the left is far worse. A sound comes from the front room. Someone comes in and talks to my mom.

"How is she?" it is Celia. I don't know why she would be here. Maybe to keep an extra eye on me. Does Lady Pescara think my mom can't keep me safe from Gwen? She must not know my mom very well. So, she's given me my bitter and angry roommate as backup. I think I would rather have Gwen around.

"She's just waking up," my mom tells Celia. "She's going to be okay. She just needs rest and fluids." Celia walks closer to my bed and stands at the end.

"Lady Pescara ordered me to be your companion," she says. I can hear in the tone of her voice that she is even less thrilled about this than I am, if that's possible. "I will be staying with you for at least another week. Mrs. Marin will be able to make regular visits." I turn and look at my mom. She smiles at me, but the smile doesn't reach her eyes.

"My time with you today is just about up," she tells me while she strokes my thumb. "I'll be back again tomorrow."

"Why do you have to go?" I ask her. I don't need a babysitter, but it would be nice to have my mom with me while I regain my strength.

"You are allowed three visitors a day," Celia interjects. "Lady Pescara believes isolation will be the best to see if you are under mind control. She doesn't want anyone to be swayed by Gwen through you." I wince when she speaks, but I keep my eyes on my mom. So, this is why Celia is here. If anyone wouldn't cut me any slack or would look for signs of anything wrong with me, it would be her.

"We just want to make sure you get the rest you need," Mom says to me. "You don't need me here to interrupt your recovery." There are tears in her eyes. I know she is lying. Is she afraid my brain is affected, too? "I will be back first thing tomorrow morning." My mom leans forward and kisses my forehead. She strokes my cheek one more time before standing. "I love you darling. Rest up." She leaves my bedside, and Celia escorts her out of the apartment.

Lady Pescara thinks she is protecting me, protecting Atlantis. But I am a prisoner here. This isn't my dorm room; this is my jail cell. I'm stuck in here when I could and should be helping Atlantis. A moment later, Celia comes back into the room.

"Well, how are you really feeling?" she asks. She takes the chair my mom had been sitting in and moves it further away from my bedside before sitting down. I am not interested in spending time with Celia.

"I'm fine," I say. "I just want to go back to sleep."

"Really?" Celia asks. There is an edge to her voice. There is always an edge to her voice. "Aren't you interested in how Jack is doing since your little escapade?"

"My mom said he was in Atlantis," I mumble through the heaviness that pushes on my eyelids. "He is reporting to Lady Pescara."

"And you assume that he made it through those eels unscathed?" she asks. "You aren't the only one in recovery." I stare at Celia and wait for her to tell me about Jack. She just wants me to look like I'm selfish for not thinking about him. Maybe I am.

"Jack was burned and bruised when he brought you to shore," she tells me. "But he didn't care at all about himself. I was headed back to the sea after a weekend sabbatical when you two walked out of it. As soon as I saw Jack, I knew something was wrong.

"I swam to him and he could barely hold you up. I tried to tell him we needed to get both of you back to Atlantis, to our doctors, but he insisted on bringing you here. So, I helped him. Once you were taken care of, he finally went back to the ocean and left me here to care for you." Celia pauses, waiting for me to thank her, but I am too tired. After a moment, she realizes I won't be saying anything, so she sighs and continues with her account.

"That was three days ago," she says. "You have been in and out of it the whole time. Lady Pescara sent word that I was to stay here with you. By then, I knew enough to know that I was supposed to be your warden. I have to watch you for signs of mind control." I roll my eyes and turn my head away.

"Look, Evelyn," Celia continues. "You may not like me much and you may actually not have anything crazier than usual going on in your head, but these are my orders and I'm going to follow them." I am surprised that Celia wouldn't accuse me outright of being brainwashed. She probably doesn't want to incriminate Jack. I shake my head as my eyes droop even more.

"Thank you for your help," I manage to say, hoping she will leave. She keeps talking, but I don't hear what she is saying. Sleep washes over me, and I give in to it.

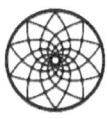

Time passes and my mom comes and goes. I finally go through the itchy stage with my burns. It's all I can do to keep from scratching. Celia is there, constantly reminding me that if I scratch, I'll scar myself forever. I almost want to scratch just to spite her. But I know it's better for me if I don't.

As I heal, I have many strange dreams about Gwen and Helios, Jack, James, and Chelsea. We are always fighting. Fighting with words and fighting with weapons. My dreams are messed up, but the sleep has still been healing. I've moved to the couch in the front room and can get everything I need for myself. Having Celia as my guard is extra motivation. I want her to help me as little as possible. No one else comes to see me. My dad, of course, is bound to the sea – leaving it would be deadly for him. But Jack and Chelsea, Lady Pescara and others I know from the ocean, even Uncle Russ, keep their distance. Maybe they are afraid to be tainted by association.

There is a knock at our door and Celia rises to get it. She has been agitated all morning, cleaning and picking up the whole dorm – even my room. It's like she is expecting company. She opens the door and I cannot see who is there, I just hear all of Celia's responses.

"She's fine," she says to the visitor at the door. "She's a little weak, but I think we can make the move anyway." *What move?* Am I being sent somewhere else? A psychiatric unit under the ocean maybe?

"I'll have her ready," Celia continues. "Tell the captain I have everything in order here." She closes the door and returns to our front room.

"Who was that?" I ask her. Celia is quiet for a moment.

"It was a messenger, Evelyn," she answers. Okay…

"What messenger?" I ask again. Again, Celia pauses before answering. She takes a deep breath and squares her shoulders.

"You and I are leaving here tonight," she says. "While you have been resting and healing, I have been working with Captain Jack to move ahead with his plans."

"What plans?" I ask. "What are you talking about?" Why is she calling them Captain Jack's plans? Is she actually ignoring orders from Lady Pescara? Celia begins pacing the room.

"After your run-in with Gwen last week, Jack tried talking to Lady Pescara," she answers. "But the general wouldn't listen. She said she cannot rely on any information from Gwen." Celia pauses her pacing to look at me. "Lady Pescara is very brave and true, Evelyn, but she can also be very stubborn. She is focused on her plans and attacks. She wouldn't listen to Jack. She accused him of being blinded by his *feelings* for you," Celia rolls her eyes. As if

Jack could possibly have feelings for me. "But Jack was persistent." She pulls a dining chair close to sit down next to me.

"Eventually, Lady Pescara had enough of Jack's perseverance," she continues. "They argued right before a council meeting. Many of the council leaders could hear them from the hall. Lady Pescara was under a lot of pressure to assert her authority. Not everyone thinks a woman is fit to run the army, Evelyn." Celia rolls her eyes again and shakes her head. "She told Jack to leave. He tried again to reason with her, but she was over it. She told him, 'Fine, take care of this yourself. But if it backfires, don't you dare leave this on my doorstep. Your plans are yours alone. If you interfere with the army in any way as you carry this out, you won't live long enough to regret it.' She opened the door and let him out into the hall. Once he was through, she slammed the door. I'm pretty sure a couple of the council members peed themselves."

Celia laughs and I give a half-smile. Celia is never this animated when she talks with me. It feels like she is trying to share a secret with me – something I am not used to. It's like we are on the same side. Though I'm not sure what side that is.

"So, what exactly are Jack's plans?" I ask. "Who was the messenger at the door? Do they have something to do with it?"

"Be patient, Evelyn, and let me finish," she says. That's more like the Celia I am used to.

"Jack didn't wait for Lady Pescara to change her mind," she continues. "He came back to our battalion and started work. He told us he was given a top-secret directive. He said Lady Pescara didn't want to know the particulars, that she knew it was dangerous and could fail. He said anyone who wanted to be a part of the effort could follow him. Anyone else could remain with the army of Atlantis and continue their service under Captain Smythe.

"Chelsea was the first of the sea group to volunteer," she tells me. "I would have volunteered first, if I would have been there instead of here."

"I'm sure you would have," I say. "But what are the plans? Who else volunteered?" Celia stands.

"We are going on a trip, Evelyn," she says. "While the rest of the army of Atlantis has been traveling across the ocean floor to the Mediterranean Sea, Captain Jack has been working on a plan to strike from land. Or rather, to strike from within." Celia starts pacing the room again.

"Jack took you to Nyobi's palace, Evelyn. He is going to take more of us. We are going to create a diversion before the army of Atlantis arrives. We are going to attack from within."

"And what about Gwen?" I ask her.

"What about her?" Celia says. "Captain Jack said her power is nothing compared to her mother and grandmother. With my report on your progress and his persuasion, Lady Pescara said she felt satisfied that you aren't under mind control. You get to join us in the Mediterranean. Once we stop Ceto and Nyobi, Gwen will be easy to deal with."

I wonder if Jack was in the same conversation I was in with Gwen. Did he not understand that she has gained power of her own?

That she understands how to use it against her family and anyone else who opposes her? It's also been at least a week since our confrontation with Gwen. She could be anywhere and planning anything by now.

"Gwen is more of a danger than Jack realizes," I tell Celia. She walks to the door before answering.

"*Captain* Jack knows what he is doing, Evelyn," she says. "Honestly, you should trust him more than you do. Now, I am going to start packing and getting ready for the journey. You should do the same. I assume you *are* going with us, aren't you?"

I nod. What other choice do I have?

"Good," she says. "I'll help you get ready once my things are together." She goes into her room and starts packing. I get up and head to my room, staring at the tidied space Celia prepared for me. Wetsuits are already laid out on my bed. Hair ties and personal products are gathered on my desk. It looks like I am the only thing she needs to pack up.

I pull out my bag, a million questions forming in my mind, and start putting my stuff inside. I'm still tired, but I want to get as much of this done without Celia as I can. The busy work lets my mind wander. Who else is coming with us? Do my parents know what we are doing? Are they going to help us, or have they already gone to be with the traveling army? My mom must still be here, but I know my dad's current control skills will be needed to move the army so far with any real speed.

Why hasn't Jack come to tell me any of this himself? Why hasn't he come at all? Is he still mad about Helios? Still jealous over James? What has he been preparing us for? What part will everyone play? I am too recognizable. I don't think I can sneak in a second time. And what about Helios? Is he still sitting in the Atlantean holding cells?

Another knock at the door. This time, I go see who it is, and open the door wide to Helios.

"Evelyn!" he says, and he sweeps me into an embrace, I groan when he squeezes my aching body. "Oh, I'm sorry. I didn't think about your sores."

"It's okay," I tell him. And it is. I'm in pain, but I'm whole.

"Why are you here already?" Celia asks when she walks into the room

"Captain Jack sent me to help you with anything you need," Helios says. His arms are still wrapped loosely around my waist and his face is close to mine. Celia watches us closely.

"Well, I don't need anything," she tells him. "It looks like Evelyn could use your help, though." My cheeks burn and my heart is pounding. Jack must have sent Helios here to test me. To see if I really do want his lips on mine or if Helios, the memory of Gileaus, is what I really want. I am getting dizzy and lightheaded again.

"I think I need to sit down," I say. Helios walks with me to Celia's chair.

"You stay here," he says. "I'll get your bags. Where are they?"

"I can help you," Celia tells him. She walks him to my room, and I hear her telling him how to find everything that I need to pack. When she passes back by me to her own room, she raises an eyebrow at me, shaking her head and disappearing into her own space.

What was Jack thinking sending Helios here? How did he even get him out of the holding cells? Why would he do this to me? Do I really have to prove something to him? Why can't we just leave everything as it was?

But life isn't like that, especially when romantic relationships are involved. Nothing can ever go back to the way it was. Nothing can ever feel the same as it did. I will have to move forward carefully and find the path I want to take, even though it will be painful and frustrating. I can barely stand the thought of it all, but we are at war. I must move forward. I can't hide under a rock no matter how much I may want to.

I take a deep breath and head to my room to help Helios.

CHAPTER 17

I have lived underwater and been held as prisoner. I've lived off seaweed and pudding. I have been tortured and held captive in an ancient dungeon. But none of that compares to the agony of flying across the Atlantic Ocean with Helios sitting on one side of me while Jack sits on the other. We have been mostly silent for the entire flight. I've kept my arms folded to keep from sending anyone any signals. Any time my head falls to one side or the other, I sit up straight again. I'm exhausted.

When we finally land, I cannot get out of my seat fast enough. Chelsea follows behind me to help gather our luggage. I feel her thoughts reaching out to me, but I have no desire to talk. All I want is to finish what we came to do and go home. I have the sudden realization that I don't even know where my home is anymore.

We have a much larger group this time since most of Jack's regiment followed him on his quest. We are acting like a study-abroad group from FIU here to examine the effects of climate change on the Mediterranean. We check into our hotel and take a day to sleep off the jet lag and prep for our venture.

We have 7 rented boats and are working our way toward the borders of Nyobi's encampment. Today is a Holy Day. The regular fishermen aren't even on the water. We had to rent the boats for a much higher price, a premium to ward off the evils of boating on a

Holy Day, but it is worth it to not be surrounded when fishermen return to the ocean tomorrow.

There is no need for anyone to put on the dive gear we rented. Nobody will be here to see us not using it. I zip up my wetsuit and jump into the water. I don't wait for the rest of my boat. I swim toward Jack and Celia; Helios and Chelsea follow closely behind me.

"Are you ready for this?" Jack asks as I approach.

"I've never been more ready for anything my entire life," I tell him. Celia looks incredulous. But right now, I'm the one with the upper hand. I know Ceto. I've been ruined by Nyobi. I've been in this fortress before.

As soon as Chelsea and Helios reach us, I dive down. There is no need for me to spend any time thinking about this. All I want is to get what we came for. I'm heading to the treasury.

When we reach the sea floor, we spend a minute looking around. Because of the Holy Day, there are not many sea people below the surface. They are all too busy on land, worshipping the Sea Queen they call a goddess, being swindled by her mind power. There are fewer sea animals swimming in the dome to protect the city. Is Nyobi not worried that she could be attacked on a Holy Day or have a bunch of sea creatures left her service? Would she let them leave?

A few guards stand at the entrance to the city. They aren't the same guards as before; these two are smaller.

"What are you doing here?" the first guard asks. He is a little shaky and unsure of himself. I see Jack reaching for the small knife he keeps tucked in his wetsuit. I put my hand out to stop him from doing anything stupid. I can handle this.

"We are here to bow before her royal highness on her honored day," I tell him as I make I low bow before him. While I speak, I send little bits of my mind control to him. The tiny purple tendrils aren't very powerful, but they will work on a weaker mind. I send easiness and understanding. They will believe me. As the tendrils reach the guards, the second guard addresses us.

"A noble wish," he says to us. "I hope other worshippers will follow your example." He and the first guard bow before us and let us into the city. Everyone in our group gives a nod to the guards, thanking them for their graciousness. I feel everyone's energy. They don't understand that I also can manipulate minds. I'm not sure I want them to know yet.

We walk down the nearly empty road to the queen's palace. Two more guards, a little tougher than the city guards, stand at the door of the palace, lazily looking around the water. They are bored and could use a distraction and it doesn't take long for them to finally take notice of us.

"Celia," I whisper as I pull her behind a building. "You are going to be our decoy." She stiffens and looks to Jack, her captain.

"That isn't what we discussed," she says to him. Jack hesitates for a moment as he takes in the situation: two bored sea guards, overworked and probably underpaid. They probably haven't

172

had much time for socializing. They are stuck working when the rest of their squad is off celebrating somewhere.

"I know, Celia," he finally says. "But I am going to listen to Evelyn on this. We weren't prepared to have so few people down here. We expected our distraction would create mayhem so we could sneak in, but there just aren't enough bodies down here to be useful. We have to be stealthy." Celia stiffens. She looks around the scene and knows Jack and I are right. She just needs a little push to seal the deal.

"Then have Evelyn talk to them," Celia says. "It looks to me like she has a way with the guards down here."

"Look, Celia," I say. "I've been to the treasury before and I can get there again. But I can't do that *and* distract the guards. These guys haven't seen many women in a while. The villagers mostly bring boys to join the army. They aren't used to seeing someone young and beautiful. They'll be way too distracted to care about the rest of us at all." Celia's face softens. I've praised her looks and admitted she is a beauty, something I would never do under normal circumstances. It's just the kind of ego stroking she needs.

"Evelyn is right," Helios says. Celia looks irritated again, but Helios knows what to say. "You are going to wow them from the moment they set eyes on you. They'll fumble all over themselves." Celia sighs and allows a small smile into the corners of her mouth.

"Alright," she finally says. "I'll act like I am a visitor to the village. Just resting between my travels between sea cities. Since it was so busy on land, I figured I'd take advantage of an empty sea to do some exploring."

"Really lay it on thick," Jack tells her. "Really act interested in everything they say."

"I know how to catch a man," Celia answers. "It won't be that difficult. Watch and learn." She tugs at the French braid in her hair, loosening it up a bit. A few blonde strands escape and float around her face. She pinches her cheeks and puts on a dazzling smile. She gives Helios a wink. He turns red. She smiles and swims away from the group.

"I wish I could stay and watch," Chelsea answers.

"I do, too," Helios says. The rest of us look at his duped face and shake our heads.

"No time to stay and watch the magic," Jack says with a laugh. "We've got work to do."

We swim further away from the gates to the meeting point with the rest of Jack's battalion. The first notes of Celia's flirting hit my ears as we leave. It is so strange to hear someone so strict and cranky behave like a flirtatious teen. Celia could have been an actress.

As we huddle together, Jack confirms everything that we planned before arriving. He will lead a group to the armory near the new recruit cells. We want to get an idea of Ceto's and Nyobi's stockpile. We want to destroy as much as we can and take our knowledge of the rest back to the Atlantean army before they attack. Helios is with me. We are going to the treasury. The queen has more stored there than a stockpile of valuables. I want to find clues about what she is using to control her army. I want to find the jade.

Helios and I make our way through the back entrance to the treasury. The guard who was posted there weeks ago recognizes me and lets Helios and me in. Helios hands him a small jewel as payment for his secrecy. The others wait in the shadows at the edges of the palace walls. We will signal them when we are safely inside.

It takes just a few minutes for Helios and me to make our way back into the treasury. We have had to bribe several guards along the way, but they aren't oblivious to the evil of their queen. A few let us pass without a bribe.

Helios pushes the door open and I follow him into the dimly lit treasury. The room is not as full as when I first saw it. Not everyone can be swayed by Nyobi's powers. Some will do as asked with bribery and are so hardened that she cannot sway them without it. Helios swims up to a high window and waves his yellow scarf to signal to the others that we have made it inside. Their bribes will work. Then he moves about the room, gathering valuable treasures into the leather satchel he brought with him. I am only focused on finding one thing.

Once I get my bearings, I make my way to the pedestal that held the jade the last time I was here. But the jade is not there. The whole space looks different. Items have been moved around as payments to land dignitaries and government officials have been made. I reach out with my mind to see if I can sense the jade in the room. It has been two millennia since I have held the power of the jade, but I could know it anywhere.

A trickle of thought enters my mind. It is a pulsing line of color: green. I feel the ancient tendrils reaching into me as I reach out for the jade. It is here and it is close. I move slowly through the water, heading toward the color where its pulse is strongest.

PEARL…… PEARL…… PEARL……

It whispers in a voice that only I can hear. Helios is still swimming throughout the treasury, filling his satchel with the items he knows will hurt Nyobi and help Atlantis the most. I'm taking this jade for both of us. I turn my face to the voice and see the jade on a new pedestal near the center of the room. It calls to me.

PEARL……PEARL……PEARL……

Pearl is not here, I answer with my mind. To my surprise, I see my thoughts move through the water. Streams of gold move from me to the jade. I am surprised and pleased by the color. The jade is neither surprised nor pleased.

*TSK…TSK…TSK…*it hisses in my ears. *I WOULD KNOW YOU ANYWHERE, PEARL. TWENTY-FOUR HUNDRED YEARS I HAVE WAITED TO MEET WITH YOU AGAIN.*

Pearl has moved on to the afterlife, I say to the stone. *I have been separated from Pearl. She is no longer here.* I feel a movement of emotion from the jade. First, anger. The jade thinks I am lying. Then, acceptance. It can feel my heart. It can feel the difference. I know it is ready for my questions. *The last time we met,* I say, *you and I didn't have any conversation. You were quiet. Why speak to me now?* I feel contempt from the cold stone as it considers its answer to my question.

2,400 YEARS IS A LOOOONGG TIIIIME FOR SOLLLLLITUUUUDE, it says to me. *I WAS ANGRY WITH THE PEARL. I HAVE BEEN PASSED FROM MASTER TO MASTER FOR MY ENTIRE EXISTENCE. THE PEARL WAS RUMORED TO BE FREE. I WAS FURIOUS SHE DID NOT TAKE ME WITH HER. I AM BORED WITH MY MASTER. I LONG TO BE CONTROLLED BY SOMEONE WITH REAL POWER…SOMEONE LIKE YOU.*

I guard my emotions and reaction. As far as I know Nyobi first gave this jade to Abraxas who used it to control nearly everyone around him. I do not know how long it has been a force in the world. I know it is powerful, but I also do not know where its allegiance lies. It could be saying what it thinks I want to hear in order to get close to me and wreak havoc in Atlantis.

And yet, something pulls me closer to it. I cannot help but be drawn to its deeply veined, dark green surface. I move closer to it until I can see my own reflection in its curving face. But my reflection isn't all that I see. A glint of gold sparkles at the bottom of the jade. When I move closer to it, I see that the glint is another reflection. My golden and empty hamsa is floating toward the jade, reaching out as though the golden hand would touch its surface. Startled, I step back, shaking my mind clear of the impulse to grab the jade. Before I can say anything more, Helios is by my side.

"This is the last thing we will need to really do damage to the queen," he tells me. He reaches his hand forward to grab the stone for our collection. Before I can tell him to stop, that the stone is more powerful than we expected, and the door to the treasury bursts open. Helios and I both turn our heads toward the movement and duck out of sight. When I turn to Helios for direction, I see him slip the jade into his satchel.

"This way," he whispers and swims away, snaking through the pedestals and treasure chests. My throat constricts, keeping the scream inside that struggles to break free. I don't want that stone out of my sight. I've got to get Helios to let me carry it, but he's already darting away from me. I follow him, keeping as low to the ground as I can. The sounds of whoever burst into the room are all around us. Fins and armor and legs moving through the water. Soon, I hear voices.

"They must be in here," the voice says. "I know I am not mistaken in this." I freeze where I am. I know that voice. It belongs to Ceto. How did she know we were here? Could she sense our presence or did the jade alert her? Did another of the guards we bribed decide we weren't worth the risk and turn us in? I shake my head of these questions and try to follow Helios again, but he is gone. I look around, panicked, not knowing which way to turn. I can't tell one pedestal from another or one doorway from another. A voice nearby speaks up.

"I think I have something!" the young boy yells. There is movement toward a spot just ahead of me. It must be Helios and he has the jade. I cannot let them get the jade no matter how much it scares me. In a moment of focused decision, I leap up from my hiding place among the pillars and pedestals. In less than a second, I feel all the attention in the room turn to me. Out of the corner of my eye, I see Helios on the ground, opening a familiar door. I have to keep everyone's focus on me.

Just as the door opens, I gather and create all the heat I can and shoot it at Ceto. The heated water hits her in the face, but she doesn't make a move toward me. Instead, a young boy with dark skin and hair swims in front of my face. He is a village boy. He cannot be more than ten or twelve years old. He looks so much like Pearl's twin, Dom, it is startling.

"Hand over the jade and no one gets hurt," he says with his young voice. The words are stilted and cut off, like listening to a robot with limited ability for inflection. But Helios has made it out of the room with the jade. I have to give him time to get away. I move my hands protectively to the bag that I carry. It is empty of anything other than a few tools, but I cling to it like it holds the greatest treasure in the world.

"You'll never get it from me!" I shout at the boy and swim backward and away from the door Helios left through. But the boy doesn't follow. Instead, his eyes roll back into his head and his body falls, lifeless, to the floor. I shake my head, unsure of what just happened, when another boy swims to take the place of the first.

"Hand over the jade and no one else gets hurt," this one says in the same monotone as the first. I shake my head, my voice too shocked to speak. His eyes, too, roll back into his head and his body slumps, lifeless, to the floor. I keep swimming backward, a new feeling of fear filling my heart. Ceto sends her next victim.

"Hand over the jade and no one else gets hurt," the new boy says. I don't have time to say or do anything before his eyes roll back and he slumps to the floor. I look at Ceto, and she smiles. She doesn't care about their lives. She doesn't care about anything but the power and control she wants.

Then a line of boys covers her from view. One by one, then two by two, they come nearer and nearer to me. Each with the same message, "Hand over the jade and no one else gets hurt." Each boy falls to the floor. I back away, searching for a better way out. The line of mind-controlled boys is coming faster, and the room is starting to fill with their bodies. The only way I can escape is by going out the same way they are coming in. I push more heat into the room, but the uncomfortable temperature only slows Ceto a bit. Fortunately, she is too busy controlling her child army to use any of her other sea skills. I make a straight line for the door and push through the mass of her sacrificial boys. Soon, I am out the door and into the hall, but the boy soldiers have made an about-face and follow where I lead.

I shoot through the door that leads to the throne room. There, I see Celia hanging on the arm of one of the guards from the front of the palace. She is right next to the throne and her mouth falls open when she sees my face. As soon as her duped guard sees me, he comes to life. He pushes Celia behind him and lifts his spear, aiming for me. The line of boys is still following me.

"Hand over the jade, and no one else gets hurt." Slump. "Hand over the jade, and no one else gets hurt." Slump. "Hand over the jade, and no one else gets hurt." Slump. Dozens of them are falling with every passing minute. I am about to get speared, but Helios has the jade and enough of a lead. The jade is safe. I just need to get out of here. I let go of the heat I have been shooting at Ceto. My body is tired, but my mind is alert. I crouch, ready to fight the guard in front of me when his head falls to his chest. Celia holds a stone vase in her hand. She drops it to the floor and swims to me.

As more boys follow me, Celia grabs my hand and we swim for the door to the palace exit. But the other guard is there with his club in one hand and a large seashell horn in the other, holding it to his lips. Before we can stop him, he blows into the horn and the palace comes to life.

Our way out is blocked by the armed guard, and the bodies of more boys fill my view. Celia and I freeze and wait, listening to the sound of boy soldiers piling up on the palace floor behind us, both of us in battle stance – arms spread wide, weapons at the ready. Then, there is silence.

"Are you ready to talk yet?" the mindless boy soldiers speak together with Ceto. The room is full of bodies, both living and dead. I let go of Celia's hand and turn to face my foe. She is beautiful as ever, but now I can see signs of her demise.

Her green skin is not as smooth. Her hair is now in chunky dreadlocks rather than shining with movement in the water. Her lips are chapped. Her eyes are dull and listless. Her eyes. Her eyes are as blank as the eyes of the boys around her. Ceto is under mind control.

A low, rumbling laugh of an ancient woman echoes against the walls.

Chapter 18

Nyobi's eerie laughter bounces off the marble walls and I turn around trying to find her, but she is nowhere to be seen. Celia and I are trapped in here together with her mindless minions. Ceto swims to me, her long tentacles floating under her, her hair a tangled mess behind her back. Her empty eyes look deeply into mine.

"Well, we meet at last," she says.

"Hello, Nyobi," I say. Celia swims closer.

"But this…" she says. Ceto turns her face to Celia.

"This is the mindless body of my daughter," Nyobi says through Ceto. "She is weak, but useful." Ceto's empty gaze returns to me.

"I'm sorry we could not meet face-to-face, Evelyn," she says to me. "But rude as that may be, you have been even more unfeeling."

"And how is that?" I ask.

"Come now, Evelyn," she says. "You have taken something that belongs to me. I knew the jade would be too great a temptation for you to pass up. I know your history with it."

"If you knew that, why make it so easy to take?" I ask. Nyobi laughs, her daughter's mirthless eyes betraying no emotion.

"Oh, Evelyn," she says. "Did you really think it was easy? You still have the jade and I still have you. Please, tell me, what is so easy about that?" She doesn't know I don't have the jade. Helios must still be close enough that she doesn't feel the diminishing power of distance. I just smile. Ceto moves her face directly into mine, eyes wide.

"Where isssss ittttt?" she asks, spewing her spittle into the water.

"Why do you think we would ever tell you anything?" Celia says. Ceto's face moves from mine to Celia's.

"What do you know of it?" she asks of Celia. "What have you done? Where is the stone? I have ways of making you speak." Her tentacles reach up and grasp Celia's cheeks, her blonde hair making a stark contrast against Ceto's shining, black limbs. The two guards from the front of the palace swim to Celia and take her by the arms but Celia's fair face doesn't flinch. She remains stony-eyed as she stares back at Ceto.

"That is where you are wrong," Celia says. "I am the daughter of a general and another descendant in a long line of Atlantean warriors. I will not be swayed by the enemy." Ceto's impassive eyes close. She flicks her hand and the two guards take Celia from the room. Another guard holds me back when I try to swim after them.

"What are you going to do with her?" I ask the Nyobian puppet. "She doesn't know anything." Ceto's eyes open and she sees me for the first time. She blinks several times and shakes her head.

"What are you doing here?!" She yells when she regains her mind. "How did you get here? What is going on?" Her tone has changed. Her voice is scared. She isn't being controlled anymore. What happened to break Nyobi's control over her?

I open my mouth to speak when noise erupts outside the palace doors. A guard swims in, shouting at the others in the room.

"The enemy has entered the Mediterranean!" he yells. "Our spies have just returned with news of their movement and we have found their advance scouts in our city! Their troops are at the mouth of the sea and have just passed the Strait of Gibraltar and head east with increasing speed. The Queen demands all to prepare for battle!"

"Where are the scouts?" I shout. "What have you done with them?!" Ceto spins toward me, eyes inches from mine.

"You have no right to speak here," she says. "You gave up that privilege months ago." She turns away from me again. "Guards, take her to the dungeons and keep her under watch. Do not speak to her. The rest of you will prepare as commanded. We are at war! This is not a drill! For her majesty!"

"For her majesty!" the guards and living boys shout. For the first time, Ceto sees the bodies of the dead boys on the palace floor.

"What happened here?" she begins. She turns her eyes to me, but my guards are already taking me from the room.

"She did this!" I shout. "Nyobi did this to them!" A guard covers my mouth and takes me down a hallway toward the dungeons. Before I lose her from my sight, I see Ceto's shoulders slump, her body lowers to the floor, and she strokes the hair of a fallen boy.

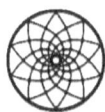

The dungeons echo with the sounds of battle preparation. Guards are changing posts, the best soldiers preparing to fight. The second-best staying to watch over the prisoners. I crane my neck to look into the small, barred windows of the prison cells. I cannot see much, but what I do see is enough. I see Celia in one of the first cells I pass. She is arguing with the guard at her door, telling him he will regret his rough treatment of her. I see scratches and perfectly arced bite marks on the guard's arms, left there by Celia's long nails and flawless teeth. I call to her and catch her eye as I am led past her cell.

"Evelyn!" she yells. "Don't tell them anything!" Celia's guard slams his club against her cell door, forcing her back a foot or two. But she swims right back up to the window as I disappear. My own guard squeezes my arms even tighter, warning me to keep quiet.

"Evelyn? Evelyn!" I hear yelling from down the corridor. It's Jack. I breathe a sigh of relief. At least they are keeping us all near each other. But my relief is short-lived as I wonder if Helios got away. Does he have the jade?

"Jack!" I shout back to him. "Jack!" My guard turns me to face him. His eyes are gray, and his face is filled with the wrinkled weathering of a life at sea. His arms are strong, like someone used to pulling heavy fishing nets over and over into his boat. He is a fisherman. His eyes narrow into angry slits, and he holds a single finger over his lips, again warning me to be silent. He refuses to speak to me at all – perfect obedience to the command of his queen's daughter. He opens a cell door behind me and shoves me in. He bolts the door and moves his body in front of its small window. I try calling out again to Jack, but my guard slams his fist against my door. When Jack tries to call out to me, the guard covers my window with a wooden door.

I am completely alone.

Chapter 19

All I hear for an hour is the sound of soldiers and guards getting geared up for a battle. If the Atlantean army reached the borders of the Mediterranean Sea this afternoon, how long until they reach the palace? It could be days to move an army of that size across the ocean floor. Would the battle even be here or would Queen Nyobi Kadul keep her forces out in the open water, thus protecting her ancient kingdom?

Within hours the hallway is quiet. The muffled noises of guards and soldiers readying themselves for battle are gone. The army is on the move.

I am sitting on a stone bench in the corner of my cell when I again hear muffled sounds outside my door. People are talking, but I cannot make out what they are saying. Then, the door handle creaks and my door swings open. I wait quietly to see who my visitor is, to see what they will ask of me, which interrogation room I will be taken to.

But I am going nowhere. Ceto has come to see me.

She ducks into my cell, her long tentacles swooping in and unfurling like a ballgown. The guard closes the door behind her. I stay on my bench.

"What did you mean," she asks me, "when you said, 'she did this'?" I stare up at Ceto, her black eyes finally seeing and understanding what is happening around her. She is not under mind control now.

"Nyobi killed the boys," I answer. "She made you kill them."

"Why? How?"

"I can't answer for the why," I tell her. "To get my attention? To protect you? To hide the fact that you were under her control? Who knows why someone kills children? But the how is more gruesome. I was trying to escape. Each boy came to tell me to stop, then fell dead at my feet."

"If they were dying," she says, "then why didn't you do as they said? Why didn't you stop?" she asks, but her tone isn't accusatory.

"I knew they were being controlled, Ceto," I told her. "I thought you were the one killing them. I knew getting out of there and back to Atlantis was the best way to make all of the horrors of war stop for our seas. I had to get out of there, Ceto. Death was chasing me. I had to get away." Ceto pauses for a moment.

"Why did you come here, Evelyn?"

"We are enemies and you're asking why I came here?" I say. "Isn't that what enemies do? Especially in war? They spy on each other. They steal from each other. They find each other's weaknesses and attack from within." Ceto moves closer to me.

"Are we enemies, Evelyn?" she asks. I cannot believe what I am hearing. Has she lost her mind?

"How could we not be enemies?" I say. "You took my father for most of my life. You held me as a prisoner in your dungeons.

You are helping the woman who stole my life from me and are trying to destroy the world!"

"But I returned your father to you, Evelyn," Ceto says. "I kept him safe with me then returned him to you when he wanted to leave. I just kept you with me to help you understand what you were missing by not joining me. And the Queen is... well, she is my mother. She was never there for me. She is here now, and I am using her to help me. To bring peace to the oceans and peace to the world." I shake my head. As she morphs into a full octopus, Ceto is losing her senses. It can't be long until she will not be able to function in any capacity of a human.

"What peace, Ceto?" I ask. "How is there peace if there is a village of boys being taken from their homes? How is there peace if those boys are lying dead on the palace floor?"

"The village takes great pleasure in serving my mother," Ceto says. "They are proud to send their boys to her army. They come daily by the dozens. More and more see the virtue of her cause and want to help her in it."

"What is her cause, Ceto?" I say.

"She tells them she wants peace in the oceans and along the coastlines, that she wants to bless them," Ceto says. "But I know better. She wants control, dominion, power, and revenge, Evelyn. She wants revenge for the life and future she lost thousands of years ago."

"If she is lying to the people, then why do you serve her?"

"Because *I* want to fulfill the promise to the people, Evelyn! *I* want to restore balance to the seas. *I* want to restore balance to the whole earth!"

"The balance you want will flood the earth," I say to Ceto. "It will destroy the very villagers you say you are serving. It will kill them and everyone else on dry land. Can't you see that?" Ceto shakes her head.

"You are wrong," she says. "You have seen for yourself that the village boys live under the water. They are first proven worthy on land by their devotion to the queen. Before they are brought to the sea, they are given a medallion imbued with her power. They can live under the sea as you and I live under the sea. Anyone who is worthy can live under the sea, Evelyn."

"But who determines their worthiness, Ceto?" I ask. "Is it you? Are you and the queen so thirsty for power you want to play God?"

"Evelyn, this is the way it is meant to be. I serve my mother so I can use her power and her resources. It was never my plan to follow her. But if you will join me, we can leave her behind. We don't need her help at all. Together, we can use the jade to bring balance to the earth."

"The jade?" I ask. Ceto pauses. "What about the jade? What do you know about it?"

"I know it aids in mind manipulation," she answers me. "I can manipulate minds without it, but with it, I can reach so many more and at much longer distances."

"Why do you think I have it?" I ask.

"Isn't that why you are here?" Ceto asks. "Isn't this why you came to the palace? To seek for the jade? Didn't you get it?" she is speaking faster and taking shallow breaths, her face is growing pale. "She said you were coming for it. She said that's why you broke into the palace. She said the jade had to be found or all would be lost! WHERE IS THE JADE, EVELYN?!"

My cell door flies open and my guard bursts into the room. Ceto passes out and falls to the floor. The guard picks her up and carries her through the cell door and out into the hallway. I wait for another guard to take his place, but none comes. After a few seconds I stand and swim to the doorway. No guard is there. The hallway is empty. I step outside and swim toward the cell across the hall where Jack is being kept. I raise the latch that bars his door and open it. As it creaks open, I hear a voice from down the hall.

"I told you the mind manipulation they used on me could be transferred to someone else." A shiver runs down my spine.

"Gwen?" I ask as I peer down the empty hall. Jack is at his doorway and I motion for him to stay quiet.

"Who else would it be?" Gwen asks as she emerges from the shadows. "I told you there was more to me than either my mother or grandmother knew, Evelyn. I moved my mind control to your guard, and he set you free. I felt my mother's energy rising, so I urged her to faint then sent him to take her from the room, leaving the door open behind him."

Jack comes out of his cell and stands by my side.

"Why do you want to help us?" he asks Gwen. She rolls her eyes.

"Why do you always assume I want to help *you*?" she says. "Honestly, Jack. You can really be very self-centered sometimes. I am here to convince Evelyn to come with me. You are safe because she would want it."

"But, Gwen, why do you even need me?" I ask. "What else can you do that Ceto and Nyobi don't know about yet?" Gwen chuckles.

"You really don't know yet," she says to me. It isn't a question.

"I don't know what?" I ask.

"I'm not the only one who can do things that Ceto and Nyobi don't know about yet." Gwen pauses and smiles at me.

"Me?" I ask. "What can I do that could be more than what they can do? They are already so powerful."

"How about you take some time to figure that out," Gwen says to me. "Until then, I'll let you and your friends go. Quite a few of you were caught by my grandmother's guards." She moves through the hall and opens the cell doors while she talks. Several of our troops enter the hall.

"This will be my gesture of good will, Evelyn. Learn more about yourself and I will be in touch. Until then, the way out is up a few flights of stairs. You won't have any trouble. The few guards still in the castle are very pliant. Just be sure to leave, Evelyn. No need to take anything else with you." Gwen turns around and swims into the darkness behind her. Jack takes my hand and together we lead the team up the stairs and out to freedom.

Chapter 20

We swim like mad through Nyobi's city. Jack hasn't seen Helios at all. I don't know if he made it out with the jade or if Nyobi took him somewhere else. So much depends on finding Helios and getting that stone, I can't make it to the boats fast enough.

"The battle has already started," Jack says as we start the engine to our boat. "The guards were talking about it just before they brought you and Celia to the dungeons. They are beyond the entrance to the Mediterranean. If we push the engines, we can get there in time to help."

My anxiety is ratcheted up, and I cannot hold still. I pace back and forth on the small deck, urging Jack to push the engines to their limit. Celia pours the remnants of the gas can into the engine.

"We won't have enough to make it back here," she says. Her arms are beginning to show the bruises she got while fighting her guards. "We'll either have to gas the boats for the return trip or leave them near the ports in Algiers."

"If we don't get there fast enough, it may not matter what happens to the boats," Jack answers. "Evelyn, see if you can coax the waves in our favor. This surface current is pushing against us."

I sit down at the back of our boat, facing the rest of the boats in our group. From where I sit, I can almost see the surface currents pushing east, the exact opposite of where we need to be. I close my eyes and speak to the sea.

Oh, divine sea, would your waves be so good as to move us west? We are moving to defeat the evil queen and restore balance to the waters of the world.

For a moment there is silence, then I hear the water speaking to me.

Reach your hand into the waves that we may know you, it says to me. I lean over the edge of the boat and let my fingers play in our wake. The water bubbles beneath my fingertips.

We cannot change the current, the water says to my mind, *your power does not extend that far. But we can urge the waves to oppose the current. Our waves will push you toward your goal for we know where the battle will be.*

Small white caps begin to form on the sea behind us. I watch them build in number as they gather to push our boats forward. Soon, I feel the little waves take over the work of our boat's engine.

"Turn off the engines!" I shout to the boats behind us. I wave my arms and signal for them to cut their engines. Jack kills our engine and the little waves move us forward, faster and faster until we are shooting through the water with greater speed than our engines could. As we speed through the Mediterranean, I let my fingers kiss the water in gratitude. I feel its gentle peace settle into my bones.

Most of the sea wants Nyobi's overthrow, too, Evelyn, it says to me. *We have struggled for millennia to free the life of the sea from her grasp. We will do all we can to help in the cause. But rest now, mighty warrior and let us do the work. You will need your strength for battle.*

I bring my hand out of the water and bring my fingers to my lips. The strength of the mighty water seeps into my body. I close my eyes and lay back on the boat's seat, closing my eyes to rest.

It is dark when the tiny waves subside. I open my eyes as our boat slows to a stop. When I sit up and stretch, I see the others waking up as well. I stand and gather my things, preparing to dive below the waves and find the army of Atlantis. A gentle breeze kisses my neck.

Why did you not seek our help, Evelyn? I feel Namaah's words fill my mind. My ancient companion tried to stop me from seeking Nyobi's kingdom before. I assumed she would refuse to help me because I defied her counsel.

I thought you were angry with me, I whisper in response. *I thought you would not help us.* Her breeze grows icy. The others around me rub their arms against the chill. Only Jack is watching me now, knowing I am speaking with the air.

Did we not carry your plane to America and back again? she asks. *Haven't we given you safe passage whenever you are over the sea?* Namaah is hurt by my actions. *We are used to being ignored by your kind, Evelyn, but we had come to love you. Your ingratitude is painful.* A pain grows in my chest, and a knot grows in my stomach.

I am so sorry, Namaah. I was headstrong and full of pride. You have been truly watchful of me and of all of us. I am grateful for your care. Can you forgive me? The cold breeze halts and we are still again. Then, a warmth opens around us.

Yes, my child. We forgive you. What is done is done. You have made the best of your decision. We will help you. We will not lead you into danger, but from it. Please do not keep us from your aid again. We were angry for a while, but our love and purpose did not change. All you need do is ask, and all that you require that is needful will be given to you.

Namaah's reassurance fills me with confidence. I know I can seek her help.

What of Helios? I ask. *I have not seen him since we were separated in Nyobi's kingdom. I have not seen a trace of him in the sea. Have you seen him?* The warm breeze slows again until I am the only one in its path.

We have seen him, Evelyn. He traveled by sail from Nyobi's kingdom. We carried his boat just a little East of here. We saw what he carries, Evelyn. He took it from his satchel and caressed its form before taking it back with him into the sea.

The jade? I ask.

Yes, she whispers in return. *The jade is a powerful force in the world. It spoke to him as he traveled west. His own ancestors hewed it from the rocks of Myanmar. The jade holds a great power when it is with him.*

So, his ancestors did create the jade? I ask.

Yes, Namaah says. *It was renowned for its power and stolen time and again before it was trapped by the queen. It recognizes his history, Evelyn. It knows he is descended from its beginning. Do you know what he is planning with it? Do you trust this boy? His scent is both ancient and new. We cannot determine his purposes.*

I do trust him, I tell her. *There is so much to explain, but he is descended from Gileaus. His ancestors have been enslaved to Nyobi for thousands of years. I do not know the extent of its powers, but I do believe the jade can help us.* A slender but strong hand grabs hold of my arm.

"Are you going to stand there and stare forever?" Celia asks. "We have a battle to fight and a war to win. We are early enough to actually be of use to Atlantis. Let's go."

She stands tall and stares me in the eye, determined to see me do the same. I breathe my gratitude to Namaah and dive off the edge of the boat with Celia. Jack follows us when the rest of the boats are also empty of the soldiers. Then he shoots past us all to be the first to the Atlantean army. He will have a lot of explaining to do.

I keep my eyes open, looking for signs of Helios. Did he go all the way to Atlantis? Is he waiting behind us where he got off his boat? Is he waiting for us or for Nyobi? A nervousness niggles the back of my mind. What if I misunderstood Helios' intentions? What if he is still working for Nyobi? If he is, then he has brought a powerful tool to help her. And I helped him get it.

Chapter 21

"So, Ceto is planning to fight against her mother?" Lady Pescara repeats. The whole war council is gathered in the tent, listening to Jack's report. It is tight and the water is tense.

"That is correct," Jack answers. "And Gwen is determined to overthrow them both."

"This is an advantage to our side, Lady Pescara," Lachlan says. "With them fighting amongst themselves they are weak." Lady Pescara nods.

"It is to our advantage," she says. "Thank you for the information, Captain Jack, and our thanks goes to your regiment for the measures taken to get it." Jack bows. "And Recruit Marin," Lady Pescara continues, "I know you were not satisfied with the measures I took in Atlantis to keep you separated from us, but those measures were necessary. I hope you can see that now."

"Yes, Lady Pescara," I say. "I have seen what the power of the enemy can do to the minds of their victims. I hope I have proven myself to you and to all of Atlantis now."

"You have," she says. "Though we have yet to see or hear from Helios. Our scouts found his boat hours ago, but both he and the jade are missing from it."

"I am sorry, my lady," I say. "I should have taken the jade myself."

"If you had, it would surely have been taken by Ceto and be in Queen Nyobi's hands right now, and you would not be here to speak of any of it," Lachlan says.

"Be that as it may," Lady Pescara responds, "the jade is still not with us and we do not know the intentions of Helios. Though he was vetted before his release from our prison, this failure is mine for letting Captain Jack take him on this mission. As it is, I can spare very few to seek him out. Nyobi's army will be here within the hour."

"Can I help to find him?" I ask. But both Lady Pescara and Lachlan shake their heads.

"We need you here in the battle, Evelyn," she says, "with Chelsea."

"With Chelsea?" I ask.

"She is more than just your companion," Lachlan interjects. "You don't know yet what she can do and with the two of you together, we have the best chance of winning today."

Lady Pescara starts to speak, but there is a disturbance at the door of the tent.

"It is time, Lady Pescara," the soldier at the door tells us. Lady Pescara's face moves from mine to the rest of the leaders in the room.

"We have trained for this, generals," she says to them all. "Gather your troops to the field, today we fight for victory."

"Come, Evelyn," Lachlan says to me as I follow Jack out the tent door. "I will take you to Chelsea and your new captain."

"New Captain?" I ask, turning to face him. Jack continues to his battalion. "But I am in Jack's squadron." Lachlan shakes his head.

"Not anymore," he says. "You were discharged from his regiment before you were sent from Atlantis."

"I know," I say, "but I thought that we would continue working together since I was allowed to help him in his mission."

"These are things that will have to be sorted out after the war, Evelyn," he answers. "Right now, you have a captain to get to and I have a battalion to oversee. This way." Lachlan swims from the tent and I follow him, glancing over my shoulder where Jack was beside me just a moment ago. Lady Pescara is busy leading her generals and preparing for the battle at hand. Her mind is already off my predicament. I will have to do as Lachlan directs.

We swim through the dark, Mediterranean waters. There are sea people and Atlantean creatures everywhere, but there is order in all of it. The armory tent is nearly empty of its stores and soldiers of every species are girding their armor. Lachlan and I meet up with Chelsea at the door of the supply tent.

"Recruit Chelsea," Lachlan says to her. She is back in her sea form, a large and intimidating sea dragon. "You are under direction to acquaint Recruit Marin with her duties in Captain Marin's squadron."

"Captain Marin?" I ask. "But…"

"That is all I have time for, Evelyn," Lachlan says to me. "I have other captains to oversee. I wish you both God's speed." He swims away from Chelsea and me and out to the open water. I turn back to my intimidating companion.

"It's kind of weird to see you in your sea form again," I say to her. Her large body is glowing in the underwater darkness around us. The gold and pink of her skin and leaves is brilliant. She is wearing a new armor, clad in iridescent shades of green and purple and blue. The armor peeks out from beneath her leafy appendages. "You are so beautiful, Chelsea." She blushes beneath the armor.

"Thank you, Evelyn," she says with a slight bow. "It is freeing to be in my proper form again. I do find the world above the water fascinating, but I am capable of so much more when I accept who I really am."

"What exactly does that mean?" I ask. "Who are you, really? Lady Pescara said they can't win without us. I know I'm not super special, so it must be you."

Chelsea laughs. "You can't expect me to believe that you are not special, Evelyn. We both know better than that. But my species are known for certain characteristics. I haven't had much opportunity to practice them, let alone use them, but if they are as good as they promise to be, then yes, you and I will be able to do great things together with them."

"I am still clueless, Chelsea. What exactly can you do?"

"Time is running short," she tells me. "Get your armor and I will explain on the way."

"You breathe FIRE?!" I ask. I actually yell it. I am shocked. My battle companion is more than just a sea dragon, she is a REAL dragon! Why would anyone keep that a secret from me for so long? I tie the last of my armor to my leg and set my weapons in their holsters.

"No, Evelyn," Chelsea tells me. "I don't breathe *fire*, but I am a dragon. I breathe super-heated *water*. But it's like I said, I haven't had many opportunities to use it, so you and I are going to have to figure it out as we go."

"Are you recruits ready?" In all my stupor over Chelsea being a real dragon, I forgot that I was assigned to a new captain. My mom.

"*You* are my new captain?" I ask her. "Since when did you want to be a part of the war effort?"

"Since I realized my daughter would be at the center of it," my mom replies. "As soon as Lady Pescara and the council fully briefed me on the situation, I was assigned my own team. This is not my first time serving the Atlantean army, Evelyn. Having you with me was one of the conditions for my assignment." My mom is suiting up in her own armor while she talks to Chelsea and me. The gold breastplate inlaid with turquoise is a brilliant contrast to her dark skin. Her strong cheekbones stand out as her native styled helmet, carved with the feathers normally worn by a village chief, sits on her shining hair. She looks the part of a leader among ancient people and I smile, feeling proud of my mom and my heritage.

"Since the two of you have not yet practiced working together," she tells me and Chelsea, "you are not to be on the front lines. I want you to hang back and work on your fighting together. When you are comfortable fighting as a team, you can move up."

My mom takes us to the back of the battle formation then leaves us to rejoin the rest of her squadron. Chelsea and I take the extra space to begin our practicing. We have only just begun when the sounds of war horns reach our ears.

"This is it," I say to Chelsea. "You're going to have to teach me fast."

"Okay," she says, "When I breathe the water, it's your job to magnify my heat. I can get pretty hot on my own, but with your ability to control water temperature, it'll be that much hotter. We will be able to stop anything in the water."

"This is insane, Chelsea. Let's do it."

Chelsea bows her head to her chest and shakes from tail to nose. When she lifts her eyes to meet mine, she blows a steady stream of water toward me. But this isn't the same, cool water I have been swimming in. This is hot water. Hot tub, hot water. The heat feels good at first but then intensifies until I can feel sweat bubbles forming on my arms. I focus my mind on the water and let my heat sensors reach into it. I gather a ball of Chelsea's super-heated water and compress it until it boils in the open water before us. Then I focus my energies on moving the ball.

Seaweed floats in the water near us and I send the boiling water to it. When the water hits the seaweed, the effect is instant. The affected stalks turn black and wither away. Chelsea and I stare at it with open mouths.

"That was awesome," she says. "Let's try it again!"

We work for an hour or more this way, falling further and further behind our advancing army. The distance finally becomes noticeable.

"This time let me on your back," I say. "We should practice our battle-ready stance."

"Okay," she answers, eager to get going.

I swim to her and climb onto her glimmering armor. It is cool beneath me, unlike the warmth of her body when I first climbed on her back.

"Alright," I say, "try again."

This time, when Chelsea bows her head down, I see directly in front of us. The two armies are gathered in full battle now. I see our troops on the front lines fighting the enemy. But the enemy are children. Young boys controlled by Nyobi's power. Forced to fight for her.

"Chelsea," I say, patting her neck. "Look." She raises her head and I feel the terror hit her.

"Those poor boys," she says. "We can't let them keep fighting. We have to do something."

"My thoughts exactly," I say, but Chelsea already knows because our minds are connected. We feel freely anything that we cannot express. We are one now and ready to fight.

This time when Chelsea bows her head, she dives into the water. We plummet at least thirty feet below our entire army. Then Chelsea bursts forward, my thoughts racing into her and hers into me. We are almost beneath the battle itself now. Our eyes move up to the fighting fins and tiny sandaled feet of thc battle. We are ready to shoot up into the fighting when I spot something in the distance. It is green and shining and I hear it calling to me. It is the jade.

Chapter 22

EVELYN! PEARL! It calls. *EVELYN, WHY DIDN'T YOU TAKE ME?! PLEASE! COME GET ME!* The pleading voice rips through my chest. I know the jade isn't fully trustworthy. I don't know if it will help or hurt our cause. But even if it is trying to trap me, I can't risk leaving it with our enemy.

"We have to get the jade!" I shout to Chelsea. "It's the best way to stop the fighting! I can use it to make everyone stop and listen!" Her mind refocuses.

"Are you sure?" she asks. "I thought it was too unstable to use."

"I know," I tell her. "But I have to try. We know it will be worse for us without it. We have to try at least to get it. We can take it to my mom or even Lady Pescara and destroy it if it is too hard to control. But we have to try, Chelsea. Will you help me?"

"I will always help you," Chelsea says in response. "I can see it." Together, we bend our bodies toward the stone. We swim faster than I knew a sea dragon could move through water. The battle rages above us for only a moment. Soon, we are beneath Nyobi's adult army. Fins and feet face the battle. Weapons are held at the ready, waiting for their turn to join the fray. Then we pass their commanding officer.

Tentacles swirl in the water above us as Ceto shouts orders to the army. She is protected from the fighting. She has her minions to do it for her. But how long can she maintain the strength to control so many of her army? Where is Nyobi?

I refocus my mind on the jade ahead. It calls to me louder and louder.

EVELYN! PEARL! EVELYN!

It shouts so loud that I cannot hear myself think. I urge Chelsea forward. She senses the call through me. She knows which way to go. Two more minutes and we arrive. Helios' satchel is floating on its side, abandoned on a blacked lava rock, the jade peeking out through the top. Helios is nowhere to be seen. Why would he abandon the jade here?

HAVE YOU REALLY FINALLY COME FOR ME?! the jade shouts to my mind. *ARE YOU READY TO END THIS WAR TOGETHER?*

I have and I am, I whisper with my mind. The jade's yelling is more than I can handle, I hope my whispering will help to calm it. I reach my hand out to grasp the satchel strap, but just before I reach it, a hand shoots through the darkness and grabs hold of my wrist.

I reach my mind out to Chelsea, but there is only silence. The glowing leaves of her body are suspended in the water around me, perfectly still and unmoving. The water, too, is still and quiet, no longer a moving and living thing. The sounds of fighting have ceased. All sounds have ceased. Everything is frozen in place.

I look at the grey and decrepit hand that holds me. Flakes of skin have sloughed off in many places, leaving the owner with rotting sores. My eyes move up the arm until they reach the body and head of my enemy. Her tentacles droop beneath her, nearly lifeless. Her snakelike hair stands on end like an evil halo of eyes searching the water around her. Her face is as grey as her arm, sores forming on her cheeks. Her eyes look dead into mine.

"Hello, Evelyn," the wrinkled lips say to me in a voice that is ragged and deep. "Our time together will be brief. I cannot hold everything in place forever. But you and I have much to discuss. Will you follow me?"

"Do I have a choice, Nyobi?" I ask. Her eyes grow fierce and angry.

"I am a queen, Evelyn. Soon, I will be *your* queen whether you choose it or not. Perhaps you would like to change the way you address me." I nod my head. It's a force of movement that I did not choose. She is manipulating my body.

"As you wish, mighty Queen Nyobi Kadul," I say through gritted teeth. The hold she has on my mind is strong. I fight for every syllable.

"That's better," she says with a disgusting smile. "Come with me."

Nyobi takes the satchel and I feel my arms and legs let go of Chelsea. I leave her behind as Nyobi drags me through the sea just a little further. As she pulls me, the unnaturally solid water scrapes against my body in its unyielding state. When we stop, I am frozen beside the queen, my head resting just beneath hers, my mind completely awake. The whole battle is like a picture in time. Legs and robes and weapons float above us without a single movement of material or skin, like we are looking up close at a giant mural of an ancient battle. Even Ceto's tentacles hover in a frozen fan in the water. Nyobi flicks her fingers in the water and we shoot through the frozen sea, the seawater scraping the exposed areas of my body. When we stop, we are outside the open door of a gilded tent, Nyobi's battle tent. She swims inside and sits on a throne. She points to a stool at her feet and I unwillingly swim to it.

Chapter 23

"I brought you here to give you a choice," Nyobi says. I sit on the stool before her, my head no higher than where her tentacles rest on the seat of her throne. "Join with me now, in this moment, or all of Atlantis shall be destroyed. Refuse me and I will end you and them with a simple flick of my finger." She holds the jade in her hand, a sure reminder of just how powerless I am. But I will not give into the darkness of her threats.

"I believe in the power of Atlantis," I tell her. "They are not perfect, but they are trying to be better. They will not stop no matter what you can do. We will always fight against you. You can't win even if you do kill me. You. Cannot. Win!"

"Ha. Foolish child. So typical of a teenager to get in over her head, believing whatever fairy tale she hears. You do not know the truth!" she says. "I have been greatly harmed. Your own family has brought me pain and misery throughout the centuries. Have you no consideration for the suffering I have felt? Have you ever considered that perhaps *I* was the victim? That perhaps *I* was innocent? Of course you haven't. That would mean admitting that your family is the blame!"

"Innocence doesn't persuade families to give up their children against their will," I say. "Innocence doesn't sacrifice those children in pride." Nyobi lifts her wrinkled chin and flakes of her decaying skin float off into the water.

"You are responsible for the deaths of those children, Evelyn. You were warned to stop. You chose not to. There are consequences to our choices, no matter how noble we think they are."

"Those children should never have entered the sea," I respond. This evil queen will not lay her sins at my feet. "You forced them here against their will. You stole them from their families. If you had left them alone, if you had left everyone alone, none of this would have happened! There would be no war, no fighting, no aching families! We could be uniting as a people, accepting each other with our differences and creating a better world! But you and your daughter…" but I don't get to finish. I am standing now and a small smile has crept into the corners of Nyobi's mouth. She raises one gnarled hand and flicks a single finger downward. A force like I have never felt before grips me. My arms are tied to my sides by invisible cords and I am pressed back onto the stool. Nyobi kisses the jade and runs it across her cheek.

"As I told you, Evelyn," she whispers, "I am a Queen. You will respect me, or you will feel the consequences." Her face softens and her influence on my body relaxes. I sit still, keeping my anger just below the surface while she speaks. "You don't understand the position you are in or what is owed to me. What *you* owe to me. Let me enlighten you.

"Thousands of years ago, I was alone and bitter. Everything I loved had been stolen from me. Everyone I had given my heart to

213

had turned from me. I was powerful, yes, but the power meant nothing. In my anguish, I turned to creation. I felt so much release in creating things that were beautiful, putting a little of my own, internal destruction in each thing I made, putting myself back together piece by piece with each thing I made. I began creating powerful items from natural elements in the sea, mostly pearls." Nyobi sets the jade on the arm of her throne and leans down until I can smell her decaying flesh.

"I was at the pinnacle of my creations," she continues. "I was ready to create the perfect embodiment of my pain. A pearl so lovely and at once so powerful that it would be an emblem of my suffering in these murky depths. I swam to the coast of Greece. My heart pulled me there. I wanted to leave a piece of me in its coasts. I brought a piece of sand from my kingdom. It was black and rough, imperfect. I found an oyster patch hidden in a cave barely speckled with light. It was the perfect place for my creation, hidden mostly in the dark.

"I found an oyster, misshapen and ugly, in the midst of the patch. I sang to it and it opened willingly. It knew pain. It knew rejection. It knew suffering. I sang the wretched piece of sand into its open mouth and it closed with a snap. I smiled, knowing what I had made. I focused my singing on the oyster and sent bits of myself into it. Bits of my power, my ability to see into the minds of others, my ability to influence their thoughts, my ability to kill. I sent all of it. The colors of my music filled the oyster. Streams of purple and gold, green and blue swirled in the water. I felt the power leaving my soul and filling that oyster and growing the blackest pearl I'd ever made.

"But soon I felt a familiar presence in the water. A man I had once loved was near, drawn to my song." Nyobi runs her jagged nails across my face, drawing blood. But I can't even wince at the pain because I am still under her power. She sits back in on her throne, watching the blood ooze from the lines on my face.

"He had nearly killed me, Evelyn. I at once loved him and feared him. I silenced my singing and hid in the depths of the cave, too exhausted from my efforts to even try to speak to him. I was weak." I see the memory she shares with me. I feel her pain and see everything as she saw it.

"I watched him swim to the patch of oysters," she continues. "He pulled a knife from his belt and started stabbing at them. Digging at them with a ferocity I'd never seen in a man before. I felt each pierce of the knife as it struck the rocky home of my oyster and pearl. After an agonizing few minutes, he swam to the surface and was gone.

"I could barely breathe. I stayed in the cave for days afterward, recovering my strength. No one else came to the oyster patch. No one else came near the cave. The other fishermen all stayed out to sea. The other tradesmen stayed onshore. Only he had come so near to me. So near I could have killed him.

"When I was finally strong enough to emerge, I saw that my oyster was gone. Some of the patch remained. My heart ached again, an opened wound that I thought was healed. I cursed the patch, watching the remaining oysters shrivel and blacken, then I returned to my kingdom. I was done with the man. I was done with creating. I was done with it all. Until many years later." She glares down at me. I can barely breathe.

"Do you know the rest of the story, Evelyn?" she asks. I nod.

"I do know it," I tell her. "I lived it as Pearl. Her father, the man who took the oysters, brought them to his children. Through your curse on her mother and his theft of the oyster, she was trapped inside the pearl. She lived, trapped in that pearl for thousands of years, Nyobi. She became one with the power of the pearl, but both yearned for freedom. She called me to her. I had to free her from the prison you created." Nyobi rises from her throne until she towers over me.

"You were WEAK!" she yells as bits of her skin fall from her body. "*You* let that pearl manipulate you! *You* destroyed Atlantis! *You* brought it to the sea! *You* stole that power, Evelyn! YOU!"

"I stole nothing," I tell her. "I was saving Pearl. She was trapped in your curse…"

"So, let her stay trapped!" Nyobi yells down at me. "Let her live the punishment of being her father's daughter! Let her stay that way! Let the power remain in her perfect form! DO NOT STEAL IT!" Nyobi raises her hand high above her head. She brings it down to hit my face, to strike me dead. I close my eyes, waiting for the inevitable, but just before her yellowed nails can touch my skin, a glint of green catches my eye. Then another hand reaches out and grabs me.

Before I can even open my eyes to see who it is, I feel my body rocketing out of the tent, almost as fast as Nyobi brought me here. When we finally stop, I try to get my bearings. I am back under the battle, next to Chelsea's enormous sea dragon body. I look to see who saved me. It is Gileaus.

My racing heart freezes, and it pushes against my ribs, pressing me to him. In an instant, my lips meet his and tears flow from my eyes. The warmth of his touch is so familiar. The healing of his embrace is so soothing, kissing away the pain I feel, but this isn't Gileaus. It is Helios.

Helios.

Helios.

Helios.

And the battle comes to life again around us.

Chapter 24

When I finally find the strength to pull away from his body, Helios stares at me wide-eyed. I don't think he expected the kiss any more than I did. But our enemy is too close for us to linger in this moment or to speak a single word. I reach for the jade in his hand, grasping it in my fist then mounting Chelsea's saddle. I tuck the powerful stone into a pocket of my armor. Helios does nothing to stop me.

"What happened to you?!" Chelsea yells. "You are a mess! And where did he come from?"

That's going to be a long story, I answer to her mind.

Can we trust him? she asks.

I'm not sure. I don't know where his alliances are, but he just saved me. I think we have to take him with us and protect him.

Yeah, to protect him, Chelsea says to my mind. *I saw your lips. Tell me the truth, Evelyn. Is he trustworthy or do you just want him with you because he reminds you of someone else?*

A sharp pain fills my head and ringing pierces my ears. I hold my head, squeezing my eyes closed. Nyobi is trying to disable me, to keep me from moving, but I'm not alone now and she is the one who is weak. I open my eyes wide, harnessing the power of the jade in my armor and shoot what mind control strength I have toward the source of the pain. Her power eases and I can focus again.

We don't have time to find out, I tell Chelsea. "You have to come with us," I tell Helios. I reach my hand out to him. "Hurry!" He grasps my arm and mounts Chelsea's saddle with me. She lowers her head and we shoot through the water. I hold onto her reins, laying my head close to her neck. Helios lays his head on my shoulder, his body flush with mine.

Within minutes, we are back near the main action of the battle. Both sides have advanced into the other, so the length and breadth of the battle is larger and clouded above our heads. Soldiers have begun to fight above and below the main line of attack. A large sphere of anger and weaponry is forming above our heads.

"Where do we go to be the most help?" Chelsea asks. "I can't see a clear opening."

"I can't see one either." Then I remember the jade in my hand. "The jade!" I yell, remembering what got me here. "I think I can use it to stop this." I reach my hand into my armor, but another hand reaches with mine. Helios is reaching for the stone.

"What are you doing?!" I yell at him as I jump from Chelsea's back.

"That jade is as much mine as it is yours," Helios says in a calm voice. "I can use it to stop the fighting just as much as you can." He climbs from Chelsea's back and comes to me. All the while, the battle rages overhead.

He could be right, but I cannot let the jade go so easily. It's true that he saved me from Nyobi, but I still don't know *how* he would use the stone. The battle grows worse overhead and Chelsea swims to my side.

"It's time to act, Evelyn," she says. "Either we use the jade, or we use our own powers to stop the fighting. We can't wait." I hold my hand against the pocket with the jade. I reach inside and grab it, caressing its smooth surface. But instead of the cold I expect from stone, it is warm to the touch – too warm. I tuck it into a hidden panel in the chest of my armor and turn away from Helios.

"We fight on our own," I tell Chelsea. "But the jade stays with me until Lady Pescara decides who gets to use its power." Helios tries to argue, but I ignore him, mounting Chelsea's saddle again. "We have to do what is best for Atlantis," I tell him. "If you really want the same things we do, then start fighting for them." I nudge Chelsea's side and we swim to the center of the fighting, leaving Helios behind to choose his side.

The battle is in full force when Chelsea and I reach the center of it. "Let's stay beneath the fight," I tell her. "We won't be seen as easily, and we can hit more of the enemy from here."

Chelsea neighs her agreement, a sound I haven't heard from her before. We swoop lower beneath the battle where we can get a better view of the combatants. Looking overhead, I give Chelsea the order.

"Start your stream," I say, and a thin line of superheated water leaves her lips.

I focus my thoughts toward the tip of the heat stream and gather the first section into a ball. I compress it and take careful aim. I send it toward the legs of one of Nyobi's adult soldiers. The ball is intensely hot, and the water burns the man as soon as it touches his legs. We watch him kick frantically as his legs turn from red to white boils and then to black. It's a horrible sight. The heat was too much. It also grazed the Atlantean soldier who was fighting him, though his legs only kick and turn red.

"You have to make your aim tighter," Chelsea says. I nod and she sends out another stream of heated water. I take a smaller section this time and squeeze it more than the last. This time I aim for one of Nyobi's sharks, striking him in the belly. The heat sends the shark into shock and he stops fighting, in too much pain to focus. An Atlantean soldier spears him through the eye and the shark sinks, lifeless, beneath the battle. I wince at the sight, but I know war is not a pretty thing. I refocus on Chelsea, and we prepare to strike again.

For the next hour, Chelsea and I send superheated balls of water into the fray. Most of the time, our targets fall. Sometimes, we miss. At the end of an hour, Chelsea is exhausted.

"I don't think I can keep going," she says to me.

"Okay," I say. "Let's find a place to rest and regroup," I tell her. We make our way under the battle to the back of the Atlantean army.

"Where have you been?!" I hear my mother's voice yelling at me. "I went to check on you an hour ago and you were gone. What has been happening?!"

"Mom," I'm startled to see her. It feels so out of place. "We came here to rest. Chelsea needs to…" my mom cuts me off.

"So, YOU are the reason so many have been falling!" she yells at us. "I saw Captain Maru being carried to the tent for the wounded. His legs were burned horribly. That was an hour ago! Immediately I thought it might be you. When you weren't where you were supposed to be, it only confirmed my suspicions. I wanted to find you, but this is WAR!" She shouts at us. "And out here, I am not Mom. I am Captain Marin, YOUR COMMANDING OFFICER! And when I give an order, I expect to be obeyed!"

"Captain," Chelsea begins, but mom cuts her off.

"NO!" she yells. "You do NOT get to speak. You two may have been a help to our army today, but you did it through flagrant disobedience! Both of you head back to camp. Do what you can to help the wounded, but don't you DARE leave! Do you understand?!"

"Yes, Captain."

"Yes, Mom…uh…Captain." Mom gives me one more glare, shaking her head. She says nothing else, just turns from us and swims back to the rest of the regiment and the fighting without looking back.

That's twice in one day that I've been yelled at by a powerful woman.

Chelsea and I turn and swim back to the camp. The day has been long, and the fighting rages on. By the time we make it back to camp, there are more than enough wounded for us to help with. A nurse quickly checks my scrapes, applying a butterfly bandage to my cheek. That is all I need, so I grab bandages and any other supplies the nurses ask for in the two-worlder hospital tent. Chelsea lends her help to the sea creature hospital tent. We are both too tired and too ashamed to talk, too tired to even share our mental connection. Eventually, we are both sent to our tent to rest. Some of the fresh recruits are just leaving, heading out to the battlefield to take over for our other worn-out soldiers. Others are fast asleep, clothing torn, armor still on, resting just enough to go back to the fight.

The few cots are full. Chelsea and I swim to a back corner of the tent. She curls on the ground and I rest next to her with my head on her tail. Together, we fall into a deep sleep.

I enter a dreamworld. Everything is fuzzy around the edges as my brain tries to make sense of what I have seen and heard today. The water around me shines a luminescent green. As I swim through it, golden tendrils move around me. They flow from my eyes and my ears and my hair. Gold fills the water around me. It fills me with a sense of familiarity.

Evelyn

Evelyn

Evelyn

I feel Namaah's whisper in the water. But Namaah is air, another reason I know all of this is a dream. I search for her anyway.

Namaah. Are you there?

I am here child, she speaks to my mind. I turn around.

There is Namaah in her human form, my Namaah, standing in the water before me. She is surrounded by the golden tendrils that fill the sea. She is smiling, her lips silent as usual. Her hair flows in the water. Dark curls caress her face. But she is changed. Where once there was a long scar on one cheek, she is now covered in scars. Her face, arms, hands, and feet are covered with the telling signs of injury.

Namaah, what happened to you? I ask through the cloud of my dream. *Who has hurt you this way?* She smiles at me, sadly.

My scars are evidence of the many years I have seen, she tells me. *They live as a tapestry to all I have witnessed on the earth. All the pain, worry, deceit, jealousy, and selfishness of man. It is all etched into my skin.*

My heart aches for my friend. She is too good to be so pained and so scarred.

I am so sorry, Namaah. She smiles and walks to me, taking me by the hand.

I am not here for you to pity me, she says. *You have a difficult path ahead of you. The queen told you a great deal.*

She did, I say, *but I don't understand all of it. At the end, she was yelling at me. I think she was yelling at me for stealing the power she put in the pearl. But I didn't steal it. I do think some of the power is still inside of me, but I didn't take it and I don't want it.*

And have you decided, Evelyn?

Decided what? I ask her. *What do you mean?*

The jade, she whispers again to my mind. *Will you use it? Will you use it to enhance the powers you returned with?*

I don't know, I tell her. *If it really does come from Helios' family, maybe it won't work for me. Besides, I promised him I would take it to Lady Pescara. She can decide how it gets used.*

Remember that Helios' family is Gileaus' family, Evelyn, Namaah tells me. *That family was nearly your own thousands of years ago. I believe Gileaus would have wanted you to use the power the jade holds. Enough of his ancestral line still lives within the jade to ensure that you can use it safely.*

I feel tears rolling down my cheeks. Not just in my dreams. These tears are real. I know I am crying in my sleep, that these tears are really mingling with the ocean water all around me.

I miss him so much, I tell Namaah.

I know you do, she answers. *I feel your pain as clearly as you feel it now. But let that love lead you to choosing right, Evelyn, not pain. Let Gileaus be a part of your future. Let his family power help you in your time of need.*

But how do I do it? I ask.

Take the stone away from here. You needn't travel far, and you needn't be gone long. You only need a safe and quiet place to act on the stone.

Is that what you think I should do? I ask. Namaah smiles.

Of course it is Evelyn. But remember, you are the one with the power to choose. You must find your own path. You can choose to continue as you are. You don't need the stone to embrace your future.

And what if I return the stone to Helios? I ask. *What would happen then? What would he do with it?*

That is a question I cannot answer, Evelyn. I am connected to you, not to Helios. I believe the jade would help him as it would help you, but the choice is yours.

She squeezes my hand.

Remember, Evelyn, it is possible that this jade knows you in a way you do not yet understand. Perhaps its power will only serve to strengthen what is already there.

Before I can say anything else, Namaah lets go of my hand and steps back into the gold. I reach out for her again, but the gold takes over. Her beautiful form disappears in the haze. I reach out for her again, but instead of finding Namaah, my hand touches the fleshy belly of my companion.

Evelyn. Evelyn, are you alright? Chelsea asks me. She nudges me with her nose, and I wipe away the tears from my dream. *Could she see what I was dreaming?*

I'm alright, I whisper to her mind. *But I think I need to do something. Will you come with me?*

Always.

I smile and lead her quietly out the door of the tent.

Chapter 25

Chelsea doesn't ask why I am leaving camp in the middle of the night. She did see my dream, and it was enough for her. I fill her in on my encounter with Nyobi and her ability to freeze time, Helios being immune to the freezing, and how he saved my life. She is wide-eyed when I finally finish.

The entire time we swim through camp, we are surrounded by battle-weary soldiers and captains. My own mother is asleep in her tent. She must have crashed there sometime after reprimanding Chelsea and me. I'm glad she's safe. I'm glad she is sleeping, but the battle still rages in the middle of the Mediterranean.

Chelsea and I weave our way out of the tent city and head west, away from our army and the battle. We finally stop when the battle can no longer be heard, and we can no longer be seen.

"Are we meeting someone out here?" Chelsea finally asks.

"No," I answer. "I have to look at this thing on my own and figure out what it can do." I reach into the chain mail armor that sits over my wetsuit. The metal of my outer armor clangs in the darkness. Finally, I find the jade and pull it from its hiding place. It is hot in my hand, and I have a hard time holding onto it.

"What are you going to do with it?" Chelsea asks.

"I honestly don't know. I kind of expected something to just happen. It called to me when we were heading to the battle."

"Why don't you try speaking to it?" Chelsea asks. I nod and bring the hot stone in front of my face.

"I am Evelyn," I say to it. "You called to me, and now I am here. What do you want from me? How can we make this war end?" There is silence in the water. I look to Chelsea and she looks back to me. Neither of us knows what to do or what to expect. Until I feel a burning in my chest. Well, not inside of me, but from something resting on me.

I reach into the neckline of my wetsuit and pull on the chain that is tucked inside. It takes quite a bit of pulling, but I finally wrestle the entire necklace free. In one hand I hold the jade as it grows hotter by the second. In the other hand, I hold my hamsa medallion. She shines her brilliant gold even in these deep and dark waters. I squint my eyes to shield them from her light. But her luminescence is not the only thing that captures my attention. She, too, is growing warmer by the second. Both items become so hot that I cannot handle them anymore. I drop both at once, and Chelsea and I follow them with our eyes as they sink to the sea floor below.

The necklace and jade are only a few feet beneath us when they settle on the floor of the Mediterranean. We watch quietly as the two pieces grow white-hot. I raise a hand up to shield my eyes from their brightness, but something else is happening. The jade is moving toward the necklace. They are only centimeters apart, but the jade closes that distance in a matter of seconds.

"What is it doing?" Chelsea asks.

"I have no idea."

"But this is your necklace," she says. "Don't you know what it can do?"

I shake my head, and we both watch silently as the jade slides on top of my medallion, nearly hiding it from view. The light that has been blinding us grows dark, and I have to blink to see again. The jade is darker than ever and the gold veining that crisscrosses its surface is beginning to melt away. The gold of the jade rolls to the edges of the stone and drips from its sides, landing on the golden hand that lies beneath.

As the jade's gold melts onto the hamsa, the hamsa begins to glow. First white, then green then a brighter gold than it has ever been. It glows and it melts. Chelsea and I stare, our mouths agape, as we watch my hamsa give way to the gold of the jade. The once-brilliant hand bends and shifts. It moves first outward then curves in around the jade like a hand grasping a treasure. Then the gold melts to create a simple band at first, then out and away from the jade. But it doesn't sink into the sandy floor below. Instead, it creates a delicate and intricate pattern around the jade. Swirls and points and flourishing patterns now surround the deep, green stone and crisscrosses its edges. I feel a sense of satisfaction from the jade as the gold frames its surface.

The gold finds an ending to its metamorphosis and finally rests in the sand. Steam rises from the area as the metal cools. I want to touch it, but I am afraid I will get burned. As if it understands what I am thinking, the necklace rises from the seabed. It floats in front of me. The steam is gone. All that is left is the gold-gilt jade and the familiar chain.

"If you touch that thing, what will happen?" Chelsea asks.

"I'm wondering the same thing."

"If something goes wrong," she says, "I'm here for you. I'll get you back to the army hospital. They'll be able to take care of you."

"I'm not sure that's as comforting as it should be," I say. "Besides, how do we explain this to my mom? She gave us orders to stay put." Chelsea doesn't say anything, but I feel her nerves. She isn't sure which option is worse. The jade or my mom. I'm not sure I know either. I turn to look over my shoulder. The battle is still far enough away that I cannot hear it. No one is here but me and Chelsea. I wonder what happened to Helios. What did he choose? Where is he fighting? Or did he run away? I turn back to the jade necklace. It floats expectantly in the water.

"It's now or never," I say out loud. I don't know if I'm trying to convince Chelsea or me. Or both of us. I reach my hand up into the water and stretch my fingers out to touch the jade. Its surface is cool to the touch now, no burning rises from it anymore. My fingers brush the delicate gold frame that was once my hamsa medallion. It, too, is cooled, though I feel it reaching out to me. This gold remembers what it was and who I am. It knows me and welcomes me like an old friend. I smile and take the new medallion in my hand.

"Are you sure about keeping it?" Chelsea asks.

"I don't know what else to do with it, Chelsea. My hamsa changed herself to hold the jade. I trust her." I finger the chain that is looped through the new medallion setting, I hesitate for a moment then make up my mind. I let go of the medallion, holding the chain with both hands, and slip it over my head.

When the chain comes to rest on my neck, my heartbeat increases. The change is slight, but I notice it, just the same. My breathing quickens and I feel something inside of me. Something pulsating through me. Something that wants to be free. I open my mouth to shout, but no sound escapes. Instead, white mist floats from my mouth and out into the sea. But the mist isn't empty. People are coming through it, from my body, swimming free of my form and out into the ocean. They are all women. Chelsea reaches her golden, armored head toward the women as they fill the water before us. But instead of bumping into them, her head moves right through. Spirits. They continue swimming forward without notice of her presence and turn to face me.

When the line finally stops, a group of dark and beautiful women floats before me. Their clothing is a style I have seen in history books and even in a few family photographs. One of the women steps forward and I recognize her face.

"Ama," I say. She steps closer to me and reaches her hand to my face. I feel nothing of her touch, but a warmth fills my heart. This woman is my great grandmother. She wears the same Cherokee wedding dress from my photo album. It is beautiful and so is she.

Next is another face I recognize. My grandmother, Ahyoka.

"Grandma," I say to her. She, too, reaches to touch my face. She says nothing, but I feel her words running through me.

Sweet, Evelyn, she says to me. *Look at how you have grown. What a task you have before you. What a decision.*

"What do you mean?" I ask aloud.

The jade has much power, as do you, my Evelyn. The pearl left her mark in your heart and it is up to you to decide how you will use it. The jade will either enhance the powers the pearl left in you, the power to persuade others, to even control their minds – or it will give you access to the help of your ancestors.

"My ancestors?" I ask. "Why is that a choice? What help can my ancestors give to me?"

This jade was hewn by family, my love. No matter its past, it is still most loyal to a family line. It will grant you your desires if you seek it.

You come from a long line of Cherokee chieftesses, Evelyn. It is not a mistake that you are the one called to this task. Through the ages, we have all found the strength within us to save and serve our people.

My grandmother gestures to the many women behind her. I lift my eyes and see them, really, for the first time. First, I see my great-grandmother, Ama. Her eyes sparkle. She smiles at me and it is a smile I recognize. It is the smile I see when my mother smiles at me. I look into the faces of the other women there. I see my mother's wavy hair, her dark, beautiful skin, I see the ceremonial robes and jewelry I've heard about throughout my life. I see a chin, a hand, a regal bearing, a way of being that reminds me of my mother – her strength, her character, her power. Then I see my eyes. I'm startled for a moment. Everyone else has eyes that are dark and penetrating. But these, these are a swirling mix of green and blue, a reflection of what I see in the mirror. The woman with these eyes, my ancestor, looks deep into my soul. I feel her searching my memory. Then, she shares her memories with me.

I see love, war, loss, exile. I see pain and suffering. But I also see determination. A determination to see her family reach safety. I see ships, ancient ships, preparing for a long voyage. I see a family kneeling, asking for divine help in their journey. I see that help given in the embodiment of this woman, this ancestor of mine. I feel her strength surging through me. Then it pulls away and I again see her eyes. They are knowing eyes. They are my eyes. I know what I will choose.

"I want my ancestors with me," I tell the spirit of my grandmother. "How could I choose anything else?" My grandmother smiles and nods.

So it shall be, she whispers to my mind. Then her eyes focus on the medallion around my neck. She reaches out her hands and begins singing to the stone, moving her hands to the rhythm of her words as their meaning echoes through my mind.

The chosen one has chosen us, she sings to the stone, *she has chosen her ancestors, chosen her home, chosen her life to guide her through her journey. Let your powers reflect her choice. Fill her with the promise of her ancestral line.*

She sings and all of my ancestors join in her song. They all sing and hum together a melody that seals their words into the powerful stone around my neck. I feel their song penetrate the stone and seep into my heart. I feel their strength.

When the song ends, my grandmother and all my ancestors close their eyes. After a moment of silence, my grandmother's eyes open.

I love you, sweet child. I will always be with you. We all will.

"I love you, Grandma," I say through my tears. My grandmother smiles at me and raises her hands into the water above her. One by one, my ancestors rise and swim in a circle above our heads. One by one, they dive into the jade. One by one, they leave me until Chelsea and I are again alone on the sea floor.

"Well, wow," Chelsea says after a moment of silence. "So, now what do we do?" It is hard to speak, but I know what comes next.

"Now, we need to talk to my mom."

Chapter 26

A war council has been convened in Lady Pescara's tent. Most of our generals and captains are here to talk strategy while their soldiers rest. A cease fire is in place for the next two days, giving both sides a chance to rest and recuperate.

"I just couldn't watch those boys fall anymore," I hear one general saying to another.

"It was awful," the other returns. "So many young. I don't know why any creatures follow her. They can only all be evil."

"Or under mind control," the first general responds. "That's the whole premise of this war in the first place, isn't it? The queen and Ceto are trying to control everyone and everything until they control the whole earth."

"I don't know how much more of their control I can take," the second general says.

"Then let's finish them," the first says again. It's one of many conversations being mumbled throughout the tent. I hear bits and pieces of the same thing. Generals tired of seeing the young slaves die. Captains wanting to end the fighting to protect their fighters. Everyone disgusted that such a battle could even be taking place in the name of Atlantis.

"Mom, I have to talk to you," I whisper when I find her in the crowded tent.

"What is it?" she asks, searching my face.

"Not here," I reply. "I need to talk where only you can hear me." Standing from her chair, my mother follows me, telling the guard at the door that she will be back soon.

"Evelyn, what is going on?" my mom asks when we are finally out of the tent.

"Mom, I have to fight. I have to fight Nyobi head on, but I need you to help me figure it all out."

"What do you mean?" she asks. Her eyebrows are furrowed just at the idea of her daughter facing the enemy head-on. I'm not sure how she will react when she hears everything.

So, I start from the beginning. I tell her about seeing the jade and convincing Chelsea to take me to it. I tell her about the time freeze when Queen Nyobi Kadul tried to get me to follow her. I tell her about Helios saving me when I took the jade. I tell her about sneaking from my tent in the middle of the night to see what the jade could do. I tell her about her mother. I tell her everything.

My mom is quiet and contemplative for a moment. I see the telltale sign of tears mixing into the ocean water around her. I know she misses her mother.

"You did the right thing, Evelyn," she says after a moment, wrapping me in a hug. "You were right to choose your ancestral line. You were right to tell me. I will do what I can to talk to Lady Pescara, but you must be ready to act even if she does not lead you herself. She has thousands of followers and will rely on you to do the right thing. She trusts you, Evelyn." She lets me go then takes my

236

hands in hers. "I'm proud of you, my girl. I know you have the strength to do what will need to be done. Now, go to Chelsea. Get what rest you can then work on your skills together. You have a great power in your heritage, yes, but we do not know when you will need it. So much depends on you being ready." She kisses my cheek and swims away, back to the tent with the noisy war council of tired and frustrated fighters. Will she be able to speak in there at all? Will Lady Pescara be able to hear her in the midst of all the clamoring voices? Will anyone else listen?

I turn back to the waterway that leads to the open field where Chelsea is waiting for me. I get just a few yards onto the path when something catches my eye. I pause and turn to see what is there. At first, I don't see anything in the darkness, but my eyes keep searching until I see something sparkle in the shadows of the rolling seabed. My brain tells me to swim away, but there is no way I can leave. I have to know what is there. Or who. All I do is turn toward the shining movement when a voice speaks from the darkness.

"That was a lot of information," the voice says. I freeze where I am. I know who is there.

"How did you get here?" I ask. Gwen moves slowly from the shadows, checking the surrounding water for others who might overhear us or see her.

"It's like I told you, Evelyn," she says when she sees the coast is clear. "I am more powerful than you think. I have many followers, many covert followers, on both sides actually. Not everyone in my grandmother's army believes in what she is doing or how she goes about it. Not everyone in Atlantis is fine with life going on the way it has for centuries. I have the help I need getting anywhere I need to go. And in getting anything I need to have. Oddly enough, my needs are often tied to you." Her eyes move to my chest where the jade is hiding beneath my wetsuit.

"I've heard that anyone who owns the jade can harness its power in any way they want," she says. "When my grandmother uses the jade, she uses it to enhance her ability to control people." Gwen makes one, slow movement toward me. "But you have stolen the jade, haven't you, Evelyn? Does stealing imply ownership? Do you own the jade now?" Her voice is accusing. She isn't really asking me these questions. She is stalling.

In a flash, Gwen swims at me. She stretches out her hand and a wall of water hits me in the face. I am blown onto my back and before I can react, she is grasping my shoulders, trying to get the chain mail off of my body. She knows I am wearing the jade, and that is what she wants. She tries freeing it from its safety in my cumbersome armor.

I call out to Chelsea with my mind, hoping she is close enough to hear me. I reach for the backside of my armor where my knife waits. Gwen sees the knife and focuses her strength there. Still holding onto my armor, she aims her wall of water at the weapon in my hand. I strain to hold onto it, but her current is strong.

"I told you, Evelyn," she says through gritted teeth. "I can do all of this without you. This is your choice!" Gwen turns her face to me, and the wall of water shifts from the knife to my face. I cannot see and I cannot breathe. It doesn't take long before my grip is weakened and the knife slips from my hand. I start to lose consciousness when I feel Chelsea reaching out to me.

Evelyn, she says, *I am here. Let me help you.* I feel her pulling her heat through her body. In a moment, the burst of her heated water hits Gwen. Gwen arches away from me when the heat burns her, and I can finally breathe. I gasp, taking in as many breaths as I can. Gwen rolls away, but she is not alone.

From the shadows, a large eel joins the fight. Its jaws open wide and he shoots out an arc of electricity through the water. But he isn't aiming for me. He is focused on Chelsea. His attack hits her before I can intervene.

Chelsea screeches with pain. It's a sound I have never heard from her before. The eel's mouth opens wide again, and I am ready. As the superheated electricity leaves his mouth this time, I focus on it with all I have left in me. In a split second, I tighten the heated water into a tiny ball and aim it directly for his mouth. Just as I prepare to release the ball, Gwen barrels into my side. My aim is thrown, and the ball of electrified water grazes the eel's body, doing limited damage.

I turn my attention back to Gwen and shove against her as hard as I can. She is blowing water into my face, but she is weakened from Chelsea's attack. I lower my head and let the water cascade over me. It flows harmlessly across my armor and the friction generates more heat. I let the water warm around me. When it is ready, I pull all of it together and force it into Gwen's face. She cries out and is blown back. I leave her and return to Chelsea.

Chelsea and the eel are in a tight-locked match. The eel strikes and Chelsea dodges it. Chelsea's attacks are broader than the eel's. Even when he dodges, he cannot escape her heat. She readies for another blow and I join her, grabbing the water as soon as it leaves her mouth. I shoot it as quickly as I can at the eel. The aim is good and he is caught off guard. His skin sizzles as the heat wraps around his body. He writhes in the water and screeches before turning again to attack me, but Chelsea hits him again with another blast. The eel screeches and twists again. Gwen calls out from behind me.

"Evelyn, stop!" she yells at me. She pushes past me and swims to her eel. "Are you just like the rest of them?" she sobs. "Do you think that just because they are different, that all *inferior* sea life is less than you?!" She scoops him into her arm and shoots through the water, over our heads, and back into the shadows. Chelsea and I swim after them but are soon lost in the darkness. Gwen has vanished.

We return to the camp and report what happened. A small group of scouts is sent into the wilderness side of the camp to search for Gwen. They return empty-handed. More guards are set around the camp, keeping an eye out for Gwen or any of her followers. Anyone who could have helped her is questioned, but no arrests are made. We are watchful, but we still have to prepare for battle.

My mom speaks with Lady Pescara, telling her about everything I have seen, heard, and done in the past 24 hours. This news is devastating to our cause. If Nyobi can freeze time, then we are in even greater danger. Lady Pescara asks us not to tell anyone what we know so we can keep morale up. Besides, she reasons, we have the jade.

If we were at home, there would be more time to discover what I am able to do with the jade, but as it is, Lady Pescara and my mom are both certain that my ancestors will show me the way. Whatever it is, it will be our secret weapon when Nyobi and Ceto least expect it.

Chelsea and I are ordered to fill every moment with preparation. We need practice, we need food and we need rest. We eat, we catch whatever sleep we can, we train, and we prepare for the battle of our lives.

Chapter 27

"Evelyn!" I hear Helios shouting my name. Chelsea and I have been practicing for hours and are cleaning up our armor. I haven't seen Helios since the battle; I have no idea what he has been doing for the past two days. Chelsea nudges my shoulder.

"Yes, I heard him," I tell her. "I just didn't want to acknowledge him."

"Evelyn," Helios says again. He is at my side now. "Evelyn, where is the jade? I need it to fight." His voice is low now, a rumbling in my ear. Helios grabs my elbow and I turn to face him with a glare. "What have you done with it?" he asks again. I pull my arm free of his grip and move closer to Chelsea.

"I have the jade now, Helios," I tell him. "Lady Pescara knows I have it so there's no going back. It's mine."

"Then take me to her. I have to get it. My family harvested that jade," Helios tells me again. "It is meant for my blood. I should be the one to use it."

"And what would you use it for?" I ask.

"Evelyn, how many times do I have to tell you that I am not interested in power? I am here to defeat Nyobi for all she has put me and my ancestors through."

"But she is also one of your ancestors, is she not?" Chelsea asks. "How can we know that you won't just use the jade to help her in the end?"

"I guess you can't know that," Helios answers. "But I've been trying to prove myself." For the first time, I notice what Helios has on. He is wearing the clothing and armor of Nyobi's kingdom. His arms and legs are covered in bruises and cuts. I reach for my knife.

"Helios," I whisper. "What have you done?" He glances down at his clothing then back at me, shaking his head.

"Evelyn," he says, "this isn't what it looks like."

"Then explain what it is," Chelsea says.

"I've been hiding away in Nyobi's army," Helios tells me. "Several of her guards and soldiers are still against her, just too afraid to stand up to her. But they aren't too afraid to help me. I got this gear from some of them."

"And who were you fighting?" Chelsea asks. "That armor is recently damaged."

"I was looking for the soldiers who fight willingly with Nyobi and Ceto," Helios says. "I've been fighting them all night."

"You've been fighting them by yourself? How did you get away and back here?" I ask. "How did you know where to find me?"

"I had help fighting, Evelyn. Like I said, not everyone is happy to serve Ceto and the queen. I worked my way to the front edge of the battle," he says. "Once I was there, I couldn't escape the swords of the Atlantean army. I pretended to fall among the wounded on the Atlantean side and was brought to your infirmary."

"And you snuck out of the infirmary without anyone noticing?" Chelsea asks. "And just found us by luck?"

"Sneaking out was easy," Helios tells her. "The nurses are so overwhelmed, they don't have time to check on every patient regularly, especially the ones from Nyobi's army. And finding you," he says, facing me, "wasn't my first goal. I was listening for the jade."

I straighten my back and look at him. I'm unwilling to give him the jade. I have no way of really knowing what he will do with it and I am unwilling to give up the promise of ancestral help in the field of battle.

"I want to believe you, Helios," I say, "I really do. But there is no way I can jeopardize the safety of the Atlantean army. I won't give you the jade." Helios shakes his head.

"I know that now," he whispers. "You have become its owner now. I can feel it. That kind of power is hard to give up." I open my mouth to protest. I am not seeking for power. I'm seeking freedom from it. But Helios raises his hand to stop me from speaking.

"You don't need to tell me how pure your motives are," he says. "I already know. If I can't have the jade, then just let me fight with you. I want to be near the jade, working with it as my ancestors would have done." He waits for me to answer, but I hesitate.

What do you think? I reach out to Chelsea's mind.

He seems sincere, she answers, *but that doesn't mean he is. His past is too complex. His relationship to Nyobi makes him a suspect no matter what he does. Not that we have a say in any of it. He would have to report to Lady Pescara.*

I agree, I say. *But there's no telling what Lady Pescara would do with him if she found him.*

How about Jack? Chelsea asks. *Sure, he isn't your commander anymore, but he is still your boy...* her thoughts pause as she remembers the kiss I gave Helios not so long ago. *Well, he has some feeling for you anyway. He may be the only one willing to help. He can take Helios to Lady Pescara.* I nod and answer out loud.

"Get Jack, quickly," I tell her. "Just let him know it is urgent, that I need his help." Chelsea bows her giant head and swims away. Helios looks nervous.

"Jack? Really?" he asks me. "I don't think he actually likes me very much, Evelyn. He isn't going to believe anything I say." Helios swims close to me and takes my hand. The familiar warmth spreads through my body, but my head is in control now. I pull my hand away.

"Please back up, Helios," I say. "I can't let my head be clouded."

"But Evelyn," he says, laughing and bringing his hand to my cheek. I put my hand on his chest and push him slowly, but firmly away.

"No," I tell him. "If you want to work anywhere near the jade, this part has to stay out of it." His hand drops to his side and he moves away from me, sitting down on a rock.

"I want more than the jade, Evelyn," he says as he sits. "I want *you*. I don't know what this connection is that we have, but I feel it down in my bones. Something about you is undeniable in me. Like I've known you forever. I didn't know it was possible to feel this way about someone. I just feel, complete when I'm with you. Do you understand that?" he looks up at me with those dark, beautiful eyes. His locks of hair fall perfectly around his face. It's amazing how a heart can still feel these emotions after so much time and space. But this is not Gileaus.

"I do know how that feels," I answer. "But I don't feel that with you." I let my words hang in the water around us. I don't know what else to say. After a few more minutes of agonizing silence, Chelsea arrives with Jack and another soldier from his regiment, one of our strongest fighters, Enzo. As soon as Jack sees Helios, his face turns red.

"What is he doing here?" Jack asks. "Evelyn, Helios is wanted for abandoning our mission. I have to take him into custody." Helios looks up to me. I don't have the heart to answer.

"He claims that he wants to help us," Chelsea says. She can feel the tension in my heart. "He says that he wants to fight with the jade for Atlantis."

"With the jade?" Jack asks. He swims closer to Helios and Helios stands to face him. "Where is the jade then, Helios?" Jack's nose is only inches from Helios'.

"You'll have to ask Evelyn that," Helios answers and that's when I decide it's time to disobey my orders from Lady Pescara. I'm going to have to tell them the truth. Chelsea can't save me forever.

I reach into the neckline of my wetsuit and tug at the chain.

Evelyn, Chelsea warns my mind, but I shake it off. I can't hide this anymore. It takes a minute, but finally the jade breaks free from my body, the medallion a gold, green, and glittering beauty in the bottom of the Mediterranean Sea. I feel an emptiness in my chest where the medallion belongs.

"Where did you get that?" Jack asks.

"I got it from him," I answer as I nod toward Helios. Jack turns to look at Helios then takes a step back, leaving Enzo to keep an eye on him.

"I still don't trust him," Jack says to me, never taking his eyes off Helios. "I'll have to take him to Lady Pescara."

"I agree," I answer. "But I don't see many other options. If he's telling the truth, he can help us. If he is lying, he's a liability."

"You've put the Atlantean army in an impossible situation," Jack says to Helios. Helios just shakes his head.

"It doesn't have to be impossible," he says. "Assign a guard to watch me but let me be a part of the fight. Let me stay near the jade. That's all I want." Jack shakes his head.

"I am no longer Evelyn's commander," he says. "I can't guarantee you any space near her. I can only take you to Lady Pescara. She will decide what happens next." He takes Helios by the arm and jerks him around, tying his hands behind his back and handing him off to Enzo. Helios doesn't fight back.

"I have to be by the jade," he whispers. "I'll do whatever it takes."

"I'll be in the middle of a battle, Helios," I say. "There's no way Lady Pescara will let you near it with your history."

"You won't be in the center of anything, Evelyn," Jack says. "I've been in the war council for hours. Lady Pescara and your mom both think you and Chelsea need to stay on the outskirts of the fighting."

"What?!" I yell. "How can she keep me out of the fighting? Why won't she listen? What is she doing, Jack? Even without the jade, Chelsea and I are a huge support to Atlantis. Nobody can do what we can."

"And nobody else has injured our own side like you have," Jack says. "Do you even know how many of our own soldiers have burns on their legs? Captain Maru isn't the only casualty of your poor aim." Jack's face is red and angry. I look closer and see the burns on his leg. Only one leg but burned just the same. Burned by me.

"Jack, I'm so sorry."

"Don't apologize to me," he says. "I don't care about the pain. I've felt worse. But you have accidentally hurt dozens of our own men, Evelyn. You and Chelsea have to stand down until the timing is right."

"Does my mom feel the same way?" I ask.

"Captain Marin will be here soon to give you orders herself," Jack says. "The war council concluded right before Chelsea came to get me." Jack sighs and comes closer to me. Forgetting that anyone else is there, he lifts my chin, so my eyes meet his and I don't pull away. I close my eyes, waiting for a kiss, but it doesn't come.

"Evelyn," he says to me. I open my eyes, embarrassed, and look at him. His eyes are as blue as the Atlantic. They are strong and good. His eyes have called to me before, but now they are pleading. "Please, Evelyn. Listen to your commanding officer. Stand down." I am mortified, not just by being rejected but for the pain I have caused. I am weak and I've hurt so many people. I pull away from Jack, back into the colder, darker water.

"Don't worry, Captain," I say. "I know my place. I won't cross the line again." I swim away from him, back to my tent where I know my mom will go to give orders. I feel Chelsea following me, but she doesn't try to intercept my thoughts.

Jack and Enzo are left to deal with Helios.

Chapter 28

The fighting has recommenced. As Jack knew would happen, Chelsea and I have been ordered to stand down, but not for being weak or incapable. Lady Pescara believes we will have a better idea of where we are needed if we can see the entire battle. Chelsea and I are to watch and wait, saving our energy for the right moment. We wait over the hospital tents, viewing the entire battle from above and watching for any signs of a sneak attack.

After several hours of watching and waiting, the wounded start coming in to be treated. At first, it's a trickle. A few severely cut arms and legs. A few who have been exposed to mind control and are going crazy. A few caught in a sea-skill battle when they didn't have the upper hand.

After a few hours more, the trickle becomes a steady flow. More and more soldiers are coming in with missing hands and feet. My stomach turns at the sight. Mind control victims are the worst. They cry out for their mothers or try to attack their nurses. They think they are still on the battlefield and are being ambushed. Some of them shout at invisible monsters that loom over them. Some talk to ghosts before breathing their last breath.

A little while more and we start to see wounded from the other side. There aren't children anymore. Nyobi went through most of them yesterday. The ones we could save are being held under a guard since they still try to fight. The ones we could not save are being held in a tent at the back of camp, waiting for identification.

The sounds of fighting are growing louder. What was at first almost inaudible is now a dull rumble in the distance, like the sound of thunder rolling across the sea. There are no bombs. No gunfire. No flaming arrows shooting through the fight. The fighting is more like a sound of raging waters. Currents, temperature, weapons – all being wielded in the battle. Still the wounded come. Still the sounds of their conflict reach my ears. Still we wait.

The day turns to night and the fighting continues. The Atlanteans are exhausted. They don't have the power of Nyobi to help them. And I have chosen the power of my ancestors, I can't use Pearl's mind power to help. I cannot give them my strength and feel like I have failed my people.

Then, just as dawn is rising again on the Mediterranean Sea, the fighting changes. The armies of Atlantis have tried rotating their troops, but we've lost too many fighters. Everyone is on the battlefield and we are losing ground. Chelsea and I watch in horror as Ceto and Nyobi's soldiers are buoyed up with the morning light. I don't know where their energy comes from, I just know our side cannot handle it. Troops from Atlantis and our allied armies start to fall by the dozens at the front of the line. The battle is moving in on our territory.

"We have to do something," I tell Chelsea.

"What can we do, Evelyn?" Chelsea asks.

"We can stay away from our side," I answer. "That way we won't risk hitting any of our own soldiers. We've got to get ourselves all the way to the back of the enemy lines, so it doesn't matter who we hit."

"Aren't Ceto and Nyobi at the back of their line?" Chelsea asks.

"All the more reason to get back there."

The sounds of the fighting are gaining intensity. We aren't far from the over-crowded hospital, and the cries of the wounded are getting worse. Patients are now being left in the open water, laying on the sea floor. I look to their writhing bodies and see a familiar form.

"Celia!" I yell and swim for her body with Chelsea following. Celia was fighting in Jack's regiment. They must be in the worst of the fighting now.

When I reach her, Celia is moaning on the seabed. I swim to kneel beside her. Chelsea hovers overhead, shock echoing throughout her massive body. Celia's eyes are closed.

"Celia," I say to her. Her eyes don't open. She just keeps moaning. "Celia, it's Evelyn." Her moaning quiets and her body stills.

"Is she dead?" Chelsea asks.

"I don't know," I answer. "Celia."

Celia's head turns to me and her eyes open.

"Celia, it's Evelyn," I say again. She nods. "What happened to you? Where were you fighting? What is happening on the field?" Celia's eyes close again and I think she is losing consciousness.

"Jack," Celia mumbles.

"What about Jack?" I ask, leaning down to her ear.

"Jack and Helios," she whispers. "Fighting… Hidden… Sneaking…"

"Where are they fighting, Celia?" I ask again. "Celia, how can we help them?" I want a nod, a pointing finger, anything to point me the right way to go. I don't want to fly blind. I want to go where I can do the most damage.

"Too…late…," Celia whispers. I lower my ear to her lips. She mumbles a few more words, but I can't understand her. Then, her breathing stops.

"Celia?" I say, looking into her open eyes. But they are lifeless.

"Celia!" I shout now and I start chest compressions on her.

"We need help over here!" Chelsea starts shouting. "Help! We need a doctor! This soldier is going down!"

In less than a minute, an Atlantean doctor and mermaid are by our side, taking over the chest compressions. The nurse leans her ear down to Celia's mouth.

"There is no breathing, doctor," she says.

"Check her pulse," the doctor orders as he continues his pushing, pushing, pushing on Celia's chest. The nurse places her fingers on Celia's neck. I can only watch her, waiting for a sign that there is hope. But there is nothing. The nurse looks to the doctor and shakes her head. She pulls a red ribbon from her pocket and ties it around Celia's wrist. From across the pile of injured soldiers, another two-worlder cries out. The nurse and doctor rise to go to them.

"No!" I shout. "You have to stay here! She needs your help!" I am grabbing the arm of the doctor. He gently takes my wrist and pushes it from his body.

"I'm sorry," he says. "There is nothing more I can do for her here. If we were back in Atlantis or had less wounded, I might have a chance of saving her. But out here we are racing time. I have to go to the others, so more are not lost." He sighs and lets go of my wrist. "I'm very sorry," he says again and swims away with the nurse.

I am frozen and don't know what else to do. I look down at Celia and see her eyes, still open. Her shirt is torn, and blood is clouding around her lifeless body. Chelsea cries.

I kneel back down beside my roommate. We were never close. But I *know* Celia. We were fighting for the same side. We were on covert operations together. She cannot be gone. But there is still no movement, no breathing, no pulse, no life. Then, a feeling. From deep inside I feel it growing. It gets bigger and bigger until I cannot contain it anymore. My eyes burn and I want to find a place to hide and let everything out. But I can't. All around is fighting. The fighting never stops. I look up at the battle that is ever closer to us. Our fighters are so tired. I can see the wave of Nyobi's army pressing into them, crashing over them, drowning them in fighting. I look to Chelsea. Her eyes are red. I've never seen them look that way before. Tiny flames shoot into the water from the corners. Is this what it looks like when a sea dragon cries?

When our eyes finally meet, I feel the burning coming from her. My eyes fill with the same, insatiable heat. It burns. I feel the burning shoot through me from the center of my heart with a heat so intense, I'm afraid it will kill me. I look down to my chest. Instead of my wetsuit and armor, I see the same burning flames curling across my body. Is Chelsea doing this to me? I look to her, but her sobs are unmistakable. She is crying with sorrow, not attacking me. I start beating at my chest, trying to stop the watery flames. But the flames aren't hitting me, they are coming from me.

I reach into the neckline of my wetsuit, searching for the chain. I grab it and tug and pull until the medallion comes free. As soon as it is out in the open water, it bursts into flames. I shield my eyes and swim backward, trying to escape the heat. But the necklace comes with me. I look up to Chelsea for help, but she is in trouble, too. Her beautiful leafy tendrils are bright with flames. The jade is setting her on fire.

I swim to Chelsea and start hitting at the flames with my bare hands. Again and again I strike, trying to extinguish the flames before Chelsea is engulfed.

Evelyn! What are you doing?! Chelsea yells to my mind. *I'm okay. I'm not being burned!*

I stop flailing my arms and look at my friend. Chelsea is glowing brilliant flames into the open sea, but she is okay. She's breathing, she isn't screaming. She is beautiful. I look at the medallion floating around my neck. It is still a flaming mass, but it is not burning me. I look back to Chelsea, covered in flames. She may be the most fearsome creature on earth.

We have to go, she whispers to my mind. *This is a sign, Evelyn. It's time for us to enter the fight.* I set my hand on her neck and nod. I'm crying my own tears now, but instead of the saline mixing into the sea, I see swirling tendrils of fire. I look to Celia lying dead on the ground beneath me. I bend down to her again, setting my fingers on her eyelids, closing them for the last time.

"I'm sorry, Celia," I whisper. "I wish I could have done more to save you. We will make this right." I kiss her forehead and return to Chelsea. I mount her golden saddle made all the more brilliant by the burning leaves around her. I look up and see dozens of eyes on us. We are aflame and lighting the entire camp. I cross my arms and create fists against my chest. Dozens of arms mirror me, even the doctor and nurse who tried to help Celia.

Chelsea and I are fighting for all of them.

I lay my hands across Chelsea's neck and take the reins. As soon as I have my grip firmly in place, I nudge her forward with my foot. Chelsea lowers her head, and with a speed I've never felt in her before, we shoot through the water and into the fight.

Chapter 29

Bodies float above and below the battle. They are suspended around the fighting, a strange frame for the explosion between them. They are the bodies of the dead who died after the hospitals were full and no one could be spared to remove them. Some of them move when a soldier is pushed through the water and attacks their lifeless bodies, mistaking them for an enemy. Chelsea and I navigate the space beneath the fighting like we are charging through a human minefield. I don't see any faces I recognize among the dead. But among the living I do.

My mom is fighting with our squadron. She is covered in cuts and is bleeding into the water like everyone else. She sends her sword through the chest of a Nyobian soldier. He crumples around the blade, a look of shock crossing his features. He did not expect to die today.

My mom is tired. I don't know how much more she can do before she collapses herself. I push Chelsea onward until I hear a wild cry. My mom has seen me. She wants me to stop, I know, but I will not even hazard a glance behind me. I know what I have to do.

Finally, Chelsea and I near the back of Nyobi's fighters. We are like a glowing target down here, but we are going to fight like the ball of fire that we are. We slow our approach as arrows shoot through the depths all around us. Then, I see her.

Maybe 60 feet ahead, her long, shining tentacles float through the water. Chelsea and I seek cover from the arrows, but my eyes are focused on that body. We hide behind some rocks and I point to Ceto. Chelsea lifts her fiery gaze and rests her flaming eyes on our enemy.

"What do we do with her?" Chelsea asks. "I feel like I could burn her to a crisp right now."

"I feel it too," I say, "but we have to be smart. We don't know where Nyobi and Gwen are yet. We don't want to be hit unexpectedly."

Arrows still fly through the water, bouncing off the rocks we hide behind. "It won't be long before they get the courage to come around the rocks," Chelsea says. "We have to get to them first."

"Are you sure that's a wise idea?" I snap my head around to the person speaking to me.

"Gwen!" I yell. The arrows are still flying around us. Gwen is creeping up beside me. The arrows aren't hitting her. Aren't even coming close. It looks like an invisible shield is surrounding her.

"I love the new look," Gwen says. "The fire of it all looks amazing. So intimidating. Does it burn you? Will it burn me if I touch it?"

"I don't know," Chelsea says. "Want to be the first to give it a try?"

"What are you doing here?" I ask. Gwen crouches down on the rocks.

"I told you I was ready to fight, Evelyn," she answers. "You weren't ready to fight with me, so I went to where I knew I would have support."

"You're fighting *with* your mom and Nyobi now?" Chelsea asks. "I thought that kind of fighting was beneath you." Gwen raises an eyebrow at Chelsea, an arrow striking the rock behind her.

"I don't intend to follow them forever," Gwen responds. "But for the time being, their army is a means to an end." Gwen turns to me again. "I finally realized that if the army of Atlantis was in real danger, it wouldn't be long before you tried to come to the rescue."

"So, you're the reason why Nyobi's forces aren't tired like the Atlanteans," I say. "You are giving them added power, aren't you?" Gwen smiles and straightens.

"Maybe," she says. "I don't know that giving them my power would be the right way to put it. It's more like I am using their bodies more efficiently."

"You're controlling their bodies then?" Chelsea asks.

"Yes."

"So, they are still fighting even though they are injured."

"Yes."

"Gwen," I say. "You're killing them."

"Correction," she replies. "*You* have the power to stop them, Evelyn. Until you decide to follow me, *you* are really the one driving them to their deaths." She is the second person in her family to accuse me of killing innocent people and I'm ready to kill her for it.

"You are killing the soldiers on BOTH sides of the fight, Gwen!" I yell. I try to stand, but too many arrows are shooting through the water. I have to crouch back behind the rocks. Gwen just smiles.

"Are you ready to join me yet?" She asks. I shake my head in anger.

"We will never fight with you," I tell her.

"Never," Chelsea says, and she glows even brighter. Gwen sighs and shakes her head.

"Fine. That is your choice. I won't ask you again. Don't say I never gave you a chance to do something more in the world."

She pushes off the rocks and soars into the open water above us. I feel Chelsea growing the flames in her stomach.

My thoughts exactly, I whisper to her mind.

A large flame erupts from Chelsea's open jaws. I grasp it in my palms, the flames doing nothing to harm me. I crush the heat into a ball brighter than stadium lights and fling it toward Gwen's disappearing form. The ball flies past her and falls into the large army she controls. Her concentration is shattered, and screams erupt from the falling soldiers as the fire spreads among them. Gwen spins in the open water and shoots daggers into us with her eyes.

"That's not gonna be good," Chelsea says.

"No. It is not," I respond. "Are you ready to make a go of it?"

"Now is probably a good time to do something," she says. Gwen is looking toward what soldiers remain in her power and pointing to the rocks where Chelsea and I are hiding.

Chelsea and I catapult from behind our hiding place and rise into the water, far above the enemy, flames surrounding us both. Without any need for open communication, Chelsea and I act with one, shared mind. I feel the burning echo throughout her body. Her golden, fiery leaves grow brighter as she ignites the flame within her. This time, as the flames explode from her body, a loud roar fills my ears. The sound of a sea dragon warning her prey.

The flame erupts from her mouth and into my waiting hands. I compress the heat and send another giant ball into the mindless soldiers below. The mass hits exactly where I aim it. I feel like my brain is on fire, talking to the heat I command through the sea. We watch the fallen soldiers drop their weapons. Some sink under the weight of their armor. Others, who were blasted free from their armor, float up into the open water.

Then the command comes to aim and fire.

With one, swift movement, thousands of fighters turn to Chelsea and me. Dread fills my body as they lift their bows, aim their arrows, and let go. Chelsea and I are floating free in the open water. There are no rocks to shield us from their strike.

In one movement, I pull out my shield from behind my back. Chelsea curls her body into a ball, so her armor is the only thing left exposed, her leafy stems sweep behind her. I curl in front of her, behind my shield. All at once, hundreds of arrows rocket by. Dozens hit my shield and bounce off into the water around us. Chelsea and I both uncurl our bodies and prepare for another attack, our legs and leaves hitting scores of dead arrows as we do. The enemy reloads their bows.

Chelsea and I get our next fireball out just in time to again shield ourselves from the attack. We protect ourselves. They fall. When I open up again, Gwen is floating immediately above her minions. Her arms are spread wide and every bow is notched. There isn't time for us to get another missive out before their arrows will strike. Chelsea starts fueling the fire within her as we both crouch behind our armor and shield. We wait for the arrows to fly, but none come. After a moment of silence, I hazard a glance from behind my shield. Gwen's arrows are no longer pointed at us. Her soldiers are facing another foe. Someone under Chelsea and me. I look down and see Jack. And Helios. And Jack's entire regiment facing Gwen's followers.

We are not alone.

Chelsea reaches for the heat within her again and forces it out with a mighty roar. Several from the group below us look up, startled by the sound. I force the roaring flames into the enemy lines, but this time, two balls pummel them. I realize I can spread the heat to several places at once, and we aim again. The next blow brings dozens of flaming balls into the crowded enemy. Jack and his fighters shoot arrows and swing clubs, swords, and maces. Many are close enough for hand-to-hand combat. But they are facing an enemy who will not stop. They cannot stop.

We fight this way for nearly twenty minutes, neither side willing or able to give up on their prize. Gwen does not have control over the entire army of Nyobi and Ceto, so the battle with Atlantis still rages on the front lines. But we have managed to distract at least a part of the enemy. Jack's troops are strong and valiant, but they are also tired. Their armor is dented and torn, their weapons dark with blood, their eyes dark from lost sleep, their movements slowing. Chelsea and I continue our assault from above, but it is a dangerous place to be.

Soon, we have more than just Gwen's followers facing us. The fighting has grown more intense where we are. More of a distraction to Nyobi's fighters on the front lines. They are all beginning to notice that something is not right at the rear. Thousands of heads turn toward us. Our burning fight cannot be missed. Everyone sees us. Everyone knows we have made it to the back of the fighting. Everyone knows we will soon have the upper hand.

I look to the masses below. I cannot see their faces, but I feel their eyes on me. On us. They can see every ball of fire that Chelsea and I shoot into the water. I hear cheering from the Atlantean army, and it rumbles through the battlefield as we take aim. Everyone is watching.

Everyone.

I feel their eyes before I see them. The shiver it sends through my body stops me mid shot. I look to my right, Nyobi's elite forces are there. She is with them. She and her daughter, Ceto. They both look at me with hard faces. Ceto swims through the water, eyes on me, to the side of her ancient mother. When she stops, both women raise their arms toward me. Their eyes sparkle and their faces spread into broad grins.

They've got me right where they want me.

Chapter 30

Both armies freeze. A moment in time stops again. Nyobi is the only moving thing I see.

"Are you sure this is what you want, young soldier," she calls up into the water. "You are brave, to be sure, but is your bravery placed well? Take a look around you. What is the cost of your decision? Are you ready to take these consequences upon yourself?"

I open my mouth to answer, but someone else responds from below. It is Helios.

"I'm not afraid anymore," he answers his ancestor and foe. "I've seen enough of what you can do. I'm here to take my heritage back."

"Foolish boy," Nyobi spits into the water. "*I* am your heritage. *I* am your future!"

"You aren't my future anymore," Helios answers. "I am creating my own future!"

Nyobi swings one arm down and sends a crushing wall of water toward Helios. The ball of fire is still in my hands. I can attack Nyobi, but I won't be able to stop the rushing water she shoots toward Helios.

I crush the heat as tight as it will go. My arms ache from the effort of throwing and crushing for so long, but adrenaline courses through my veins. The heat is so intense I finally feel it burning my hands. With one swing, I send the heat directly at Nyobi where she is focused on destroying her own descendent; she doesn't even see it coming and the ball strikes her in the face. She plunges, screaming like a banshee, into the deeper water, grabbing Ceto on her way down. But, like everyone else on the battlefield, Ceto is frozen. Her motionless form can do nothing to help the wrinkled queen from plummeting toward the seabed.

Down Nyobi goes. Down Ceto follows. Nyobi's body strikes with a blow so loud and convulsing, I see the shockwaves ripple through the water. Ceto falls on top of her mother, saved from death by the ancient queen's own crushed body. As a cloud of sediment explodes into the water, the mind control the powerful queen held over the people is broken. I look to the army below me. Most are holding their heads, looking into the faces of their comrades with confusion. I begin to hear the mumbles of "What happened?" "What are we doing here?" "Where are we?" filling the sea. For the first time, they are free from her destructive power. For the first time in thousands of years, Queen Nyobi Kadul does not reign in the Mediterranean. The queen is dead.

As realization dawns on the armies, a new cheer erupts from our forces. I look to Chelsea. She is smiling, the flames that surrounded her are gone. Her power is exhausted. I throw my arms around her neck and hold her in a tight embrace. She buries her enormous head into my shoulder, grateful that our efforts have not been in vain. But then I remember Helios.

I shout out his name and dive into the water below. It takes only a few seconds to reach him, but those seconds are like an eternity. Everything moves in slow motion as I see his body sinking into the water. It feels like he is running away from me. All I want to do is reach him. To save him. But he just keeps sinking.

"Evelyn," I hear Jack calling my name. I know he is swimming after me, but I cannot stop. I have to reach Helios.

I finally reach his body just as it touches the sea floor. I lean over him, calling his name.

"Helios," I say. "Helios." His eyes are closed, and his chest is motionless. The Atlantean armor he now wears is crushed, the force of the water enough to mangle his breastplate. I watch him closely, but there is no sign of life. "Helios," I whisper again. I reach my hand down and caress his cheek. He cannot be dead. I lower my lips to his forehead and press them into him. I kiss his face again and again, but no response comes. I feel a hand come to rest on my shoulder. It is Jack, but I am too distraught to notice anything else.

I rest my forehead against Helios' and watch as my lifeless medallion slips down its chain and through the water. It comes to rest on Helios, finding the only remaining descendant of its first owner. I close my eyes.

All of a sudden, Helios' body jolts beneath me. A loud gasp escapes his lips and his eyes spring open. I sit up and watch the life pour back into him. A single, golden tendril floats from the jade to his heart.

"Helios," I say a broad grin spreading across my face.

"Evelyn!" he shouts at me. "Watch out!" he raises his arm and shoves me away. When I lift my head, I see a half dozen arrows hit the ground. Gwen. I forgot about Gwen.

I jump from the sea floor and turn toward her. She is still floating above the army as before, but her strength is diminished. The power lost when her grandmother was destroyed hurt her. She isn't controlling as many as before, but she isn't alone. Rising from the ocean floor from what should have been her grave, Ceto appears. Her hair is filled with rock and debris. Her arms are covered in scrapes. Her face is already swelling, bloody, and bruised. One of her tentacles has nearly been torn off. But she is alive. And she is only focused on me.

"You thought you could destroy me!" she shouts through the water. "But you are no match for me, Evelyn Kai Marin. I thought once that you would make me stronger, but now I know better. All I needed was to rid the world of my mother! Now her power is mine, alone!" She opens her arms wide and lets out a peal of laughter so unearthly it makes me cringe. No cackling witch could match that laugh. It is the laugh of pure evil.

"Gwendolyn!" she calls to her daughter. "Join with me child and live the heritage you were born for." Ceto keeps her eyes on me, waiting for her daughter to come at her command.

I look up at Gwen. She hesitates over the men she controls. What will she do? On her own, she is powerful. But with her mother, she could be unstoppable. I see the wheels turning in her head. Slowly, the soldiers beneath her lower their weapons. She has made up her mind. She lifts her chin, eyes on me, and floats down to her mother. Ceto takes her by the hand and together, they raise their arms over head.

I look around me, their army is not under any control now. They are watching, confused, waiting for what will happen next. The army of Atlantis lifts their shields, readying themselves for an attack. Jack raises his shield over his body and Helios'. Chelsea dives to me. I stand.

The first strike is a blow I have never felt before. Ceto's power over currents is only made stronger by her daughter's help. I go rolling backward through the Mediterranean, head over heels. I see shields and armor, heads and fins, rocks and sand – all swirling past me as I am thrown through the water. By the time I come to a stop, I am beyond the borders of Atlantis' camp. I search the water frantically.

Weapons, armor, shields, bodies, tents, poles, cots, everything that made camp is strewn all over. I search for a face, anyone I know. A shimmer catches my eye. Chelsea.

I swim for her, but she is still. I reach out with my mind, but she does not answer. Chelsea.

When I make it to her body, I see her breathing. Thank goodness. She is only unconscious. She will be okay, but I can't say the same for everyone. Lifeless bodies float throughout the water. The wounded from the hospital are either dead or crying out for help. Doctors and nurses are scrambling to their patients, looking for supplies and shelter. But I look to the battlefield.

Soldiers are regrouping and creating barricades with their bodies and shields. Our strongest current control fighters are lined up in front of the barricade. Together, they aim for Ceto and Gwen. Their forces are strong, but not strong enough. Ceto's current is still pushing west, only slowed by the eastward currents of our army. I rush to the fight, this time without Chelsea. I join with the other water temperature fighters, trying to help in any way I can.

It feels so strange, gathering heat without Chelsea. I've grown accustomed to the feel of her next to me these past several days, heat rising through her belly, drawing her weapon from within herself. Even when fighting with the other temperature control soldiers, there is only so much heat that can be found. We draw all we can from the ocean water. I feel the shiver of the water as we steal too much of its heat. We haven't been careful.

Ice crystals form on my arms and face. The bodies of my fellow fighters are just as iced. I call out to the sea creatures on our side, seeking their help. Dozens of fish, sharks, and other sea life swim to our ranks. They begin swimming back and forth under our feet, building the heat in their bodies. We draw from their heat, and they swim harder and harder, faster and faster.

The heat we make is being thrown at Ceto and Gwen's army. They are not a large contingency of two-worlders, but a mass of people and sea creatures serving under mind control. But Ceto isn't prepared to face us alone. Very few of her soldiers have any underwater skills, and they begin to shrink under the pressure of the hot water pelting their faces. Several pass out as their bodies are drained of water in our current of heat. The rest press forward toward us.

Ceto rises above the heads of her fighters, facing our battle lines. She pulls her arms behind her then throws her power into the water. Our current control is overtaken, blown back by the blast Ceto sends. As our current controllers fall back, Ceto's soldiers press forward, brandishing their weapons, striking wherever they can.

The temperature line is safe, too far to the side to be hit by Ceto's water. But that cannot last long. Ceto continues to blast her current, we blast our heat, but her army still presses on. She will not stop until we are destroyed. Then, out of the corner of my eye I see something rising in the distance. It looks like an ancient wall, but it is really a wall of rocks and debris. Gwen floats behind it, arms poised to direct her missive. I call out to everyone to cover just in time. Gwen throws her arms forward and the rocks come flying at our temperature fighters. Everything from car-sized boulders to small pebbles rains down on our shields. I feel the cries of the sea creatures swimming beneath me, unable to hide beneath a shield. I feel the life energy extinguish in many of them and I feel the excruciating pain of others. I scream at the top of my lungs. The pain is too much to bear.

When I open my eyes, all I can see is Gwen, staring at me and smiling.

Chapter 31

The pain from the sea creatures and the anger over everything that has been stolen from us all is more than I can contain. I feel the burning rumble of the fire within me. I feel the heat of the jade as it lights up with my own indistinguishable flame. My eyes grow wide and this time when I scream, a torch of fire comes from my own lips instead of Chelsea's. Gwen's smile falters.

I call out to what is left of the current control group.

"Get me over there as fast as you can!"

Without hesitating, I swim toward Gwen. She is my target now. I feel the surge of water behind me as the current controllers push me through the water. I shoot like a bullet, arriving within twenty feet of Gwen before I slow down. By now the fear on her face is satisfying. She's been smiling over us for long enough. I let out a yelling ball of flames so long, I don't have to compress it. Gwen covers her face as a line of her mind-controlled followers shoots up to cover her with their shields. I watch their legs writhe from beneath their shields, unable to do anything to save themselves as long as Gwen has them in her control. But I can't let their suffering stop me. This is war.

I swim up so I can attack above their heads and over their shields, directly at Gwen. But their shields move just in time to cover her. I don't let that stop me as the wall of flames continues to shoot out of my mouth. I start focusing on the shape of the flames and bend them with my hands until the superheated jets melt the shields. Gwen screams as the molten-hot metal hits her head and arms and legs. I am almost through the barrier when a wall of water hits me from the side. Ceto has joined the fight.

The armies below begin their hand-to-hand combat again as I charge back to Gwen and Ceto. Atlantis' current control line fights to get me there. I feel power coursing through my body as I propel through the water. I ready my flames and take aim, this time ready to strike with my super-heated ball of fire. But I have forgotten something. Ceto also has water temperature control skills. Just as my ball is ready, Ceto shoots it from the ocean with an icy blast. The flames are extinguished immediately and the water cools drastically. I know what her next move will be, so I dive down to the army below us. And I'm not a moment too soon.

An icy blast shoots into the fighting, right where I dived. Soldiers from both sides are instantly frozen around me. I feel the iciness, but my own burning heat keeps me from freezing where I am. Still, I must find a better vantage point. I must go up.

I shoot up into the water, praying that Atlantis' current control line will know what I need and they do. I feel them pushing me through the water, faster than any normal human could rise without being crushed by the pressure. Below, I feel Ceto trying to push into their current with her own, but I have too much of a head start. She can't stop me or slow me down, so instead, she follows me.

The Atlantean fighters give me all their strength. I power through the water until I am only a hundred feet below the waterline. Fifty feet. Twenty feet. Ten feet. And I'm free.

I shoot out of the water like a rocket and head straight to the clouds above. There isn't a soul on the Mediterranean. No one to see the two-worlder rising from the sea, a water spout a thousand feet long lifting her into the air. Just behind me, however, Ceto is coaxing her own waterspout to follow me. Overhead is a massive, billowing storm system, ready to pour over the water below. Perfect. This is what I need.

Namaah! I call out to the air around me. *Namaah! I need you!*

I am here, my pearl, she whispers back to my heart. *I will not leave you.* My heart fills with courage. I hope she knows what this means to me.

Namaah, I say. *Ceto is right behind me. Can you force her back to the ocean?*

Without saying a single word, Namaah sends a torrent of air behind me. Ceto is blown off-course and starts falling, head over tentacles, back toward the Mediterranean Sea. But the air didn't just knock Ceto off course. My waterspout, already weakened by the distance I've traveled, is also knocked askew by the phenomenal wind. I start my fall from the sky. The black clouds spin in and out of view as the Mediterranean grows closer and closer. I call out to the water.

Mighty waters! Will the waves deign to help an unworthy ally? It is all I can do. I don't have time to properly address the water as it deserves and expects. All I can do is hope my plea will be heard and found acceptable.

We see you, I hear the waves beneath me speak. *Do not worry. We will catch you.* I don't have time to utter a response when a massive wave barrels across the Mediterranean. It rises 75 feet or more into the air until my feet kiss its surface and I slide safely down the slope.

Thank you, mighty sea, I say to the waves. *Can you still help? I am fighting a foe to us all.*

Yes, the surface water whispers. *We know who you fight. You have killed her mother. The evil Queen Nyobi Kadul tortured those whose only desire was to live peaceably in our sea. We are grateful for your service and want to keep our waters free. We will help you.*

I let out a breath I didn't know I was holding.

I thank you, I say to the water. *You cannot know what this means to me.*

We can know and we do know, the water responds. *But we must warn you. Not all of our kind feel as we do. The water beneath the waves has been tempestuous. They liked being in control of all life. We will be forced to fight them.*

No sooner does the surface water finish speaking to my mind than another waterspout surges out of the ocean, this time with Ceto and Gwen both at the top. My heart falls at the sight. I have only fought Ceto above the water. I don't know what Gwen can do here. I'm not eager to find out.

Urging the waves around me, I rise on the water's surface. It takes me into the sky where I am face-to-face with my enemies.

"You think you can beat us here, Evelyn," Ceto says in her cruel, smooth voice. "But you are wrong. Together, Gwen and I cannot be stopped. We will annihilate you!" Ceto sends some of her waterspout toward me and it hits me dead-on. I am blown off-balance, but the waves keep me up.

"I am not afraid," I tell her as I get back up on my feet.

"That will be your mistake and undoing," Ceto says in response.

"You are alone, Evelyn," Gwen calls out. "You could have joined us, but you have chosen your fate. Now you will pay for it."

Gwen narrows her eyes at me and starts speaking in words I haven't heard in over two centuries. Then I see them. The colored tendrils of mind-control begin snaking their way toward me. They are colors that I know. Colors I used myself when I inhabited Pearl's body. I gave up the ability to use them when I chose my ancestors' help. What I would give to have them now. If they reach me, I will lose my mind. I will be forced to see a world that does not exist. I will believe what is not real. I will end my own life.

Please keep me away from those things, I call to the waves that hold me aloft. Without warning, my stomach lurches and I am weightless. For a moment, I feel like I am flying. Then I feel the falling.

The waves catch me before I can slam into the steely-grey surface of still waters. Waters that reflect the darkening sky above. I slide again to the surface of the sea. The tendrils are still coming. Every color of the rainbow snaking through the sky on the way down to me, ready to drive me to madness. I dive beneath the surface and swim as fast as I can. But there is no current control help now. I am too far away from the Atlantean army.

I keep swimming beneath the waves, constantly looking behind me. Then I see them. The bands of color break through the surface of the water and continue their path to me. I swim up and call to the water's surface.

Please! I yell and the water understands. The waves rise into the air, leaving the deadly, colorful tendrils to continue their path into the depths. Gwen and Ceto are hundreds of feet away.

I must get closer to fight them, I tell the waves. *Please, take me there.*

The waves roll me along and I ride them like I am surfing. I have no board, but my feet skim the water as though it were solid. When I can see Gwen's face again, it is laced with anger. Ceto lets out a laugh and spreads an arm in front of her daughter.

"My turn," she says. She raises her hands to the sky above and calls out to the clouds.

"I am here, faithful friends! All we have planned is coming to fruition. This girl is the only thing that stands in our way. Destroy her and the entire earth will be ours! We will cover the earth with your watery might and we will rule together!"

Instantly, shards of icy rain pelt my face. Then the rain turns to driving snow, then to hail. I reach for my shield, but it is not there.

Namaah! I call out.

I see you, my child, she whispers back. A massive wind blows from the east, knocking the hail off course. I fight to maintain my footing on top of the wave.

Ceto's face doesn't show the slightest disappointment. She only smiles. Then she reaches forward to the waterspout that holds her and her daughter aloft. Moving her arms in arcs and waves, she speaks to the very deepest water. She is changing the current.

She forces us to fight ourselves, the waves say to me. *Our sisters of the deep are pulling us further away.*

My feet start slipping as the waves roll beneath me. They are being pulled back by the current and push to keep me in the air. Ceto lets out a laugh.

"Now, my daughter," she says, and Gwen starts her singing again.

Namaah blows fiercely into their faces. The colorful tendrils snake toward me, but they are bent in the racing wind. Ceto coaxes the current to bring me closer to the driving hail. My waves beat fiercely back.

How long can this continue? How long can we keep up this back-and-forth? How long until I am too tired to keep going? How long until I fail?

"Why have you not come to help me?" I cry out in the wind. "I chose the help of my ancestors! Where are you?!"

Ceto's laugh pierces the storm.

"You are all alone, Evelyn," she screams into my mind. "You cannot stand forever. I will overcome you." Her laughter fills my soul. Her darkness fills me with dread.

Will help ever come? Will I perish alone?

You are not alone, Evelyn. We are here.

Chapter 32

Time stands still. The raging wind freezes. The waves are sculptures of their motion. The hail suspends in the air around me. My enemies are grotesque statues of hatred and revenge. Nothing else moves. Nothing but me.

"Are you really here?" I ask of the stillness. "Have you really come?"

I feel a low burning from my chest. I look down and see the jade floating free from me. It hovers in the stillness before me, glowing with beautiful hues of gold and green. A tear escapes from the corner of my eye as a golden mist pours from the jade. In it, I see familiar shapes, familiar people, familiar spirits.

One by one, my ancestors leave the jade. One by one they turn to face me, smile, and take their place in front of me, creating a family shield between me and my enemies. The last to leave the jade, again, are my great-grandmother, Ama, and my grandmother, Ahyoka.

I told you we would be with you my child, my grandmother says to me. *You have done all you can do on your own. We have watched you with great pride, a true descendent of the rulers of our nation. We have blessed you with our strength while we could not be seen. Now, all will know that you are a true descendent of our power.*

She lifts her hand to my face. Again, I do not feel the pressure of touch, but the warmth of affection from one who came before me.

"I love you, Grandma."

And I love you, my child, she whispers in return. *Now, shall we call your mother and finish the chain?* I smile and nod.

My ancestors reach their hands toward the sea and sing to the silent waves below. A hole opens up in the water's surface and my mother rises through it atop a column of water. She is still as she rises, a statue added to the frozen picture in time. She comes to rest before Ama, her grandmother. Ama reaches her hand to my mother's face. The etched feathers on my mother's helmet break free from their metal cage. A headdress made for a chieftess rises up from her dark and wavy hair. The beads and feathers so sacred to my ancestors, shine out from her like a fearsome mane. When the warmth of Ama's spirit reaches into my mother's soul, my mother blinks, then blinks again. She turns and sees me.

"Evelyn," she says and reaches out her hand. I extend my hand toward her, and though we are too far apart to touch, I feel a surge of power connecting us.

We have come to help you, sweet Marisol, Ama says. Her voice is low and soothing. My mother turns to her.

"Grandmother?" she says. Ama nods.

Time is of the essence, my grandmother says. Ama turns to her and nods.

Indeed, it is time, she says, then turns back to my mother. *Do not worry, my granddaughter. We are with you. We are all with you.* She motions to the ancestral line behind her. Their backs are to my mother, but their form is so like her own that their relationship is unmistakable. She knows who they are.

"The way of the chieftess," my mother says to Ama and Ama nods.

The way of the chieftess, she repeats.

Ama and Ahyoka turn from us and find their place in the center of the line that separates us from Ceto and Gwen. Ahyoka calls out a command in Cherokee. I do not understand the words, but I feel their power. All at once, my ancestors take a battle stance. Some hold weapons. Weapons imbued with ancient power. Others hold shields. The rest raise their hands high or out in front of them, facing our foe. Ama speaks and time returns. The wind nearly knocks my mother from the sky, but once Namaah recognizes her, she moves her currents more gently around her.

Gwen's mouth opens wide. She sees my ancestors, too. Ceto's eyes open wide. Her nostrils flare and she bares her teeth in a monstrous grimace. She opens her mouth wide and lets out a piercing scream. Instantly, the hail turns to shards of ice and they all aim for my mother. Mom raises her arms above her head. At first, I think she is trying to shield herself from the attack, but then she brings her arms forward and yells back at Ceto.

I've never heard that sound from my mom. In all the chaos that has ruled my life over the past year, I have never asked my mother what she is capable of under the sea.

The shards spin in wild circles and stop only when they all face Ceto.

My mother sends them toward Ceto, but Ceto turns them back. As my mother attacks again, the line of our ancestors strikes. Every weapon and powerful chieftess aims at Ceto. All at once, a line of blue light shoots from each of my ancestors. The power joins in front of Ama and Ahyoka. The mother and daughter link hands and send the stream of power into our foe. As the light hits Ceto, a scream of pain erupts from her lips. The shards of ice spin to face her again.

Before the ice can hit its target, a brilliant line of white light leaves Gwen. Her mind powers. She is shining them at my mother. My mother's concentration falters as the first tendril snakes its way toward her, and she drops the ice into the sea. But the other tendrils are slow. Our shielded ancestors move in front of my mother, linking their arms together. More tendrils reach the shields. Even though shields of my ancestral spirits are not solid, the tendrils cannot penetrate them. The first tendril turns from white to black when it reaches the shields. It falls and disintegrates into a thousand falling flakes of mind-control ash. Gwen screams and aims again. Again, her tendrils fail. Her mother's screams turn to a roar.

The line of light that hits Ceto subsides. My ancestors' spirits turn to face me and my mother. They all soar through the air, around and through me, until their line stands behind me and my mother.

"What is happening?" I ask my grandmother's spirit. "Where are you going?"

It is time for you to finish this task, Evelyn, she says. *We have shown you where you come from. Your heritage is in you, Evelyn. It always has been. We came before you and we stand behind you. You can do what is required at your hand.* She brings her hand to my cheek again then passes through me.

I turn to my mom. She smiles at me and I smile at her. Our ancestors sing together in an ancient chant, giving us their strength, wisdom, and determination. My mom and I both turn to Gwen and Ceto. Ceto is weak from the attack my ancestors made against her, but she still has a powerful relationship with the water above the ocean. She calls out to the dark clouds above, begging them to give their all to defeating me. I call to Namaah.

Are you ready, my friend?

Need you really ask? She answers. I smile.

Beautiful Namaah, I say to her, standing on my mountainous wave. *It is time for us to end this fight. Give all you have to them.* I feel her reply in the rushing wind around me. She moves around me with the strength of a hurricane, aiming solely for one creature, Ceto.

But Ceto has been making deals of her own. Her icy shards are aiming only at my mother. The wind does not hit them. Instead, my mother wields her own power against the ice, stopping them midair in a war with our enemy.

Evelyn, you must keep your eyes on all before you, I hear my grandmother whisper. I turn to face Gwen just in time to see her sneaking, green tendril reach my ankles. I cannot get away. The tendril wraps around my ankle and I am victim to the hallucination.

Suddenly, I am surrounded by hissing, seething snakes. Somewhere in my head I know they are not real, but I cannot escape their existence. The snakes, long, black, and with hooded heads, strike at my legs. With every strike, I feel their venom burning in my veins. I begin aiming balls of fire at them, shooting them dead. But for every snake I hit, three more take its place. The only thing I can do is run.

I turn and race away from the snakes. I see a large tree ahead of me, if I can just reach it, I can be safe. I'm almost there. I jump.

And I am falling. Falling through the sky. The tendril breaks free of my ankle and the hallucination disappears. The snakes are gone, but the water is rushing toward my face. Right before I slam into the deadly water, a wave reaches up to catch me. It is not early enough to keep me above the surface, but it slows my fall and helps me slip beneath the waves rather than crash through them to my death. I plummet through the watery depths and cry out. Every nerve aches and stings, the remnants of the hallucination still prickling my body.

Evelyn! I hear. But I cannot tell who is calling out my name. All I can do is send vibrations of pain. I am in so much pain.

Then, without warning, I feel a living body beneath me. My dive into the water is stopped by a giant creature. As soon as my skin touches her leafy tendrils, the stinging is relieved. Chelsea has come for me.

Evelyn, are you alright? she asks. *I am here with you. What do we need to do?* Relief floods through me. I wish I could savor this moment and close my eyes and sleep, but Chelsea nudges my consciousness. I am forced to wake up.

My mom, I manage to say. *She is fighting Gwen and Ceto.*

Alone?

Yes, alone, I answer. *But with Namaah.*

Then let's get up there, Chelsea says. She pushes me upright then dives beneath me, coming up so I sit on her saddle.

Are you ready? She asks. She sends me her clarity and my mind is refreshed. My mother is up there fighting my enemy. I have to get going.

I'm ready, I manage to answer, my mind gaining clarity with every second.

Chelsea shoots up through the water, catapulting us into the air. I call to the waves and they reach us before we can fall. But I hear screaming.

My mom is wrapped in flaming red tendrils of Gwen's hallucination. Ceto is sending her shards of ice into the swirling red tornado around my mother. The icy knives cut through the tendrils and my mother's arms and legs. I feel the flame leaving my body before I am even aware that I created it. Chelsea feels its power and unites her inner burning with mine.

I reach my mind out to the waves and beg them to bring me to Ceto so we can end this. The waves hear me and send Chelsea and me soaring through the sky. When I am within fifty feet of my worst enemy, she turns her attack on me. She smiles as her icy knives fly toward Chelsea and me. The knives hit, but they do not cut, Chelsea and I are too heated for that; instead, the ice melts and drips down our bodies. A look of fear crosses Ceto's face and I smile.

Chelsea's flames erupt from her at the same time mine are taking shape. Instead of one flaming torch, we are two. I spread my hands wide and coax the flames into a single, bullet size ball. I shoot the ball at my enemy.

Ceto tries to duck, but the bullet is too fast. The blazing weapon strikes her in the chest and bursts open into flames. Ceto lets out one, hysterical scream. But the scream dies almost as soon as it touches my ears. I watch as Ceto's tentacles are dried and engulfed by the flames. They curl like a flower petal burned with a match. Before long, Ceto is nothing more than dust tossed about by Namaah's wind.

All of these things happen in just a few moments. We rise. We fire. Ceto dies. Done. But the fighting is not over yet. My mother still screams.

I look to Gwen. Her mouth is twisted with anguish and surprise. It's a look that doesn't last long. She turns to me, wielding an evil smile I thought only her mother could conjure. I see confidence written on her face. But this time there is a slight chink in her armor. She is surprised that I have killed her mother. Surprised, but not sorry. She thinks I have gotten rid of another obstacle. She still thinks she can win.

Roaring like a lion hunting its prey, Gwen lights from the inside. Fire pours from her eyes, her mouth, her ears, and down her skin. The flames turn red and smokey tendrils leave her flaming body. She is still holding my mom in a hallucination.

I race to my screaming, writhing mother and reach for her, trying to take the hallucination from her. Anything to stop her suffering. Even if I am hit by Gwen's attack, the singing of my ancestors will be enough to strengthen my mom and she can finish the fight. I am within only a few feet of her and I reach my arm out to grab her, but she lunges at me. Chelsea tries to dodge her, but I urge her to hold steady. My mom will not hurt us. In a flash, my mother reaches my body.

"I'm here, Mom," I yell through the sound of her screaming. "Let me take the tendrils! You can finish Gwen!"

Mom's face turns to me, her eyes are wide and filled with fear. I try to pull her to me, to hold her and take the pain away, but she reaches her hand out again and grasps the chain around my neck. The red tendrils that encircle her body snake up her arm and wrap around the chain. I reach to stop her, to take her hand away from my neck, but I am too late. The chain snaps and falls from my neck. I grab my mother's wrist and try to catch the necklace, but it slips through my fingers. The jade falls to the ocean like a rock, too fast. I watch in horror as it plummets into the waves. My mom pulls away, the hallucination taking a vicious turn within her.

I turn to face my ancestors. They can help me. They must. But they are gone. Their help was granted by the jade. The jade is lost and so are they.

We can still do this, Evelyn, Chelsea says to my mind. *Just because you can no longer see them does not mean they are no longer there. We are strong together and they are with us. We were made for this.*

I don't know if you're right, I tell her. *But I am nothing if I don't try. Let's go.*

We race forward on the waves toward Gwen. But Gwen's smile still covers her face. I feel Chelsea's burning rising to the surface. I try to burn, but the feeling is gone. I cannot produce a flame. Did that disappear with the jade, too? Stung, but unphased, I focus on Chelsea's heat. When the fire leaves her mouth, I pound it into obedience, forcing it into an intense ball of flame. I shoot the flame directly at Gwen's face. It bursts and she is engulfed. I feel a momentary sense of joy until I hear her laughter through the flame and smoke.

"Like I said, Evelyn," she calls through the flames. "I have more power than *even you* can realize."

The flames clear and I see Gwen's face focused on mine. She still haunts my mom. Anger is still my companion. I urge Chelsea forward and pull out my knife. I am close enough to run her through. But Gwen flicks her fingers and a blue line, so faint I can hardly see it, reaches for me. Just as the glimmering line touches my forehead, I see a glowing figure rise from the sea. Is this part of the hallucination? I try to look away, but my eyes are transfixed. I feel Chelsea grow rigid beneath me. She is captured, just like I am.

Gwen laughs and says something to me, but I cannot hear her. I am focused on the figure. It grows larger as it rises into the sky. I see a chariot made of gold, drawn by four golden horses. In the chariot is a young man holding a bow and arrow. I've seen his face before. Recognition dawns. Helios.

The jade hangs from his neck, burning bright as the sun. His eye catches mine for just a moment and I smile. My smile distracts Gwen and she turns to see what I see. Her spell against me is broken. My mother stops screaming. Gwen has let her go. My mom falls from the tops of the waves. They catch her and carry her down to the surface of the sea where she can rest safely. I turn back to the fight in front of me. Helios' body is muscular and majestic, like a sculpture of a Greek god. He lets his golden arrow fly straight at Gwen. It hits her in the chest and shoots right through her. She doesn't make a sound but lifts her hands to Helios. Black tendrils snake out of her fingertips.

I will not let her harm Helios. The deepest water in the Mediterranean may have been serving Ceto, but it is still subject to my control over water temperature. I reach to the water with one, last command.

Freeze her.

The water is angry and does not want to obey. But I am descended from rulers, from a long line of chieftess leaders. The sea cannot deny my authority. Reluctantly, the water gives way to my power. It rises even farther in the air until it surrounds Gwen. She is engulfed by the sea. Her tendrils sneak out from the water, but a tiny waterspout reaches out to them. Everything freezes.

Gwen tries to sneak another tendril out, but the water is too fast. A wall of ice blocks her attempt and reflects the tendril back on its creator. Gwen is struck by her own hallucination as a box of ice closes around her.

The ice is heavy, and Gwen is high. The water gives way and she falls to the salty water below us.

Chelsea and I are right behind her. Helios shines like the sun beneath the clouds.

Chapter 33

"Evelyn, the council is ready for you," my mom says when she peeks her head in the door. "Oh! I'll wait in the hall for you." She closes the door and Jack's face is bright red. She caught us mid-kiss. Jack pulls away.

"Oh, no you don't," I tell him, then I pull on his collar until his lips are right where I want them, firmly on mine. Jack laughs a little then wraps his arms even tighter around my waist. I run my fingers through his hair and take in his scent while the familiar taste of his lips fills my mouth.

That's one perk of having an office in the Atlantis government buildings. I have a door. Whenever Captain Jack needs to "discuss" something, we can have the quiet and private time "talk." I just need to be better at locking the door or listening for knocks.

I finally pull away after just another minute. We do have a war council to get to after all.

"How about we eat dinner onshore tonight," Jack says as he kisses my forehead. We can even take a boat out to watch the sunset."

"Mmm... Sounds good to me," I say. "Can we have Greek food?" Even though I'm getting better at moving past my life in

Ancient Greece, I still love that part of myself. Eating their food brings me a joy that I miss.

"Anything for you," Jack says. "I suppose I should get going. I have to pick up something from my office before the council."

"Alright," I tell him and he leaves my office, mumbling something polite to my mom in the hall, then heads to prepare for the meeting.

I smile at my mom when she comes in and I pick up my own papers from my desk.

"So," she says. "How are *you*?" I feel my face go red.

"I'm doing well, Mom," I answer. "Let's get going." She gives me a jab in the side when I pass her, and I laugh out loud. Life is so good – finally so good.

The past several months have been spent slowly rebuilding our underwater world. When the dust finally settled in the Mediterranean, we spent several weeks helping the wounded rebuild their lives and government. Returning the surviving children to their families was the most difficult. Many families were ashamed that Nyobi's army lost. They felt certain their sons were not faithful enough. I can only hope that the effects of her mind control will wear off before it is too late for their sons.

As for Nyobi's underwater kingdom, the sea creatures there have formed their own government. They are wary of two-worlders or anyone else in human form. I can't say that I blame them. We have done so much damage, I wonder if they will ever let us return. Lachlan travels back and forth between Atlantis and the

Mediterranean, trying to secure an alliance with the freed city. His efforts have not brought much success yet, but he is very hopeful that in time an agreement can be secured.

Our allies remain devoted to Atlantis. We are all weary from the toll of war. We are all working for lasting peace, trying to secure the devotion of all sea creatures, no matter their species. That is why I am headed to the council today.

Since the fighting, I have risen in the ranks of Atlantean leadership. I am on Lady Pescara's Council for the Inclusion of All Sea Life. As a new captain in Atlantis' forces, I have greater say in the council. Even the generals listen when I speak. We are slowly changing minds and building a new Atlantis where all species have equal opportunity and respect.

I fold my letter to Helios and seal the envelope, handing it to my secretary who takes it to the delivery station. Helios is more than I realized. His ancestors didn't just mine the jade, they ruled in the skies long before they were sent to earth to enlighten mankind. With the jade, Helios can order life above the seas. He is a two-worlder, like me, but he serves in a different kingdom.

The Greeks used to believe the sun was pulled across the sky by a god-driven chariot. They didn't understand two-worlders. As a sky two-worlder, Helios can talk with and work with birds, clouds, and Namaah. It doesn't take a special skill set or talent. All sky two-worlders can communicate that way. But Helios is from a family line the other sky two-worlders thought were extinct. They welcomed him when his chariot burst out of the ocean. He was made a leader in their kingdom.

At first, Helios asked me to join him in the sky. He even offered to live life on land, so we could be together. But I wouldn't take that new life from him. I loved Gileaus too much to let his descendent miss out on living as his true self. I wished him well and promised to write as often as I could. We will work together for a unified earth once things are settled in Atlantis. But our future together will not extend beyond that. He kissed me goodbye before mounting his chariot again. For the first time, I didn't see him as his ancestor, but as himself. Helios, my friend.

Mom and I head down the corridor to the council room of the ancient building. I have learned so much about myself, my life, and the world in this place. It is still sometimes surreal to know this is the life I have chosen – to be a part of something bigger than myself, to watch myself grow into someone so capable – it is a life I am proud to call my own.

We pass my dad's office and I peek my head inside. He is busy at work, sorting through the massive paperwork that war creates. He was spared from the fighting, too weak from his time as a prisoner to be allowed in battle. Now he organizes and cares for Atlantis' prisoners.

"Hi Dad," I say. He looks up from his work, a broad grin spreading across his face. He swims to me and wraps me in a hug. Then he lets me go to embrace my mom and give her the kind of kiss I was just giving Jack. I clear my throat.

"Um, we'd better get going, Mom."

"Off to the council?" Dad asks.

"Yep. What are you doing?" I ask. He sighs, letting go of my mom and pointing to the papers in his hand.

"I've been going through the prisoner files here. I just finished writing a letter to James' parents." My heart drops a little. James lost so much of himself in all of this. Once he finishes serving time as a prisoner in Atlantis, he will be exiled from the sea. He won't even be able to vacation at the beach.

"How are they taking the news?" I ask my dad.

"As best as any parent could," he answers. "They understand the choices their son made. They are more ashamed than anything. They are seeking counsel from a trusted advisor. I hope they can find a way past their shame so they can love their son, for his sake." Dad squeezes me close.

"I love you so much, Evelyn," he says as he kisses my forehead. "I could not be more proud of you."

"I love you too, Dad." I squeeze him back then let go. "We'd better get going. Just wanted to say hi." Dad wishes us luck, and Mom and I head back into the hall.

"Dad and I are going to dinner tonight," Mom says. "Café Filet. Want to come with us?" I shake my head.

"No, thanks," I answer. "I'll be going onshore tonight." The guard opens the council door. The sound of scattered conversations reaches my ears. Lady Pescara and Uncle Russ talk together. Uncle Russ hasn't smiled much since the victory in the Mediterranean. He and Aunt Cynthia were devastated by Celia's death. He wears a medal of honor with her name inscribed on it. He is such a good man, it hurts to see him lose someone he loved so much. I hope he is proud of her memory. Celia may have been difficult to live with, but she was dedicated to Atlantis. She gave her life to protect what she believed in.

My mom and I look for our seats. The round table is full except for two open chairs. One of them is next to Jack. He stands and smiles at me. I smile back. My mom pats my shoulder.

"I'm sure you won't be going onshore alone," she says teasingly. I smile again.

No, I won't be going onshore alone. I think I may spend a lot of time onshore with Jack. And time in the ocean. And time for the rest of my life. Whatever happens, I am so content with my life and future. I am at peace. I am whole. I am growing into who I want to be. It is going to be a beautiful adventure.

The end

Acknowledgments

One of the biggest things I have learned in this industry is how willing people are to give freely of their time and knowledge. It is an incredibly supportive community that I am so proud to be a part of. I only hope to pay it forward like these wonderful people have done for me.

First, I owe a tremendous debt of gratitude to TJ Mackay, Founder and Publisher of InD'Tale magazine. TJ is a pro in the business of independent authors with a rich treasure of knowledge and expertise. If anyone has made me a better author in all of this, TJ, it is you. You have patiently read through my cringe-worthy, early drafts and guided me to a stronger voice and better story. You didn't hold back, and in so doing, have helped me grow in ways I would never otherwise be able to do. I know I have miles to go and so much still to learn. I am so grateful to have you as a mentor. Thank you.

Second, my Mindee. Mindee Dziuba of JoobahStudio.com has been with me from the start. She reads my mind as she creates each beautiful cover for my books. She is professional in every way but has also come to be a trusted and valued friend. Thank you, Mindee, for being my cheerleader. I love you.

I have the best beta readers in the business. Sarah Bleyl, Anna Simkins, and Erin Salvesen read my early drafts and give me their honest opinions. From texting me in the middle of the night with excited words over the plot line, to finding answers to historic questions that I need answers to, to letting me know they 'just don't like Jack,' these women help me mold my story and characters into something better – something you will love reading. I could not be more grateful for your love, support, honesty, and friendship. Thank you all so much.

I have been blessed on this journey to have the support of a wonderful copy editor. Penny Friday Baker of Baker Blooper Editing has been the eyes that find the grammar, punctuation, spelling, and other errors that my tired eyes cannot see. Penny, thank you so much for your guidance, professionalism, organization, and friendship. You help me perfect the work I have spent countless hours on. Thank you.

As I mentioned before, the people in this business are incredibly giving with their time and talents. That is the case with Christy Frazier – teacher, author, and speaker. Ms. Frazier has a full schedule but still took the time to read my work and provide me with a review. She encapsulates the selfless sharing of the many authors and editors and other professionals in this community. Thank you, Christy.

I am so grateful for my daughters. Ashleigh, Evelyn, and Chelsea have been excited for every inch of progress I've made. They each out-write me and have more talent than I will have in this life and give me the enthusiasm to keep going. I am so proud of each of you, my girls. The world is your oyster and I am eager to see the pearls you create in your life. Thank you for being happy for me, cheering for me, and being my greatest creations. I love you.

My husband is my best and truest companion. Thank you, Steven, for having faith in my dreams, supporting my desires, and giving me every inch and opportunity to grow. We grow together and we grow better. I love you.

And finally, my readers. Thank you for supporting me, reading my work, being excited for each new installment, and reading some more. You make me an author and for that I am grateful. Here's to a complete trilogy and more books on the horizon!

About the Author

EJ Pay loves spending time with her family and at the beach near her home. She gets ideas everywhere and writes most of those ideas on her bathroom mirror. Her goal is to create original, engaging stories with strong, female leads that her daughters can emulate. Find out more about EJ by visiting www.ej-pay.com, Instagram @ ej_pay_author, or on Facebook at EJ Pay. You can find all three of her books, <u>Called</u>, <u>Trapped</u>, and <u>Released</u> on Amazon.

www.ingramcontent.com/pod-product-compliance
Lightning Source LLC
Chambersburg PA
CBHW031250170626
46807CB00001B/75